ALSO BY BILL LOEHFELM

THE DEVIL SHE KNOWS

BLOODROOT

FRESH KILLS

THE DEVIL IN HER WAY

THE DEVIL IN HER WAY

BILL LOEHFELM

SARAH CRICHTON BOOKS   FARRAR, STRAUS AND GIROUX   NEW YORK

Sarah Crichton Books
Farrar, Straus and Giroux
18 West 18th Street, New York 10011

Copyright © 2013 by Bill Loehfelm
Printed in the United States of America
First edition, 2013

Library of Congress Cataloging-in-Publication Data
Loehfelm, Bill.
    The devil in her way / Bill Loehfelm. — 1st ed.
       p.   cm.
    "Sarah Crichton Books."
    Sequel to: The devil she knows
    ISBN 978-0-374-29885-2 (hardcover : alk. paper)
    1. Policewomen—Fiction.   2. New Orleans (La.)—Fiction.
 3. Suspense fiction.   I. Title.

 PS3612.O36D45 2011
 813'.6—dc23
                                                2012029704

Designed by Abby Kagan

www.fsgbooks.com
www.twitter.com/fsgbooks • www.facebook.com/fsgbooks

10   9   8   7   6   5   4   3   2   1

For New Orleans

I have love in me the likes of which you can scarcely imagine and rage the likes of which you would not believe. If I cannot satisfy the one, I will indulge the other.

—*MARY SHELLEY*

THE DEVIL IN HER WAY

1

The punch caught Maureen flush in the temple, striking near her right eye.

The big bony fist drove the rim of her sunglasses into her cheek, knocking them askew but not off, and put a faint buzz in her right ear. She yelped at the blow, a comically loud and clear *ouch!* A lucky shot, she thought, thrown by a guy she'd been dumb enough to give a free one, to let for half a second step into the blind spot over her shoulder. The punch did get her adrenaline cranked up and pumping double-time, something she hadn't thought possible, not with the way her skin had throbbed and hummed as she'd barreled up the metal stairs outside the two-story apartment complex and charged down the concrete walkway toward the muffled screams coming from behind the thick metal door of Apartment D.

Her assailant, a skinny black man, barefoot in dirty jeans and a food-stained green tank top, staggered out of that apartment doorway as if he were the one who'd been hit. He stood about half a foot taller than Maureen, putting him at almost six feet. Weightwise, he carried only a ten-, maybe twelve-pound advantage over her.

Maureen braced herself against the balcony's rusty iron railing and drove her heavy boot heel into the man's knee, slamming it hard sideways. The man, who hadn't escaped in his half second of opportunity but had instead started babbling something apologetic, screamed like she'd stabbed him in the eye. He wobbled but didn't go down. No problem. Maureen didn't need him to fall. Not yet. She just needed his chin to drop into the range of her right cross, which it did as he struggled for balance, his face bobbing into perfect position.

Setting her feet, she brought her fist from behind her hip and snapped her arm forward, using force from her hips and her back like a baseball swing. She connected well, grunting as the punch landed. A sharp pain shot across her knuckles and the back of her hand like an electric current. The shock died at her wrist. There and gone in an instant. A flash.

Her assailant dropped to his hands and knees on the concrete balcony, coughing. Hell of a shot, Maureen thought, if she did say so herself.

"On your face, motherfucker! Now!"

When the man did not immediately comply, she kicked one arm out from under him. He collapsed face-first onto the concrete. Snapping her cuffs free from her belt, she dropped to her knees, straddling the man's hips. She bent one arm behind his back, cuffed that wrist, and then bent the other arm, shackling his wrists together, the metal handcuffs grinding like machine gears as she locked them. The man didn't resist, his breathing fast and wet.

Maureen leaned her forearm into the back of his head, squashing his nose into the cigarette-ash-and-piss-stained concrete. "Do not fucking move. You are done moving. Done."

She rose to her feet, the four other cops who had arrived on the scene gathering around her. Nobody said a word.

Maureen took a deep breath, trying to calm down. Getting up for a run-in was never a problem for her. Getting her control back, that was where she needed practice. In front of the stone-faced cops surrounding her, she felt exposed and raw, almost as if they'd walked in on her getting laid. Under her uniform, sweat slicked her whole body. Salt stung her eyes. Her heart kept right on racing, punching at the inside of her bulletproof vest.

From behind her dark glasses, Maureen studied her fellow officers. They were hard-bodied men her age or younger. They looked ready and eager to step in and take over for her. She worried that this guy at her feet constituted an informal but important field test, one that concerned a lot more than proper technique with a pair of handcuffs.

Pop quiz, hotshot.

Sad and frail and cuffed as he was, stinking of shitty weed, and sweat, and cheap booze, and Taco Bell, the sad bastard at her feet had hit a cop. Even though she was a rookie, and even though he hadn't done any real damage, hitting a cop was more than bad news—it should be a one-way ticket to traction. That was what she'd heard, at least. Or had she heard that it used to be that way but wasn't anymore? She blinked the sweat from her eyes.

She was only five weeks out of the academy; as a condition of her rookie probation she could lose her job over anything, no questions asked and no chance to argue her case. Twenty-first-century police department or not, plenty of cops didn't like women on the job. Her being from out of town didn't help. She'd heard rumors she was a plant, from the FBI, from the DOJ, both of which had an active eye on the New Orleans Police Department. She didn't know these guys surrounding her. She didn't know them as cops, or as men. She couldn't trust them. Not yet. One brutality complaint, the wrong kind of gossip or rumor in the wrong ear, and she'd be out of a job, maybe even up on charges of her very own, all before she'd even had a chance to wrinkle her uniform.

These days, zero tolerance in the New Orleans Police Department started with the police themselves. Every arrest, every report, every stat—anything that outside eyes might see got scrutinized. Maureen's instructors at the academy had hammered CYA into her head. Forget Protect and Serve, they said; *Cover Your Ass* was the department mantra.

Looking down, she noted that the man at her feet was breathing better now, steady and less shallow, though a small pool of blood had collected

on the concrete by his mouth. Had she knocked out a tooth? Did they
have to find it if she had? She stepped to the side of her perp. As her
adrenaline drained, Maureen started to think less about stomping this
guy and instead worried that she'd get shit over the kick in the knee or
the punch in the mouth.

She heard telltale heavy breathing heading her way along the balcony and came back to herself, back to the present. Along the balcony
came Preacher Boyd. Her training officer. The man who had the last word
on whether she'd ever get to be real police. Preacher was large and heavy,
with close-cropped dark hair, skin the color of cork, and hooded green
eyes. Freckles like red-pepper flakes dusted his broad nose and full cheeks.

Wow, Maureen thought. He was actually out of the car. And had
climbed a flight of stairs.

"Make a hole, you sweaty pricks," Preacher said. "Special fucking
occasion."

Two of the officers eased by Maureen, stepping over the handcuffed
man, staring him down from above. They'd be knocking on other doors,
canvassing about the original call, a midday domestic. One of them, another rookie fresh from the academy, released a "Nice shot, Coughlin,"
under his breath like a belch that embarrassed him. She wasn't sure, but
Maureen suspected he was the guy whose nose she'd broken during
hand-to-hand training.

The other two officers entered the open door of Apartment D, talking
to the bloody-nosed young woman on the couch, a wailing baby on her
lap. One of the officers spoke into his radio, requesting that a female officer be sent to the scene to assist with the victim. Maureen, insulted at first
by the request, realized she was not the best person to console and reason
with the victim, considering she'd nearly knocked out the woman's companion. Served him right, the fucker, for beating a woman, a woman
holding a baby in her arms. That the vic held a baby, Maureen remembered, made for an even more severe set of charges on the man in cuffs.
Good. He was getting everything she could think of, assaulting an officer
not the least of them.

The woman in the apartment outweighed Maureen and the perp combined. She'd watched everything through the open door. She glowered at Maureen with hateful, teary eyes, her blood-crusty nostrils flared. She seethed like she'd known every violent thought that had crawled through Maureen's head. Through her dark glasses, Maureen glared right back.

She wanted to smack that dirty look right off the other woman's face, bloody nose and tears be damned. She wanted to grab her by the shoulders and shake her. Maureen felt her cheek starting to swell where she'd been hit. She opened and closed her mouth, working her jaw muscles. Maybe she'd been hit harder than she'd thought. Anger rose in her again.

Maybe if you'd thrown him that attitude you're throwing me now, Maureen wanted to say to the woman, he wouldn't have hit either of us. Not today, at least.

Easy for you to say, Maureen imagined the woman replying, you, with your gun, and pepper spray, and Taser, and boots, and your four boys backing you up. Easy for you to fight back, with all the shit that you carry.

"Enough with the eye-fucking," Preacher said.

Despite the fact that he spoke while leaning into the apartment door, with his thick finger pointed at the woman on the couch, Maureen knew he was talking to her as well.

"Ma'am," Preacher said, "please do what you can to help these other officers, officers you called, if you remember. We'll be taking in your . . . whatever he is, here. You'll be able to find out how to reach him."

"I already know all that," the woman said. "And I didn't call no police, neither. It's not my fault can't nobody mind their own business around here, so don't go puttin' that on me. You *better* get him a doctor. That's what needs to happen. That's who you need to be calling."

"If he needs a doctor," Preacher said, "he'll get one."

Stepping back from the doorway, he turned to Maureen, tilting his head to study her swelling cheek. "Your first throw-down. You never forget your first time. Congrats."

"It does beat paperwork," Maureen said.

"I can't get up," the man said.

"Sir, what is your name?" Preacher asked, hands on his ample hips. He made no move to help the man to his feet.

"Arthur. Arthur Jackson."

"Mr. Arthur Jackson, please stand up so we can have a look at you."

"I can't stand," Arthur mumbled into the concrete. "She busted my knee. She ruined my one good one."

"And it hurts so bad," Maureen said, "that you haven't moved or made a sound in several minutes."

"I was in shock," Arthur said.

"And now you're better," Preacher said. "Get up or Officer Coughlin here will be forced to throw you over the balcony railing down to the parking lot. We sure as shit ain't carrying you. My knees ain't all that, either. And if you're gonna make us call an ambulance, we're gonna make it worth it. That shit costs city money."

Maureen leaned down and grabbed Arthur by the cuffs and high on one arm, dragging him to his feet. He whined and protested about the pain in his knee. He did seem to have real trouble standing. Despite his struggles, Maureen got him propped up against the wall.

Preacher leaned into Arthur's face.

Arthur turned his face halfway away, blinking furiously. His chin was slick with blood and a long tendril of red spit hung from his bottom lip. Above his right eyebrow, Maureen saw a bump the size and color of a plum rising under a nasty scrape. From when she'd kicked his arm out from under him, she thought, and he'd hit the concrete face-first. She'd done visible damage, a serious no-no. Yes, he'd hit her first, but she'd been careless at the apartment door and allowed it to happen.

Preacher turned and over his shoulder his eyes met hers for a split second. Maureen saw the anger flicker across his face. She knew they were having the same thoughts. She'd made a mess; she knew that. She'd admit it, but later. Not in front of Arthur. She was at least smart enough to know that much.

"He can barely stand," Preacher said, his voice low.

"That's what I was tellin' you," Arthur said.

"You shut up," Preacher said. He keyed the radio mic on his shoulder and calmly called an ambulance to the scene. He grabbed a fistful of Arthur's tank top and steadied him against the wall. "Sit down and wait. And stay quiet. Go back into shock."

"I ain't done nothin'. I don't deserve this. You heard her. She didn't even call y'all. There wasn't even a problem till y'all showed up." Working around his injured knee, Arthur slumped against the wall. "Y'all got a cigarette?"

Preacher walked away without answering either the accusation or the question.

Maureen followed him down the balcony to the top of the stairs. She wasn't exactly hanging her head, but she was prepared for a scolding.

Preacher reached into his pocket, brought out Maureen's pack of cigarettes from the car. "Smoke one where he can see you, the prick. You all right?"

"Fine. You do know he hit me first."

"I saw. It'll be in my report."

Maureen pulled a smoke and her lighter from the pack. She lit up with a long, long drag. The hot smoke burned her lungs. "You did? From the car?"

"I said I saw. That's what you need to know."

Maureen watched the Washington Avenue traffic slide by, the cars slowing in both directions to study the police action, the cruisers parked at angles, their blue lights whirling. Up and down the street, people stood clustered in front of their houses, smoking cigarettes and chatting and watching the goings-on at the Garvey Apartments. Maureen didn't quite understand the fascination. Police activity at the Garvey, or anywhere on this stretch of Washington, really, was hardly an anomaly.

"I can't believe you called an ambulance," Maureen said. "Arthur needs an ice pack and an Advil and that's more than enough. You know that as well as I do. Why are we making a fuss over this?"

Preacher adjusted his crotch. "He's bloodied up. He's having trouble standing. He has to go to the hospital first. Personally, I could give a fuck about the state of him, but lockup won't take him like that. Those sheriff's department bitches won't take anyone we bring in with as much as a hangnail. We'd be wasting our time. Believe it." He took a deep breath, held it for a beat, then let it leak out slow as a faint whistle. "We'll hang a drug warning on him, too. Say that's why we called in a medical. We were worried he was too high for the sheriff to handle, a danger to himself and others, some shit like that. We'll make it work."

"It's probably true."

"Likely enough, anyway," Preacher said. "Everybody's gonna smell that weed stank on him. And he did hit a cop. Plus, it's that much more paperwork to wade through for anyone crawling out from under a rock to complain about him being marked up."

"I'm charging him with everything I can."

"Please do. Charge him with 2-Pac. I give a fuck?" Preacher, grinning at his own wit, again studied her cheek. "Speaking of ice packs, I think it's done swelling. In a day or two it'll be hard to see if you didn't know you'd been hit." He took his cell phone from his pocket. "Show me that cheek."

Maureen turned her face slightly toward Preacher and he took the picture. "Can't hurt to have that," he said. "I'll attach it to the report. Let me know when you're done writing it. Make sure some of the other guys get a look at the bruise. Sooner the better, while it's fresh and ugly."

Maureen took another long drag of her cigarette. She finally felt her brain and her insides downshifting to somewhere near normal. Though she knew that biologically nicotine did the opposite, she felt her heartbeat slow. God, tobacco was amazing. How was it that a stimulant mellowed you out so much? How would she ever give it up?

"I should've waited for the second unit," she said.

"I told you that when we pulled into the parking lot. They were practically around the corner. Less than a minute behind us."

"But she was screaming," Maureen said. "You could hear it clear as day."

"She was screaming *at* him," Preacher said, "not screaming for help. You gotta know the difference."

"You could tell that from the parking lot?"

"You gotta know what to listen for."

"I didn't think he'd answer the door," Maureen said. "I thought it'd be her. Or they'd refuse to answer altogether."

"Good thing he answered," Preacher said. "*She* might've hit you, too. Harder. Looks like she'd like to."

"At first he was just hollering, I don't even know what he was saying. Just yelling and flailing his arms."

"He got the first shot in," Preacher said. "That's a problem."

"He pushed by me," Maureen said. "Just kinda stumbled really. I thought at first that maybe she'd hit him in the back and pushed him out."

"Not unreasonable."

"I think when he heard the other units arriving, he meant to run, not fight. I really do. That wasn't a 'I wanna fight six cops' kind of punch that he threw. Something in him saw the opportunity to knock me down, maybe he saw me standing between him and the stairs, I don't know. I'm not sure how much he meant it. I think it was panic. If what that woman said is true, about not being the one who called us, his shock at seeing me makes more sense."

"The thing of it is," Preacher said, "if he had a knife in his hand, or a bat, or a pipe, or a gun within reach, and panicked the same way, and everything else plays out the same, then that's your blood on the concrete over there. Panic is dangerous. For everyone, whether it makes sense or not. You have to avoid it." A siren wailed not far away, closing in on them. "Otherwise we're calling that ambulance for you. He can't get behind you. No one can. Ever."

Maureen stared across the street at the park and the playground and the basketball courts.

"Ever," Preacher repeated. "Anybody home, Coughlin?"

"Yes, sir," Maureen said. "It'll never happen again, sir."

"I ain't lost a probie yet," Preacher said. "Not to the rules and not to the streets. And, girl or not, you won't be the first. I'm the good kind of selfish, the kind that's gonna make you a good cop. Live it. Believe."

In her peripheral vision, Maureen noticed movement beneath her in the parking lot. Glancing down, she saw that a young boy, maybe eleven or twelve years old, had drifted out from under the stairs. She wondered how long he had been down there.

The boy wore an oversized white T-shirt over faded cargo shorts in a blue, white, and gray camouflage pattern. He wore them low. Standard uniform for the neighborhood. His knobby shoulders rounded, his hands in his pockets, he looked up at Maureen and Preacher at the top of the stairs, watching them with one eye half closed, as if peering at a slide through a microscope.

Maureen caught Preacher's eye and tilted her head, directing him toward the boy.

"Hey there, son," Preacher said, peering off the balcony. "Do me a favor, take your hands from your pockets."

His hand drifted to his hip, to his weapon. Maureen's throat tightened.

"Preach, he's, like, eleven."

"I'm twelve," the boy said.

"Hands, son," Preacher said. "Let me see them."

The boy did as he was told. He slid each hand free slowly. In each hand he held a smooth wooden stick, drumsticks. He didn't say anything. His mouth was tight and twisted, as if he had something to say but couldn't find the right words for some big thoughts kicking around in his head.

"There something we can help you with?" Preacher asked. "Something you need?"

The boy took a half step toward the foot of the stairs.

"You can come on up here," Preacher said, waving the boy toward him with the same hand that had reached for his weapon. "We don't bite."

"Do you live here?" Maureen asked. "Which apartment are you in?"

The boy opened his mouth to say something. A sharp whistle, like the sound of a man calling a dog, stopped him from speaking. The boy dropped his gaze. Maureen spotted the whistler standing across the street.

An older boy, eighteen, nineteen years old, wearing baggy jean shorts and a black Bob Marley T with the singer's laughing profile emblazoned over a giant pot leaf. The older boy had his hair in short twists that were bunched like the candles on a birthday cake by an old-school terry headband. He wore a cowrie shell necklace tight around his neck. Black aviators hid not only his eyes but also most of his face.

"Yo! Shorty!" he yelled, with as much command, or maybe it was warning, in his voice as there was in his whistle.

The younger boy turned away from Preacher and Maureen. He didn't even look to see who had been yelling to him. He already knew. He tucked his sticks in his pockets and slunk away across the apartment-complex parking lot. He didn't look back at Maureen and Preacher.

When the boy hit the sidewalk, the whistler turned and headed up Washington Avenue in the opposite direction, talking on a cell phone. Mission accomplished, apparently.

"You know what," Maureen said, watching the whistler walk away, "gimme a minute."

"For what?"

"Hey!" Maureen yelled across the street. "Hey! Hold on a second."

The whistler looked back over his shoulder, just to let Maureen know he'd heard and was ignoring her command. Cell phone to his ear, his lips moving, he continued walking away.

"Bob Marley. Wait right there a second."

"Coughlin, what're you doing?"

"I want to talk to that guy," Maureen said, three steps down the staircase. "I wanna ask him what he thinks is going on."

Something had happened between the two boys. Maureen could feel it buzzing in the air around them, but she couldn't decipher what it was.

"It's just regular 'don't talk to the cops' street bullshit between kids," Preacher said. "A chance to show us up. Maybe they're brothers. Forget it."

Maureen watched the younger boy walk away in the opposite direction.

At the corner he fell in with two other boys the same age and size and dressed in the same style, big T-shirts, big shorts slung low beneath hips and butts they didn't have. She watched as the three of them bumped their small fists and talked. Maureen felt comforted that the kid had hooked up with friends. He looked them in the face when they spoke to him. She grinned at his amateur gangsta lean. She wondered what they talked about.

At a break in the traffic the trio crossed the street and meandered into the ballpark, more of an open field with tilted bleachers and a battered softball backstop. They appeared headed for the basketball courts or maybe the new playground beyond the courts, but in no hurry.

Maureen looked around for the whistler, but he was gone.

A commotion had started building in Apartment D, raised voices, then shouts, then something breaking—a lamp or a mirror. Maureen jumped back up the stairs, headed in that direction, but Preacher grabbed her by the arm as she moved past him.

"Give it a minute and let those boys work," he said. "Stay right here. We're guarding the only escape route."

The woman screamed. The sound was more like a roar, really, Maureen thought. She was afraid of what might come out the door.

"Oh, man," mumbled Arthur from his spot against the wall. "Now y'all gone and done it to me."

Red-faced and dripping sweat, two officers dragged the woman out the front door, one officer gripping each of her thick, gelatinous arms. Her hands were cuffed behind her back. Inside the apartment, the baby wailed at top volume. The woman flopped about on the balcony like a giant hooked fish, unleashing a stream of profanities the likes of which Maureen, even in all her years in the bar business, had never heard. When the woman had exhausted herself, the officers eased her facedown on the balcony and released her arms. They checked her breathing and stood.

One cop, a burly unibrowed Hispanic, stretched his lower back. The other, a tall, thin blond with a big nose, walked over to Preacher and Maureen.

"What the fuck happened in there, Quinn?" Preacher asked.

"You won't believe it, Preach," Quinn said, his chest heaving as he struggled to recover from the effort of subduing the woman. "In the dish-washer. Like, two pounds of weed in a garbage bag. And three guns in a shoe box." He smiled. "A fucking bust and a half and we fucking fell right into it."

Preacher's eyebrows jumped up his forehead. He threw a quick glance at Maureen. "Yes, indeed."

Quinn shrugged. "Ruiz was the one that spotted the washer was un-hooked and leaning half outta the counter. He went in there for a glass of water."

"Tell ya what," Preacher said, turning to Maureen. "Now I believe it wasn't her that called us here. These two clowns are no dealers. They're holding for someone else, under orders, I'm sure, to stay away from the cops."

Maureen scanned Washington Avenue in both directions. The three boys and the whistler were gone. I don't know what it is, she thought, but we're missing something here.

2

Sitting in a back pew of a dim and empty church, soaking wet and taking a break from running in the driving rain, the stained-glass shadows spreading like puddles all around her, Maureen stared at her white hands, her fingers thin and spidery in the dust-cloudy half-light. She wiggled her fingers, watching the digits move as if they were underwater, or unattached to her, or she to them. So white, she was. Always had been. Like plaster. Like marble. Like porcelain, or clouds. She made fists. Squeeze. Release. Squeeze tighter. Release again. She watched the blood rush in and out of her knuckles. The punch that had dropped Arthur Jackson to his hands and knees, that had left his blood on the concrete, hadn't left a mark on her hand. She wanted that punch back. She wanted a do-over on the Garvey Apartments. For reasons that had nothing to do with Arthur Jackson's health.

It could have been, Maureen thought, it *should* have been *her* finding the weed and the weapons in that kitchen. She had no doubt she would've spotted the crooked dishwasher. Had she controlled the scene like she should have, like she'd been trained to do, she could be crowing about what she'd done, letting that goof Quinn buy her a beer at the Bulldog. Instead, while everyone else went out after work, she was learning from Preacher how to gracefully fudge a trip sheet. The art of mitigating self-inflicted damage was a lesson he felt she really needed to learn. She'd felt like she was back in high school detention all over again.

At the Garvey Apartments, she had exploded from the patrol car looking to bang some heads. She had to admit that. She hadn't given a second thought to controlling anything, especially herself. She'd make up for it, though. She'd find out who had really made the call to the police about Apartment D. She'd impress Preacher with her initiative. Prove she was more than a blunt instrument.

In the last days before she'd moved to New Orleans, late at night through her mom's living room window, while the rest of the neighborhood slept, Maureen had watched a spider spin a vast web that stretched from the branches of a spindly birch tree to the curbside streetlight. She remembered the sight of the silken threads, pale and wispy in the lamplight, drifting in the breeze with one end unanchored. It was marvelous, it really was, in the truest sense of the word, how that solitary spider built that web one strand at a time, something so tiny and determined building a trap so intricate and beautiful, so strong and deadly—all of it starting from one slender and delicate thread—and the spider, skilled and smart, avoiding getting caught up in her own trap.

And when birds or the wind or boys playing ball broke the web during daylight hours, out came the spider at night to rebuild. Every time.

Maureen crossed her hands and locked her thumbs together, bending her fingers into the eight legs of a spider, like she used to do as a kid making animated shadows on the wall.

Fragile, loose threads were what her thoughts, what *she*, felt like too often these days, like those first few strands of the web—unmoored, untethered and blowing loose in the breeze.

She hadn't told a soul the whole truth about that dark time last winter on Staten Island, when a twisted, murderous psycho named Frank Sebastian had hunted and brutalized her. Maybe keeping her mouth shut had made things worse for her, had let the anger and bad memories linger. Her mother knew a few things. Detective Waters knew others. Throughout the spring after the incident, Maureen had dated a cute, kind, and dumb younger guy named Derek, and she'd told him some of the story. Not all of it, but enough to explain why she sometimes flinched when he touched her or whispered her name, and why she sometimes woke up panting and screaming in the night, ready to throw fists.

Derek knew that Maureen had been a victim of violence, though, no, she hadn't been raped. And he knew that she had saved herself, mostly, from the perpetrator of that violence. The fact that Sebastian was dead, and that she had killed him, and not just him, that detail she kept to herself.

Another thing Derek never knew was how he put the idea of New Orleans in her head with his talk about the Saints and their miraculous Super Bowl run. He couldn't stop talking about how if the Saints could find a way, the dead-in-the-water Saints, the goddamn 'Aints, for chrissakes, couldn't his beloved New York Jets do the same? Maureen didn't care much about football, didn't care much for the boy, to be honest, but the idea of a new city, a new place, a wounded place deep in the process of remaking itself, that idea she liked a lot.

Somewhere else she could be *someone* else.

The concept had lodged in her brain, where it grew, like an infection.

New York City slashed its budget, killing the police academy class she'd already enrolled in. It killed the one after that, too, leaving her with at least a year of her own to dispose of before she could become a cop. She had to leave New York. It was sad. She'd been so sure at first blush, when she first decided to be a cop, that she wanted to wear the hometown colors, to wear its badge, but she couldn't wait. She wouldn't survive the delay. She knew herself. She'd be back on her feet with a drink tray in her hand, bumping coke off her house key between rounds and thinking about everything great and healthy she'd do if she could just get a few days off.

Researching other opportunities, she discovered that New Orleans,

THE DEVIL IN HER WAY 19

flush with federal grant money, was announcing its first academy class in three years. She started reading about the city and the police department in the online version of the New Orleans newspaper. Even six years after Katrina, she kept seeing words like *remake, recover, reinvent,* and *rebirth*— things she wanted and needed for herself. A new, reform-minded police commissioner had rolled into town not long ago and now sat at the right hand of a popular mayor. Firings, forced retirements, and indictments battered the department. Everything from murder cover-ups to faked traffic tickets. Cops going to jail every month, it seemed. All the scandal only heightened her attraction. She saw opportunity in it. She applied. She got in, with an offer of a city job until her academy class filled up. Just as she'd suspected, the NOPD was hot for fresh blood, eager to recruit from beyond the city and the state. And then all that was left to do was to fire her therapist, pack the car, and kiss her mom goodbye.

Here in New Orleans, it was so far, so good.

She sniffed, her nose itching. Her eyes watered, and she fought off a sneeze. *Tell us about your father, Maureen. You were only eleven when he left. Don't you think that matters?* That was what the shrink had asked her. Right, she'd thought, and that's why I want to play a boy's game and run around with a gun in my hand. So Daddy will love me. Whatever. Fuck you. Believe it or not, Doc, it's not always about the one with the penis. Selfish prick that he was, her father wasn't the problem. Maybe the girl just wants to kick some ass.

The therapy, her mother's idea, had proved costly and pointless, nothing more than an excuse to take expensive pills that gave Maureen diarrhea and headaches. The medication worked, though, in a way. She thought less about her past when she worried in the present about not soiling herself in public like a toddler. She gave up on the therapy and the medication within weeks. She had other options, she knew, and liked none of them: ill-gotten opiates, Irish whiskey, various combinations of both. Old and tired, all of it.

She hated the fog and the hangovers that trailed her into her days when she indulged in chemicals the night before, found them even more debilitating than the nightmares. Cultivating a Xanax addiction didn't seem the best way to launch a law-enforcement career. She'd done the "just to get by" thing with coke in the past, when she was waiting tables. It was bullshit, lazy self-deception. She'd known it then and believed it now. Plus, she'd watched her mother use white wine to numb her own wounds for years. Alcohol and its sister drugs only preserved the pain. They retarded its natural disintegration. Though she was unsure which part of her was broken, Maureen feared that fate. She didn't fear a fight. She didn't fear pain. She feared, had always feared, stasis, paralysis.

Confession is good for the soul. That was what her old high school track coach, a Catholic priest, had told her. They'd talked on occasion, though never in detail, the spring after everything happened, after the insomnia had kicked in hard. She'd gone back to her old high school campus to run endless late-night laps around the school's outdoor track. But the old priest assumed that it was guilt that had Maureen running in circles, guilt about something she'd done, like cocaine or married guys, or something she hadn't done, like get married and have babies. The priest assumed that she suffered from the want and need of forgiveness. But she wasn't sorry for what she'd done, at least not the thing that was keeping her up at night.

Of course, she'd never said anything to dissuade the priest. She hadn't expected real help from him; she just liked hearing there was hope for her. She liked the warm sound of someone else's faith in the dark. Maybe that was why she liked this old church, why she'd picked it as the rest stop and turning point for her evening runs. She liked catching her breath amid the shuffling steps and murmured rosaries of the neighborhood widows. According to the handwritten signs out front, she wouldn't be able to do it much longer. The city had shrunk since the storm. The diocese was dying, literally. The church was to be deconsecrated and locked down in the coming weeks, its valuables shipped away or sold at auction. Maybe, Maureen thought, she wouldn't let that stop her from coming. Maybe the church would be even more beautiful without all that Catholic suffering and guilt getting in the way.

It would shine, maybe—like a newly minted divorcée.

Over Maureen's head, the rain pounded like a stampede on the slate roof of the church. Thunder rumbled as if God, embarrassed over her thoughts, were clearing his throat. It doesn't rain this hard at home, Maureen thought. Ever. The rain, it's another one of those things, like the heat, like the light and the air, elemental things, that was different about Louisiana, about New Orleans. Which was home now, by the way, Maureen reminded herself. No more Staten Island. Forget the living room window. Forget the itsy-bitsy spider.

Maureen had always figured the rain stayed the same wherever you went, if she could credit herself for thinking about such things, or places other than New York City, at all.

Around her in the empty church, in the spaces between her thoughts, Maureen could hear the drops falling from a leak in the roof, miniature heavy-bellied, dirty-water suicides. One at a time. No rhythm to them. She couldn't hear them release from the ceiling, couldn't hear them fall. But if she listened, she could hear the impact. That fact meant something to Maureen that she couldn't put her finger on. It bothered her that all she could hear was the end.

3

Maureen stood with her back pressed to the heavy wooden doors of the church. She watched the rain pound the gray-veined marble of the steps. Thunder boomed again overhead, more angry than embarrassed this time. Despite the shelter of the doorway, Maureen stood in a puddle, the water seeping through her sneakers. She picked up one foot, shook it, then did the same with the other. Nice work. Fucking waste of a perfectly good afterglow. Great idea this, she thought, standing around in a king-hell thunderstorm while back at her apartment Patrick slumbered away in postcoital bliss, warm and naked. Yeah, *that's* the way to seek solace for your troubled soul. Leave the cute naked boy in bed and run two miles in the 'hood.

Hopefully, Patrick took instruction as well after sex as he did during and he'd still be there, still naked, when she got home. She brushed wet clumps of hair from her face, skipped out into the street, and continued her run up Constance Street.

Running along the narrow street, she dodged ankle-snapping potholes, nodded at wet dogs barking at her as she passed their gates. She thought again of her mother's place back on Staten Island, the last place she'd lived before moving, another place rich in potholes and barking dogs.

In some ways, cities were the same. Some things, she figured, you couldn't leave behind, no matter how far away you went or how strange a city you picked. Unless you left people behind, too, and Maureen figured she wasn't ready for that quite yet. She wanted another shot at life before she struck out for the yawning wastelands and built her Unabomber shack.

The night before Maureen had left for New Orleans, as he'd driven away from her mother's house, Derek had cranked the car stereo, blasting some classic number by one of those '80s hair bands he liked and knew she didn't—one thing she definitely wouldn't miss about him was screwing to the romantic musings of Mötley Crüe.

As she headed up the stairs from the foyer to the kitchen, her mother popped the cork on a new bottle of wine. Maureen was happy that Amber drank less wine these days. She was also happy that Amber finally drank decent if unspectacular bottled wine and no longer defended those shameful tragedies that came in a box. And, of course, Amber never hesitated to share.

Maureen pulled out a chair and sat at the kitchen table.

"Did you tell him?" Amber asked, her back to her daughter as she poured two glasses of white at the kitchen counter. When Maureen didn't answer, she glanced over her shoulder, skeptical eyebrows raised. "You didn't, did you? Christ, Maureen, you're leaving tomorrow."

Amber brought the wine to the table.

"Ma, it's not that easy," Maureen said, reaching for her glass. "I'm trying to pick the right time." She tilted her head, raised her glass. "And now, it does appear that time has run out."

Amber's eyebrows arched high on her forehead as she took the seat across the table from her daughter. "MMM-hmmm. As soon as you decided to move, as soon as you got into the academy in New Orleans, those weren't good times?" Her stern gaze softened, and she reached across the table to cover her daughter's hand with one of her own. "I'm not saying this to be mean, but—"

"Here we go."

Amber hesitated, as if rethinking what she had planned to say.

Maureen knew it was an act. Just get on with it, she thought.

"You are doing to Derek," Amber said, "what your father did to us."

"That's ridiculous," Maureen said. "And you know it. Derek and I aren't married. We don't have a kid. We're nothing like you and Dad. We're certainly not in love. Not even a little bit."

"Thank the Lord for small favors," Amber said. "But what you're doing isn't right."

"We've been dating for a few months," Maureen said. "I hardly know the guy."

Amber raised her hand. "What this boy lets you get away with."

"He had a good time. He knows what he's doing."

Maureen was not about to admit to her mother that, in truth, Derek had dumped her not an hour earlier, only minutes before she'd had the chance to tell him she was moving away for good. He'd dumped her, in fact, while she had her hand in his pants. Did it get any worse than that? They'd taken a walk in the neighborhood, over by her old grammar school. She'd backed him into a dark doorway behind the playground, where she'd planned on giving him a quick farewell blow job to ease his passing into her history. Before she'd even gotten him out of his jeans, he'd started in with how he knew she was using him, how he knew that her heart wasn't in their relationship. He'd let her have it pretty good, actually.

Maureen had been so stunned by the turn of events that she'd almost started defending herself, forgetting for a moment that she was leaving town forever in less than twelve hours. Not the kind of story you share with Mom, no matter how unfair she was being.

"You don't care about Derek any more than I do," Maureen said. "You've been against this move from the beginning."

"That's me," Amber said, waving a dismissive hand, "ridiculous old

Mom. Against everything her daughter wants, all the time. I live to punish you."

"Don't make this personal. It's not personal."

Amber gazed around the kitchen, her mouth hanging open in exaggerated shock. "Don't make it personal? Maureen, you're my only child, you're moving fourteen hundred miles away. You're *all* my family. What's *not* to take personal? Like father, like daughter, I guess."

"That's friggin' cruel, Ma. I'm not like him. That's not fair."

Amber raised her eyes to the heavens, entreating the divine powers. "Jesus, Mary, and Joseph." She looked again at Maureen, meanness in her eyes. "I always thought you were more Fagan than Coughlin. Like your grandmother, like me. Maybe I was wrong about that. I hope not."

"You always do this," Maureen said, struggling with her temper. "You get so mean."

Her move was hard on her mom. Maureen knew this. And when Amber hurt, when she really hurt, she struck to kill, fierce and quick as a rattler. Maureen knew this, too. She'd grown up with it. Her mother's lashing out wasn't, Maureen thought, recalling her own admonishments, personal. But, damn, it was hard not to take it that way.

"You always try to get me with Dad leaving us," Maureen said, "when you can't argue logic. And you turn cruel, and you stop making sense, like what the hell's Nana Fagan got to do with this conversation?"

"You remember Grandpa Fagan?"

"No."

"Me neither. Not well."

"So . . . what does that mean? What are you saying? Grandpa left Grandma like Dad left you. This is not news. It's got nothing to do with the current conversation. You're completely illogical, Ma."

"What's logical about a thirty-year-old woman becoming a police officer in the most dangerous, backward city in the country, when that woman already lives in the safest big city in the world, protected by the greatest police force ever? Where she'd be a legacy, sort of? Where she could stay home?"

Maureen couldn't hold back a giggle. "Greatest police force ever? You know what you sound like?"

Amber crossed her arms tight across her chest. "This oughtta be good."

"You sound like a woman whose boyfriend is a cop."

"Ex-cop," Amber said. "And you didn't answer my question. What's wrong with New York? What's wrong with staying right here? You grew up here."

"My point exactly," Maureen said.

"But it's not personal."

Maureen drank down her wine in two big gulps. "You already know the answers. There's nothing wrong with New York. There's nothing wrong with you. I love New York. I always will. You know the problem is me, the things I've done here. They make life here, make moving on here . . . difficult. Impossible, really."

"It's a big city," Amber said. "People forget."

"When?" Maureen asked. "When I'm thirty-five, when I'm forty? My life is already starting way too late. And what about me? When do I get to forget?"

"It's been less than a year."

"I have no control over my life here."

"You're a hero for what you did," Amber said.

Maureen shook her head. "So you say. So say the girls in my kickboxing class who have figured it out some. I don't feel like a hero. I feel like a complete wreck."

"That SOB got what he had coming."

"That one night, it's all I am anymore. And I'm not talking about other people. I'm talking about me."

"If more people like you had badges and guns," Amber said, "this world would be a better place."

"That's nice of you to say." Maureen grinned. "So I'll start with making New Orleans a better place and go from there. They can use the help."

"Good luck with that," Amber said. "I've been Googling, you know. I can do that now. I figured it out. Well, Nat taught me. Murder, drugs, poverty, corruption. And that's just the police department. New Orleans sounds like some third-world empire. I don't understand the appeal for you, I really don't."

"They need me down there."

Amber raised her hands in surrender. "I'm done trying to talk sense into you. You always did do whatever you wanted no matter what anyone else said. Go clean up. Nat'll be home from his walk soon. He's bringing pizza."

"I thought he started walking to lose more weight."

"Then don't eat it," Amber said. "Have some more rice cakes or whatever."

Maureen laughed out loud. "Ma, I've never eaten a rice cake in my life."

"I know," Amber said, her cheeks flushed. "This talk of leaving, it makes me emotional. I don't know what I'm saying. You're going away. I hate it."

"You're coming to my graduation in June, right? We talked about this. You guys said you'd come."

"We're coming," Amber said. "I promise we are. I don't have anything against New Orleans as a place. I just don't understand wanting to live there."

"You don't have to live there," Maureen said. "I do."

Amber pushed up from the kitchen table. "A cop in New Orleans. Christ Almighty, where did I go wrong? Why not just run for sheriff of Atlantis?"

4

The next afternoon, standing on the hot sidewalk a few blocks up Washington from the Garvey Apartments, Maureen set her coffee on the roof of the patrol car. She lifted her ponytail and pulled it tighter, hoping to catch a breeze up from the river or down from the lake on the back of her neck. No such luck. The August sun broiled her bare nape, her forehead and forearms. The cooking would continue until the daily late-afternoon thunderstorms arrived. She checked the skies. Not yet. Nothing but that hot white ball bleaching the blue out of the sky. The storms wouldn't bring much of a break, anyway, not this late in the summer, early August. After the rains, she and Preacher patrolled an outdoor sauna instead of an oven. Six of one . . .

She pressed her sunglasses into place with her finger, touched the tender spot on her cheek. Through his bulletproof counter glass, the store owner had offered to make a fresh pot of coffee for her. Maureen declined. When she had tried paying for the coffee, he had noticed her cheek and offered her ice. She'd declined that, too. The bruise was yesterday's wound; no need for ice. She worked her jaw from side to side. By her next shift the mark would be gone.

Sweat now tickling her collarbone, Maureen wished she'd taken the ice from the store owner for her temples and her throat, or for the back of her neck. She sipped her coffee, burning her tongue. Even in this brutal heat, she preferred a fermented cup of burnt Community. As with good bourbon, she wanted to really feel it going down. Only one thing was missing.

"Preach, I'm gonna smoke one before we move on."

Preacher sat behind the wheel, tapping with fat fingers at the laptop anchored beside him on the front seat. His postshift cigar peeked up from the pocket of his blue uniform shirt. "Knock yourself out."

Maureen set her coffee back on the car roof. She pulled the pack from her pocket and lit up. "You having any luck with that number?"

Preacher, who was frowning at the laptop screen, didn't look at her. "Powerball's not till tomorrow."

"Not the lottery," Maureen said. "That phone number, from the Garvey Apartments thing. Did you get through to dispatch? Find out if that nine-one-one call really came from Apartment D?"

Preacher looked at her. "I was gonna do that? Why would I do that?"

Maureen took a long drag of her cigarette, releasing the smoke, dragonlike, from her nose before she spoke. "We were gonna find out who made the call. See if the call was a setup."

Preacher shook his head. "I passed the idea along to Quinn. He seemed to think it was a good one."

"Quinn? Why give that tip to him? Double-checking that call was my idea."

"And it's a good one," Preacher said, "but it wasn't your bust. You didn't find the stash and the guns, Quinn and Ruiz did. The detective and the DA handling that case will be talking to them about it."

"What about me?"

"What about you? If Jackson gets indicted for whacking his baby momma in the nose, then the DA will give you a call. I wouldn't hold my breath on that. They've got a lot more on him now. Just move on."

"That's not fair," Maureen said. "I took a punch on that bust. Quinn and Ruiz just cleaned up after me. They had it handed to them."

"Sounds fair to me," Preacher said. "They shouldn't have been cleaning up after you in the first place. There shouldn't have been a mess."

Maureen turned her back on the car, took a few steps away from it. She was furious with Preacher, mostly because he was right. She'd let a manageable situation explode in her face. She had to let it go. After the shift, she'd find Quinn or Ruiz and offer her help. She'd show she could be a team player. She crushed her cigarette out beneath her boot and returned to the car.

Before climbing back into the cruiser, she glanced across the street. She almost dropped her precious coffee. What she saw had to be a joke.

Across the street from where she stood, not thirty feet away, a man worked hard with a screwdriver to muscle open the hood of a parked car. In broad daylight. Right in the middle of Washington Avenue. Right in front of LaSalle Park. Was this guy serious? Did he not see the blue-and-white cruiser parked across the street from him? Or did he just not care?

Maureen stepped around the cruiser, off the curb, and into the gutter, frowning behind her sunglasses. She looked closer at the guy working the car. She knew him. She'd arrested him before. Last week. For burglarizing the same car he worked on now. Unreal. She searched her memory for his name. It was in there somewhere. Repeat offenders, she chided herself, are the people you need to remember.

She backed up to the patrol car and leaned down into the open driver's side window. "You see this?"

Maureen knew Preacher felt her stare, but he refused to look away from the computer.

"You're seeing this, right?" she said. "Across the street?"

Preacher didn't respond. Because he wouldn't look, she knew he'd seen.

"Tell me you see this," Maureen said, standing and rolling her shoulder, vest sitting heavy and crooked on her frame. Sweat trickled

down her spine. She was gonna be one of those cops that gave up wearing the vest, she could tell already.

"I ain't seeing nothing," Preacher said, "except the clock." He patted his cigar pocket. "And that says our shift ends in an hour, which means it speaks a lot louder than you, louder like the fucking bells of Saint Vincent's, so I don't hear nothing, either. You got reports to write."

Like a father he sounded, telling her she couldn't go outside until she finished her homework.

"We can't let this go," Maureen said. "Half the street's lookin' at us. People see me seeing it, right now, as we're standing here. What're they gonna think when we let this go? I mean, Preach, sir, we're coming outta the doughnut shop, for chrissakes."

If I get in the car now, Maureen worried, they're going to think I'm afraid of getting hit again. Word would circulate. Talk like that would only make the next guy she had to brace more anxious to throw down. With the drugs, the booze, the panic, and the friggin' heat, nobody needed any additional inspiration. One surprise that had come in the academy: being a woman made her getting hit more likely, not less.

Preacher raised a finger in the air, his eyes glued to the laptop as if crucial information crawled across the screen.

"Correction," he said, tipping his finger in her direction. "You are coming out of the corner store, which is really a po'boy shop and grocery by the way, and if you wanna be a detective someday you really oughtta get more observational, not to mention learn the local lingo, but anyone looking at us and seeing you is probably thinking, I hope to God that girl bought herself a sandwich while she was in there 'cause she sure could use it.

"In general, I wouldn't worry what anyone in this neighborhood is thinking about us. Opinions are beyond salvage levels. Believe."

"That's harassment," Maureen said, amusement creeping into her voice, "making jokes about my weight."

She glanced across the street. The man had the hood open. He was leaning into the engine.

"You're skinny," Preacher said. "What's the world coming to when telling a woman she's skinny gets to be harassment? The truth is harassment now? You know what, Coughlin? Look in the glove box. The sexual-harassment complaint forms are in there. Right under the map to someone who gives a fuck. You make no sense to me sometimes."

"Help me out here, Preach."

"You're fat, Coughlin. That better? Get your fat cottage-cheese ass in the car, please. You're lettin' the AC out."

"Officer Boyd."

"Coughlin, please, we got shit to do. Like go home in one piece. How many times you wanna get hit this week?"

"That man is stealing."

"So he is," Preacher said. "And so he was yesterday and the day before that. You know what's on his calendar for tomorrow, rook? Fucking stealing. I guarantee it. Leave us some crime for tomorrow. I need this job."

The man had now attracted an audience of three young boys. The drummer boy and his two friends from yesterday. Perfect, Maureen thought. She wanted to talk to them anyway. She wanted to hear what Drummer Boy had wanted to say to her and Preacher. She wanted to know about the whistler. This incident was shaping up into a real opportunity; she had to take advantage.

"I'm going over," Maureen said. "You coming?"

"Fuck me," Preacher said, tapping a few computer keys. "Yeah, yeah. I'm right behind you. You are a slow learner, Coughlin."

Maureen checked the traffic then started slowly across the street.

The perp was another thin, middle-aged black man, this one wearing baggy gray Dickies and a filthy white T-shirt. He was tall, close to six-six. They haunted the neighborhood like disconsolate teenagers, men like this one. Men like Arthur Jackson the baby-momma beater, ranging in age from thirty-five to fifty-five, bored and sullen, conditioned to violence and insult, dishing out and enduring both from all directions as regular the summer thunderstorms. The shit that had happened yesterday, it was happening today, it would happen again tomorrow. They had records of petty crimes that went on forever. They knew cops, city attorneys, criminal court judges, and, if they had kids, civil court judges by their first names.

Maureen had attended a handful of Preacher's court dates at the Broad Street courthouse, from arrests he'd made before her time. The hearings came off like office reunions. The cops, the crooks, the lawyers, everyone knew one another. The proceedings were convivial, the participants re-signed to their roles. The scene reminded Maureen of a movie she and her mother had watched about a pro wrestler, the part about how even the sworn enemies in the ring were actually friends behind the scenes, everyone with his part to play so the show could go on and the paying customers went home satisfied.

The man's name popped into her head: Norman Wright. She could see it on the arrest report. She'd filled it out herself.

Wright hunched under the open hood of an old green Plymouth. The screwdriver lay on the pavement at his feet. He was elbow-deep in the engine, twisting and yanking at something, grunting with the effort, as if trying to jerk a resistant weed from a garden. Involved in his work, he had his back to the street. He didn't see Maureen approaching.

The boys stood close together on the sidewalk, their backs against the park fence, watching him work. They didn't warn him of Maureen's approach. Letting her catch him unawares made for a better show. Maureen nodded at the kids. The boys smiled, mugging for her, trying to make her laugh and give herself away to Wright. One put his finger to his lips, making Maureen think of see, hear, and speak no evil.

"Mr. Wright," Maureen called out. "Officer Coughlin, on your six."

Wright shot up at the sound of her voice, smashing his head on the Plymouth's hood so hard his knees and hips gave out halfway on impact. Arms out for balance, he staggered away from the car in a twisty dance step. Maureen almost rushed to catch him, but Wright corrected himself well and turned, easing his weight back against the Plymouth's grille as if he'd intended every move he'd made. He crossed his long arms, trying to look casual. He smiled, but his eyes watered from the blow to his head. His dry, flaky knuckles bled from his work inside the engine.

"Officer, good to see you again," Wright said. "Call me Norman."

"I'd rather not," Maureen said, hooking her thumbs in her gun belt, a habit she knew she'd picked up from TV. She couldn't help it. She stayed aware of the screwdriver.

"Ooooooooooh, snap," piped in one of the kids, his chin shiny from the orange drink that he'd also dribbled down his T-shirt. He belched a puppy belch. "She said, 'Fuck you, Norman.'"

"Do you have to talk that way?" Maureen said. She'd grabbed some napkins with her coffee, for the two ounces she knew she'd spill in the patrol car. She pulled those napkins from her pocket and handed them to the orange-drink kid. "Who's teaching you manners?"

The drummer's friends shrugged. They glanced at each other, then looked back at Maureen as if she'd started stuttering and they were waiting for her to form intelligible words. Neither took the napkins.

"Well, nigga," the other kid finally said, "wipe your face." He winked at Maureen. He actually winked. And, though she knew better, it was everything she could do not to smile. This one was taller, Maureen noticed, and seemed a little older than the drummer and the orange-drink kid. "You hafta excuse him, Officer. He's half retard and half crackhead."

"Am not," Orange Drink said, but he took the napkins and did as he was told.

"And the other half is plain stupid."

Orange Drink tilted his chin up in Maureen's direction for inspection.

She gave a nod of approval, and Orange Drink tossed the fistful of dirty napkins in the gutter. Maureen growled. The drummer stepped forward and picked up the napkins. He handed them to Maureen. She thanked him.

"Boys, I'm Officer Coughlin," she said. "You're gonna be seeing a lot ῀ ῀e around the neighborhood. We should get to know each other. Tell ῀"

The boys glanced at one another, then looked back at her, their expressions sphinxlike. Blue uniform, Maureen thought. White skin. Progress would be slow. Another day. Wright was her concern.

"Beat it," she said. "Go find the playground. And watch your mouths from now on."

The taller kid punched Orange Drink in the arm, hard, and took off running down the street, his victim on his heels in pursuit.

"I'm gonna remember your faces," Maureen yelled after them.

The drummer, silent this whole time, lingered. A serious look frowned up his long face. He studied Maureen the way a kid might study an exotic zoo animal. He seemed pretty fearless, at least when it came to cops. She threw a quick glance up and down the street, looking for the teenager with the shell necklace. No sign of him.

"What am I gonna do with you guys?" Maureen asked him. "We're gonna be sharing this neighborhood. We should help each other out."

"Officer," he said, "don't hate the playas, hate the game."

"And what's your name, playa?"

The kid lifted his chin at Wright. "Please lock up this here sorry-ass nigger for good, 'fore he get himself kilt for messin' with Bobby Scales's whip. He *been* told."

"Don't you worry about what I been told," Wright said to the kid, "or what I ain't been told. You don't know."

Bobby Scales, Maureen thought. Okay. Not a name she'd heard before, but one worth knowing, obviously. It was important enough that this kid assumed that she, being a cop, already knew it. Mr. Marley in the shell necklace? She didn't want to ask straight up and give away the fact that she didn't know the name.

"I'm just sayin'," the drummer said. "Mr. Bobby and his boys be out here fucking with it under the hood early most *every* morning lately. Piece of shit don't ever run, but he out here tryin'."

"What're you doing out early every morning?" Maureen asked. "Helping with the car?"

The kid shrugged and turned to walk away, his parting words cast over his shoulder, dismissive, as he picked up his pace. "People that know shit *know* Bobby."

The kid was half a block away before she realized she hadn't asked who had called to him from across the street, or if he knew who'd called the cops on Arthur Jackson and his woman. And he hadn't answered a thing that she had remembered to ask. She hadn't even learned his name. Outwitted, she thought, by a twelve-year-old. Yup. Undercover. Detective. Super-fucking-intendent. She was ready.

Could she at least remember seeing someone working on that old Plymouth?

She saw cars worked on at curbs throughout the neighborhood. She hadn't noticed this particular car, or anyone paying particular attention to it, other than Wright. Good job being observational, she thought. The neighborhood was a busy one. People were on the streets most of the night and day. Lots of people didn't work. A lot of them worked nights or odd hours, like she had for over a decade. People spent considerable time outside, working on cars or houses, hanging out in the front yard, talking, grilling, playing dice, cards, and dominoes.

To the untrained eye, the neighborhood looked chaotic, but most people did the same things every day. They tended to the same flower bed, worked on the same old beater in the driveway outside the house. Played the same games with the same friends. Maureen knew she needed to see the particular neighborhood patterns. Without knowing those patterns, she'd never notice the aberrations.

Wright watched, shaking his head as the drummer jogged up the street after his friends, throwing one last glance at Maureen over his shoulder.

"You know those boys?" Maureen asked.

"Neighborhood brats," Wright said. "It's a damn shame, what's happened with kids these days. No respect."

"This is your idea of setting an example? Stealing engine parts in broad daylight?"

"Wright's jaw dropped. "Officer, what are you talking about? That's just

"Is it?"

"This is my cousin's car. I was about to bring the battery over to the auto parts store so they could match it up with a new one and get rid of this one, as this here one has run out."

"Step aside for a sec," Maureen said. Wright shimmied to the corner of the front fender. Maureen looked into the engine. "This battery in here is brand new."

"You would think that," Wright said, "to look at it. But it's a lemon."

Maureen straightened. "'Scuse me?"

Behind her, across the street, she heard a storm door thrown open. She backed away from the Plymouth, keeping an eye on Wright but bringing the doorway into her peripheral vision. A tiny black woman, rail thin and maybe five feet, wearing a blue caftan and a matching head wrap, stepped out her front door and onto her small concrete stoop. She settled into a rickety lawn chair and lit a long white cigarette. She stared hard at Maureen and Wright as she smoked.

Mother Mayor. The doyenne of Washington Street. Preacher had pointed her out on day one of Maureen's training. Fantastic.

Maureen wished she'd listened to Preacher and stayed in the car. Had she done so, she'd be taking a cool shower back at the district by now instead of standing in the hot street getting eye-fucked for doing her job by the self-anointed neighborhood watchdog. And Maureen knew that Mother's neighbors, people passing in and out of the corner store, people in the park, they watched her, judging and assessing her. The new cop. The new girl. She had to come strong in front of the block. Had to. Because if she didn't, the next time she came around looking for something, she'd get ignored, or worse. Hell, maybe even Preacher was paying attention. She had to impress him, too.

"Why you harassin' this innocent *black* man?" Mother Mayor demanded loud and clear from across the street. For a small person, she had a resounding voice.

Maureen held a hand up high against the interruption, regretting it right away.

"Oh no, you didn't," Mother Mayor said. "I axed you a question. I seen him nearly fall over. You hit him like you did Mr. Arthur?"

Maureen's head snapped around. "Oh, you *saw* that? So then you saw him hit me first. We're looking for witnesses to that event. I need to come over there and talk to you? Maybe you can tell me whose stash that was we took. I'll be right over when I'm done here."

Mother Mayor said nothing. She hadn't seen a damn thing at the apartments. She didn't move well, and rarely left her stoop, as far as Maureen could tell.

"Yeah, that's what I thought," Maureen said. She threw a glance at the patrol car. Fucking Preacher. Couldn't he at least go over there and keep Mother Mayor occupied? "Please, ma'am, give me a minute."

She turned back to Wright. "This is Bobby Scales's car and everyone knows it. He works on it all the time. He's gonna kill you for messing with it again."

Wright huffed and puffed, trying to decide which of Maureen's claims to disavow. He looked to Mother Mayor, hoping that she'd raise a ruckus and come to his rescue. "Why would you say stuff like that? Call me a liar and all? You believe them brats over me? You hear this, Mother Mayor?"

"'Cause you are a liar," Maureen said. "Last week I caught you stealing out of this same car."

"Naw."

"Yeah," Maureen said. "And I arrested you for it. The reason there was a new battery in it last week is because you stole the old one the week before. Officer Quinn busted you for *that*. Three times in this car now that's not yours to be in."

"Naw."

"So you're calling me a liar?" Maureen said, stepping closer to Wright. "That wasn't you I arrested last week? You knew me when I walked up to you just now. It ain't from the library. You calling me a liar or you calling me stupid?"

"I ain't calling you nothin'."

"I didn't think so."

Maureen turned to Mother Mayor, who from her chair had watched the arrest last week, roaring about the injustice of it to anyone who'd listen. "What about you, Mother? Anything to add while we're at it?"

Mother Mayor leaned forward in her chair, wrapping her hands around the stoop railing, narrowing her eyes at Maureen. Even from across the street, Maureen could see the wheels turning in the old woman's brain. Mother Mayor was loud, she was dramatic, and she was racist, but she wasn't stupid. She took pride in being an irritant, and because of her sex, her size, and her age, she could say things other people could not. Might even provide a public service that way, Maureen thought. She gave voice to things other people might think and feel but would never and could never say. But, as Preacher had told Maureen, Mother Mayor never filed formal complaints, never put her name on anything. She took care not to make real enemies of the police. Not when she, or some niece or cousin or neighborhood kid, might need a cop's help someday.

Cover Your Ass. It wasn't just the rule in the NOPD. It played in the neighborhood, too.

If she wanted info about the Garvey Apartments, Maureen thought, Mother Mayor was the person she needed to talk to. Of course, that meant she needed to be nice to the old bat.

"It's my job," Mother Mayor said, "to keep track of who you arrest around here?"

She dropped her half-smoked cigarette into a soda can, shook it, and rose from her chair. "If you can't keep count your own selves, maybe that's something y'all need to think about. I know we all look the same to you."

Mother Mayor disappeared back into her house with a loud slam of the storm door.

Wright groaned with disappointment. There's an interesting turn, Maureen thought. Mother was not monitoring Wright's arrest all the way through. Why abandon him? Mother wasn't falling over impressed with the new skinny white-girl cop, that was for sure. Wright was on the outs with Mother, then. What had he done to get there?

Wright blew out a long sigh, scratching at his forearms, his ragged nails leaving gray trails on his dark brown skin. One thing was for sure, Maureen thought. No point in asking Wright, whose attention was waning and whose eyes were glazing over, what he'd done wrong.

Maureen knew he had planned on having that battery boosted and sold by now, probably at the body-and-rim shop a few blocks away. She had fucked that up. He was itching in places much more demanding than his arms. He would soon go from frustrated and impatient to desperate to stupid. Just like Arthur of Apartment D had done. She had about another minute and a half to make use of being the lady officer before Wright's need for a fix transformed her into *that bitch cop*. She couldn't let things turn violent again. She did not need another bruised black man in cuffs on her record.

Behind Maureen, a *whoop-whoop* from the patrol car. Okay, so Wright wasn't the only one on the block getting itchy and impatient. Preacher wanted his cigar.

Wright turned, assuming the position against the front of the Plymouth. Maureen left her cuffs on her belt. Play this one different, she thought. This wasn't Arthur Jackson: The Sequel. Wright hadn't hurt anyone, hadn't even threatened anyone. Why not show some smarts, show the flex and discretion that she hadn't shown the day before? Here was an opportunity, right away, to show Preacher that she'd heard his message, that she was growing up as a cop. No punches, no blood, no drama. Rookie or not, sore cheek or not, she was a better cop, a smarter cop, than that. She'd prove it to Preacher and the neighborhood at the same time.

And then they could all go home and have a cold bath and a big whiskey and chain-smoke half a pack over a day well spent and a job well done.

Okay, maybe that last part was just her.

"Turn around and face me," she said to Wright. He did so. "You can't treat Bobby's ride like your own personal ATM. It's not legal. It's not safe. I can't look away when you do it. I can't ask other cops to look away. What if you get one grumpier than me? One who doesn't know you? And don't think Scales can keep looking away, either. Don't think he doesn't know."

"You *told* him?" Wright asked, showing real fear. "How could you do me like that?"

"Tell on you?" Maureen asked. "Why would I . . . What is this, fourth fucking grade?"

She reached into her pocket, pulled out the change from her coffee. Three crumpled ones. Not a lot of flex for her to work with.

"What're the body shop guys gonna do when they find out you're putting them on the wrong side of Bobby Scales? Or when they find out you and your stolen goods led me to them, with detectives in tow for a peek at their inventory? Don't look shocked, I'm a troublemaker that way. What if Bobby misses when he shoots at you and hits one of those kids? Or Mother Mayor?"

"Aw, that's low down."

Maureen raised her shoulders, her hands in the air, as if daring Wright to contest the truth of what she'd said.

"Stop stealing," she said, slipping Wright the bills from her pocket. "At least for today."

Wright tucked the money into the pocket of his pants as smooth and quick as if he'd picked the bills out of someone else's pocket. It was the only graceful motion he'd made since Maureen had rolled up on him.

"Close the hood on the car," she said.

Wright did as he was told and stepped over to the sidewalk. He clasped his hands behind his back. He had to be eager to bolt now, Maureen thought, for the fix, or for whatever Plan B he had for scoring enough cash to get the fix, but because he had taken the money, he waited to be officially dismissed. Maureen realized that without even trying she had started cultivating her first informant. May as well put him right to work, she thought.

"Tell me what you know about Bobby Scales."

Wright rolled his shoulders, tried to gin up a charming grin. "C'mon, officer. What am I gonna know that you don't?"

"Humor me."

Wright took a deep breath. His eyes wandered over the block. "Due respect, but that ain't a three-dollar question. Know what I'm sayin'?"

"I'm good for more," Maureen said. "Down the road."

Wright laughed at her. He offered his wrists. "I'd rather go to fucking lockup."

Maureen believed him. He was, in his way, telling her at least some of what she wanted to know: Scales was dangerous. "One question, then. Within your pay grade. Does Scales wear a shell necklace and a white headband? He a big fan of Bob Marley?"

Wright shook his head. Maureen wasn't sure if the headshake was her answer or Wright's refusal to give one. She was out of cash. Because of Wright's need, her time with him was short. Considering his history, she thought, they'd cross paths again soon. She'd do better next time.

"This car," Maureen said. "It's off-limits. I don't ever want to see you so much as look at it again. Understand?"

Wright nodded, backing away down the sidewalk.

"Tell me you understand," Maureen said, following him, keeping within a few steps. She wanted him thinking she might still change her mind about busting him. "I don't wanna be out here, chalking you up some night."

"I got it," Wright said. "Don't worry about me. Forget about me. I never even liked that car." He turned and hustled away, headed in the same direction as the three kids. "Ain't nobody got to worry about me."

5

Maureen returned to the patrol car feeling like she wasn't getting her money's worth out of anybody. She wasn't entirely sure that Preacher, still planted in the driver's seat, had stayed awake during her encounter with Wright.

She grabbed her coffee off the roof and climbed into the car. "Thanks for nothing, Preach."

"What's gonna make you look tougher?" Preacher said, yawning. "Me huffin' and puffin' across the street, me screeching up in the car, lights and sirens wailing, or you handling things on your own? Which, by the way, you seem to have done admirably. I ain't got nothing to prove. I'm all about you, Coughlin. Your personal growth, your success. That's what matters here. That's how a partnership works."

Preacher hit the lights to make them some space and pulled the car out into traffic.

"I'm your training officer," he said. "I can't do the job for you. How will you learn if I'm always there to fall back on?"

Maureen lifted the lid on her coffee, sipped. It was cold. She flicked the lid onto the floor of the car, rolled down her window, ignoring Preacher's complaints about the heat, and dumped the coffee. She ground her teeth. Don't do it, she told herself. Don't send Preacher back to the boys' club griping about this moody bitch he got saddled with; don't give him that satisfaction.

She crushed the paper coffee cup in her fist and spiked it onto the floor. She left the window down, glaring across the car, daring Preacher to utter one more complaint. He didn't.

"Who's Bobby Scales?" Maureen said.

"Who's asking?"

"Me."

"He done something we need to know about?"

"I don't know. That's why I'm asking about him. His name came up back there."

Preacher sighed, shaking his head. "Make sure you go right to the top brass about this guy, they love a probie getting investigative right out of the academy. Especially about an auto burglary interruptus with no arrest."

Maureen bit her bottom lip, looked away. Punch your FTO, she reminded herself, and you're back to waiting tables. Swallow it. For now. He's like your period. He's temporary, necessary, and you'll be glad that it happened when it's over. Two more shifts. One, really, since this day was almost over. She could stand his foolishness for one more day.

"What?" Preacher asked. "Am I harassing you again? Was it the interruptus?"

"One of the kids mentioned Scales," Maureen said. "That was his Plymouth that Wright was messing with. For the third time. I'm thinking maybe Scales is the guy in the shell necklace, from yesterday."

"Because this necklace guy seems like the type to get intense over a beat-down Plymouth that's older than him?"

"Okay. No."

"Listen, I'm sure this Scales character is grateful to you for protecting his property," Preacher said. "It is your sacred appointed duty as an officer of the law. I'm sure he's dropping a thank-you card in the mail as we speak, but remember this, 'cause it'll save you a lot of time. Anyone we need to know out here, they will be revealed to us soon enough. They can't fucking help it. It's one of the great ironies of criminality types, they can't stay away from the cops."

They idled at the busy intersection of Louisiana and St. Charles, waiting for the red light to change. Maureen watched a legless black man in a wobbly wheelchair push himself through the crosswalk in the direction of the twenty-four-hour Rite Aid, his gray-whiskered lips working over toothless gums. An old foam daiquiri cup was jammed in his crotch, the cup's edges chewed. She knew there were dollar bills squashed into the bottom.

That beat-down Plymouth, she thought, was not the car of a man who wanted people thinking him dangerous. Then again, Scales's name made Wright bad nervous. More nervous than he'd gotten over her. Of course, Maureen would only take him to jail, which was another day in the life. Scales, on the other hand, might stomp his sorry ass over the car. Because Scales could whip some ass, that didn't make him a criminal. And who in the neighborhood, on either side of the law, didn't scare a thieving junkie like Wright? He lived his whole life afraid.

"Do me a favor," Maureen said, "and turn the car around."

"What for?"

"I want to talk to Mother Mayor. Five minutes, tops. A couple of quick questions."

"What makes you think that woman will even open her door if you come knocking?"

"How am I gonna know if I don't try?"

"Questions about what?" Preacher asked. "We established that Apartment D is not your gig. You missed your chance with that. Live with it."

"She acted funny when I was talking to Wright," Maureen said. "She gave me practically no shit."

"So you've got Mother all figured, after five weeks on the job. Congrats."

He shook his head. "Don't be vague with me, Coughlin. Save the mystery shit for your boyfriend."

"I'd like to see what she knows about Scales, about the car, maybe."

"And if the subject of Apartment D comes up, well, so be it." Preacher looked at her across the car. "Am I right?" He cracked a smile. "You think I'm new at this? You're smart, and you're crafty, Coughlin. I like that about you, but you're still new."

"I swear on my brand-new badge," Maureen said, raising her right hand, "that anything I learn about Apartment D, should the subject even come up, I will deliver willingly and joyfully to Quinn and Ruiz. I want to find out about Scales, and find out who that drummer kid is. I still think he's got something on his mind."

"About Apartment D?" Preacher asked.

Maureen shrugged. "That is where he first approached us."

The light turned green. The legless man was only halfway across the street. A driver a few cars back leaned on his horn. Maureen told herself the honker couldn't see the cause for the holdup: thus his behavior. He leaned on his horn again, this time longer. Maureen tensed, her hand drifting for the door handle. She could enlighten the impatient motherfucker as to the cause of the delay. She hated that shit. The selfishness. Because this prick and his car and his legs had somewhere to be. Didn't everybody? Her ticket book sat on the cruiser's dash. She had a mind to make Mr. Selfish a few minutes later and a few dollars lighter. Because of who she was now, she could do something about people like him. Right, she thought. As if that asshole was any more reachable than Norman Wright. As if he'd act differently in this situation the next time. He'd blame her, and the guy in the wheelchair. The horn again. But that didn't mean she wouldn't enjoy breaking his balls.

Before Maureen could make her move, Preacher hit the light bar and the honking stopped.

"It's a great way to shut people up," Preacher said. "Especially minor people not worth getting out of the car for. Those lights have power. More than the badge, more than the gun, I think sometimes. You get out of the car with your ticket book, that shitheel will cry all over you about not knowing what he did wrong. But somehow, they always seem to know when the lights are for them."

He turned his eyes back to the road. The man in the wheelchair had stopped to fix his zipper. The police cruiser, lights going, shielded him from oncoming traffic. Cars squeezed by in the other lane.

"You ever had a dog?" Preacher asked. "A good dog that knows better? Say its name once, loud and sharp, and that's enough. A smart dog knows when it's fucking up. The lights work like that. The master's voice. Just another valuable tidbit for you. They come fast and furious sometimes."

Maureen watched two teenage boys in matching Xavier Prep polo shirts help the legless man, zipper difficulties corrected, thank God, maneuver his wheelchair onto the sidewalk. They turned away, though, returning to the bus stop when he started talking to them, smiling and shaking his cup.

The old man safely landed, Preacher waited one more beat, as if daring another blast of the horn. He slowly rolled the patrol car into the intersection. Cars passed them now on either side, the drivers throwing dirty looks their way. She wasn't used to it yet, Maureen decided, the public identity she now carried out into the streets every day. Nor had she adjusted to people hating her on sight because of that identity. She lived now with a new form of bigotry—everyone in that blue uniform was the same, and that one part of them, the uniform, trumped everything else, as if *cop* were a race and not a job.

Preacher palmed the wheel, whistling Led Zeppelin's "Kashmir" while making an illegal left through the busy intersection and onto St. Charles.

Maureen craved a cigarette. "I need another cup of coffee."

"That high-octane shit you like," Preacher said, "that they make with the espresso maker. The grocery on Sixth is where you get it?"

"They close at six," Maureen said. "It's five after."

"They'll do it for us," Preacher said.

"No. I hate doing that. I used to—"

"Yeah, you used to wait tables," Preacher said. "Yeah, you've mentioned that a time or two. But that ain't you no more. That badge on your chest, don't tell me you wear it for the salary. That's the case, you must've been a shitty waitress. Let's get you one of those nuclear coffees. On me. But you gotta go in and get it. And spot me a bag of Zapp's for the ride back to the station."

"Okay, yeah, yeah," Maureen agreed, mostly to shut him up.

So she'd let him let her get herself a coffee. When she was in the service industry, she'd stayed late, done extra for cops, for firefighters, and for vets. It was a thing you did. It was neighborhood etiquette. Having cops hanging around at closing time when the cash was being counted was a good thing. It hadn't stopped being a good thing because she was the cop and no longer the one wearing the apron. And this was her neighborhood now.

"After we get coffee, before we go to the station," Maureen said, "can we go back to Mother Mayor's?"

"Tomorrow," Preacher said. "Shift's over at seven and we got paperwork."

"It's practically on the way."

"Tomorrow, Coughlin. I said tomorrow. People need our paperwork so *they* can go home. Night tour needs the car. Show some respect for the system."

Maureen said nothing, chewing her bottom lip as she gazed out the window. Bobby Scales was just a name, not an immediate danger or an impending threat. She could let it go till tomorrow. She glanced over at Preacher. As if she had a choice.

Traffic bunched on St. Charles and Preacher slowed the cruiser. Storm clouds were rolling in from across the river, weighing heavily on the city like Maureen's bulletproof vest weighed on her. The hot, heavy air filling the police car smelled of growth and decay, of what Maureen imagined might be the scent of dead flesh anointed with exotic oils, or some terminally ill harem girl, sick on the inside but gorgeous to the eyes and tasty on the tongue.

She slipped off her shades, wiped at the perspiration under her eyes with her fingertips.

Man, she thought, it's too fucking hot in this town. A deep inhalation told her she stank.

6

Late that night, frightened awake by nightmares, Maureen sat in bed, naked in the dark, chain-smoking, the red glow of her cigarette the only light in the room. She'd kicked the top sheet onto the floor, where it lay in a tangled ball. Despite the smoke, she could smell all around her the phantom scent of blood as fresh and strong in her nose as a puddle of spilled paint. She felt the imaginary blood slicking and sticking to her, like the sweat she wore at work these days as a second, liquid skin.

She didn't need to remember her nightmares to know what they were about.

When she awoke smelling blood, she had dreamed of Sebastian.

She pressed her back against the wall, splayed her legs out in front of her. The damp backs of her knees stuck to the bottom sheet in the heat. The window unit didn't work worth a damn unless she ran it all day and night on high, but then it rattled like an old bus. The blinds glowed in faint yellow squares from the streetlights outside, and she watched for shadows moving behind the blinds, her cell phone gripped tight in one fist.

Beads of perspiration trickled down between her breasts as she took deep, steady breaths. Opening the windows, with their screens full of holes, only let in mosquitoes. And those other things. The flying cockroaches. Loud as bottle caps hitting the windowpanes, flying around in the dark all night. It didn't help that the building's handyman stored the garbage cans right under her windows.

She could hear the roaches out there now, tapping like the fat fingers of someone trying to attract her to the glass.

Five blocks away, somewhere out on St. Charles Avenue, a streetcar rattled along the neutral ground. Uncanny, really, she thought, how those old trolleys could sound like the commuter trains that ran across Staten Island. Weird. Like spirits rattling their chains. She shivered. She felt too old to be afraid of the dark. She'd had a night-light once, a plastic lady-bug her father had given her, but she'd thrown it away long before she'd moved. What she really wanted to do was get out of bed and get her gun.

These days she either woke in the night terrified or woke in the morning halfway to furious. Sometimes she woke up like that for days on end. Some weeks, she wondered if her bed even had a right side to wake up on. It wasn't how she wanted to feel, and she hated the raw fury that swirled inside her. The rage was like a virus—she could feel the jagged-edged individual cells drifting around inside her veins. Most of the time she hated it. Sometimes she loved it. She wished it away and then lamented when it left, feeling empty inside to the point of tears.

At first, she had tried not to bring the bad feelings to work, but they proved too useful to leave home. The anger was like an engine humming inside her, a second, stronger heart. On the job, she could let her feelings run riot on the inside, she figured, as long as she controlled what she did, and as long as she controlled what she allowed other people to see. There were times she was good at all that, other times not so much.

She opened her cell. At some point in the night, Patrick had called. There was a message. She didn't listen to it. She had someone else on her mind right then. Two in the morning. That meant three a.m. back in New York. He might be up, might have his cell on and handy. He was as much an insomniac as Maureen. If he didn't answer, no harm done. She found his number and hit SEND. It took him only two rings to answer, as if he'd been waiting.

"Evening, Officer," Nat Waters said. "I had a feeling it was you."

"Am I that predictable?"

"Spend a few decades as a detective," Waters said, "and you learn some things about people."

"How's my mom?"

"She's good. She misses you."

Maureen heard the scrape of a fork across a plate. Faint voices in the background. Ah, the diner. She knew Waters had cut a slice of waffle with his fork and then swirled the slice in a pool of melted strawberry ice cream. They'd shared this meal often in the days before she'd left New York.

"She sleeps right through my nightly wanderings," Waters said. "It's a blessing for both of us."

"Mom knows you're eating waffles and ice cream at the Dove? This is allowed?"

"She pretends she doesn't, but she knows. And I pretend I'm getting away with it. I'm terrible with leaving evidence behind. She also knows there's worse things a man could be out doing than eating waffles and ice cream at the local diner. Long as I keep it to once or twice a month, the waffles, I mean, and don't talk much to the waitresses, she lets it slide."

Maureen tapped her fingers above her heart. "Just don't overdo it, for the sake of the ticker."

"I won't," Waters said. "I promise. How's work?"

She touched her cheek. "I had my first throw-down yesterday. Took a punch in the face."

"That's a big step." Maureen could see the smile lighting up his sad, droopy face in the bright diner. "You win?"

"What? Of course I fucking won."

Waters laughed at her. "Of course you did. That's my girl."

"Only needed one shot," Maureen said. "A right to the jaw." The hairs on her forearms stood up. *You shoulda seen me,* she wanted to say, feeling like a little girl just off the diving board and treading water in the deep end, foolish as it was. *You shoulda been there. You shoulda seen.* "Well, I only needed one shot after I took out his knee."

"What was the call?"

"Domestic," Maureen said. "He came through the front door at me, got a punch in."

"Weapon?"

"Nope."

"Lucky for you," Waters said.

"So I've been told. You sound like Preacher." Was she whining? She worried she was whining. There was no point to it; Waters always took Preacher's side, anyway.

"How's it going with him?"

"Same. He's got me writing tickets, writing reports till my fingers cramp. Forget bullet wounds. I have a better chance of getting carpal tunnel and paper cuts."

"I know you hate writing tickets," Waters said, "but you can make good collars with traffic stops. They're a valuable tool. Learn how to use them."

"Nat, he's killing me."

"I told you that you'd meet guys like Preacher. You gotta live with it. And you can learn from him. Guys like Preacher, they survive because they know the system and the politics. They know the people who are good to know. Keep him on your side. Do that, and you'll get to know those people, too."

"I don't want any part of that boys' club, or their politics," Maureen said. "That's not what I'm here for."

"You can't go from 'A' ball to the major leagues in five weeks. That's a good thing."

"Nat, I'm already thirty. I'd like to make Homicide before I'm fifty, for chrissakes. Writing tickets and babysitting road blocks at basketball games won't get me there."

"A smart cop uses every advantage," Waters said. "Like the treasure trove of information buried within her much more experienced training officer, for example. You got the badge on your own. You earned it one hundred percent. Top of the class. You're in the club now, take advantage of the privileges. You've *earned* them. I promise you, every other cop, including your future competition for Homicide, they're doing it right now."

"Everybody's doing it," Maureen said. "That's your justification? Are you serious? I can't waste any more time than I already have."

Waters laughed. "You haven't put any time *in* yet, Maureen. No time spent on the street with your eyes and ears open is wasted. Learn. You're a smart, capable, tough young woman. Once you pay your dues, you'll get fast-tracked up the pay grades. But you gotta put your time in. There's no shortcut around that."

"I don't care about rank," Maureen said, "and I don't care about pay grade. What I care about is the work, and I want to be Homicide."

"Then make sure your trip sheets are letter-perfect," Waters said.

"Paperwork. Christ, you're worse than Preacher."

"What good is a homicide cop," Waters said, "who can't get it right in court? And if it didn't happen in your paperwork, it didn't happen on the street. Them's the rules all over."

"Shift reports aren't homicide case files."

"No one's gonna let you near the second," Waters said, "unless you prove you can do the first. Like it or not, your department's a shambles. Unfortunate, but to your advantage. The fact that you're honest and can write in complete sentences makes you invaluable. Buy some ADA in a tie a drink, he'll tell you the same things."

Maureen's phone buzzed in her hand. "Hang on a second, Nat." She checked the screen. Work. In the middle of the night. That was weird. "Nat, let me call you back. There's another call." Without waiting for an answer, Maureen switched over. "Coughlin."

"Sergeant Willis, Sixth District. Officer Coughlin?"

She got out of bed and turned on the light in the ceiling fan. "Yes, sir, Sergeant?"

"Did you question a Norman Wright this afternoon? Black male, about forty-five years of age. In Central City."

"Yes, sir." She could see Willis at the night desk, her trip sheet from that afternoon in his hand. She thought of Waters and smiled. She was pretty sure she'd done everything right.

"About what?" the sergeant asked.

That was on the sheet, too, Maureen thought. A test, then. Wake her up in the middle of the night, see if she had her shit together.

"Suspected car burglary, sir. Nothing came of it. Minor neighborhood thing. If my report or my description of the incident needs adjusting, I'd be happy to take care of that."

Should she offer to come in now, hours before her next shift, or would that be too much? If Sergeant Willis had any feelings about her situation, he betrayed none.

"Officer Coughlin, your presence is requested at a crime scene in Central City. Intersection of Washington and Dryades." A pause. "Sound familiar?"

"Yes, sir." Very near where she'd confronted Wright.

"Report to Detective Sergeant Christine Atkinson. She's the rank on scene. You can go in plainclothes."

"Thank you, sir," Maureen said. "I'll be there in less than ten. Anything else I need to know?" Willis obviously did not enjoying playing messenger to a rookie, but Maureen couldn't bite her tongue. A detective, a *female* detective, was asking for her. Forget Preacher, now *that* was a useful connection. Her adrenaline was pumping hard. She was wide awake and fearless. "I haven't met her yet, is the detective sergeant property crimes or persons?"

"She works out of headquarters."

Maureen drew a blank. Then her heart dropped out of her chest. Headquarters. She'd messed up on something bigger than paperwork. What had she missed? Should she have arrested Wright? Was it Arthur Jackson? Had he returned to the apartments looking for payback? Or had she done more damage to him than she'd thought? She thought of Waters, of what had always been his greatest fear as a cop. "Internal affairs?"

An exasperated sigh from Willis. "Good Christ. And what the hell would the Public Integrity Bureau want with you? You're still in diapers. The detective sergeant is with Homicide. *They* operate out of HQ. PIB has a separate address. Wasn't that on the test? Unless you really loved data entry, get a move on, rookie."

Maureen snapped closed her phone, breathed a sigh of relief. She dropped to the floor and did a dozen push-ups to clear her head.

7

Maureen had to park her Honda a couple of blocks from where she'd spotted Wright that afternoon. The crime scene wasn't hard to find. The bright blue cruiser lights flashed over the cottages and shotguns lining this stretch of Washington, jeweling their front windows with blasts of sapphire. Within the clouds of blue, Maureen could see the white klieg lights and flashlight beams of the officers on the scene. Red flares burned in the street, a ruby trail of bread crumbs, or blood drops, leading to the cluster of lights. None of the neighborhood onlookers she passed said a word to her.

As she got closer to the corner, walking up the middle of Washington Avenue toward the flares, Maureen saw a small crowd gathered against the storefront of the locked-up grocery where she'd gotten her coffee yesterday. The crowd was mostly older men in ratty bucket hats and stained fedoras, forty-ounce bottles in their hands or at their feet. They wore their slacks loose and their plaid shirts buttoned high despite the heat. Their eyes shone like rain puddles in the orangey glow of the storefront's overhead lights as they watched Maureen approach.

A uniform she recognized from the weight room, a heavyset guy younger than her by five years maybe, walked out of the emergency lights and met her. He lifted the crime-scene tape so she could step under it.

Over her shoulder, he eyed the crowd by the store. "You're Coughlin. The new girl. Nice work on that fuckup Arthur Jackson."

"That's me." She didn't know the officer's name, couldn't read his name tag in the dark. The new girl? Had he really just called her that? She let it go. She put out her hand.

"Officer Maureen Coughlin. Pleased to meet you."

The uniform didn't shake her hand. He didn't state his name. "You can hang your badge on your belt." He grinned. "You know, wearing your ID at a crime scene, just a thought."

Maureen took out her badge, pleased that she'd be able to wear it. "Thanks for the tip."

"That way, those of us working tonight don't have to waste our time stopping you every ten feet." He jerked his thumb over his shoulder. "Atkinson is over there by the ambulance across the street. The Amazon blonde."

"Thanks again for all your help," Maureen said. Prick.

She spotted the detective sergeant standing by the back of the coroner's van, her hands in her pockets. Heading Atkinson's way, Maureen walked around the circle of red flares marking where the first cops on the scene had found the body. She counted three of the small numbered cones that marked where bullet casings had been recovered. The screen used to conceal the body from the public was gone, which meant the body was off the street and in the van. Inside the flare circle would be the chalk outline of the corpse. Maureen wondered about the first time she'd chalk up a body. Not something a normal person should look forward to, she thought.

Atkinson was a blonde, Maureen saw, and a light one, at that. Looked natural, too. Couldn't have helped her any on the way up, Maureen thought. Unreal how many men bought into that bullshit about blondes. The detective sergeant didn't extend her hand as Maureen approached. She crossed her arms over her chest.

"So you're Coughlin. I thought you'd be bigger."

Atkinson wore a brick-dust-red man's dress shirt with the sleeves rolled up over well-muscled, freckled forearms. A thin gold bracelet shone on her right wrist; no rings. She had huge hands. Her shirttails hung over ancient faded jeans. The jeans ended at a pair of battered cowboy boots. Maureen hadn't been in the South quite long enough, but the boots looked like alligator skin. Reptile, for sure. Even without her boots and the inches they added, Atkinson probably made six feet, easy. She wore no makeup. No earrings. She wore her gold shield on a chain around her neck.

"Yes. Sorry," Maureen said, as if it were her fault she stood shorter than Atkinson, who was by far the most intimidating cop Maureen had ever met. She resisted the urge to move her T-shirt hem away from her badge, to let it be better seen. She worried she was staring at Atkinson's shield.

"I mean, I thought you'd be bigger," Atkinson said, "for someone who put a woman-beater in an ambulance."

"Wow. You heard about that."

"I asked about you and was told. There's a difference. Now that I know about you, tell me about Norman Wright."

"Well, I saw him working on the hood of this old Plymouth. Green. Dirty. I don't see it now, but it was parked right around here at the time. I came over from across the street"—she turned and pointed to the grocery—"he had his back to me so I identified myself. Then I—"

"I said tell me about Norman Wright," Atkinson said. "Not about you. If I need to know more about you, I'll ask. Tell me about Norman Wright."

Maureen took a deep breath, reconsidering Atkinson's demands. She opened her mouth to start a physical description of Wright, but then the gears caught in her mind. That's not what Atkinson wants, either. "He's a drug addict. Heroin. A petty thief. That's his record, anyway. Theft and possession. Never got popped holding any weight. No kind of dealer. He seems . . . lost. Alone."

"Family?"

"He talked some about a cousin this afternoon, said it was the cousin's car, but I didn't buy it. I don't think he's homeless. He gave an address when we arrested him last week. I never checked up on it."

Maureen paused, thinking she should give Atkinson a chance to speak, to ask more questions. The detective said nothing. She had a stillness to her Maureen found unnerving.

"He shaves regularly," Maureen continued, the detail arriving by surprise, "even if he doesn't bathe much. I think maybe he shares a place around here, maybe with a couple other junkies. But then again I never did see him with anyone else around the neighborhood."

"You saw him often?"

"I guess I did." Maureen found she couldn't recall a shift when she hadn't seen him shambling down the street or loitering outside a store. When the hell had she noticed he shaved on a steady basis? But he did. Regular as Preacher and more regular than she shaved her legs.

"So you busted him last week," Atkinson said. "Simple burglary, simple possession for a foil of dope. More charges on a very long list of priors."

"That's right. I did." She felt guilty, for the first time, for the severity of the bust. Preacher had encouraged her to pile on the charges, talking about recidivism and court pay and getting out of the heat. "I wrote him for everything I had on him."

"And today?"

"I let him walk."

"What changed? Why let him walk today?"

Maureen's mouth went dry. She looked down at her feet, which stood in the middle of a murder scene. No fucking way. Her luck couldn't be this bad. It wasn't possible that the drug-addled bum she'd let walk that afternoon had gone and killed someone that night. She'd seen Wright's record. Petty violations. Monkey business. Nothing violent. Nothing even felonious. And now this shit.

Preacher had told her, he had practically begged her to leave it alone. But, no, she knew better. She had to do the right fucking thing. It took everything Maureen had not to break down and beg for mercy. Stick to the detective's questions, she thought. For once in your life, do as you're fucking told.

"After what happened with Jackson," Maureen said, "my training officer and I talked about discretion. We talked about getting a reputation. That maybe it's not always best to be so gung-ho." As she spoke, she kept her eyes on the night sky over Atkinson's shoulder. "I thought giving Wright a break might pay off down the road. It defused the situation, and looked good in front of the neighborhood." She splayed her hand over her collarbone. "I don't want to send everyone off in an ambulance."

"You were being watched?"

"Aren't we always?" Maureen said. "There were these kids hanging around. Three of them."

That fact caught Atkinson's interest. "Three kids. How old?"

"Twelve or so. Middle school age."

"Where do they fit into this?"

"They were taunting Wright for breaking into the car. Some guy named Bobby Scales owns it. The kids, well, one of them, said Scales would be pretty pissed at Wright for messing with the car."

"What can you tell me about Scales?"

"Not a thing," Maureen said. "I didn't ask."

"Explain."

"The way the kids talked about him," Maureen said, "they assumed I knew who he was, so I played along. They talked like he's well known around the neighborhood. I didn't want to look ignorant."

"Did you take the names of these kids?"

"No, Sergeant, I didn't. I shooed them away. They weren't involved. They were just wising off."

"You're familiar, I assume," Atkinson said, "with the concept of a lookout?"

"But they didn't say anything when I walked up. They let me come right up on him without a word."

"As far as you heard."

"With due respect, Detective," Maureen said, "you should've seen the way he banged his head on the hood of the car. He had no idea I was coming."

"Okay, what's that tell you?"

"That they weren't working for Wright," Maureen said, the light-bulb going off. Why had she argued the lookout point? Way to put your boot in your mouth, rookie. "They were working for this Bobby Scales?"

"Did you see a cell phone on these kids?"

"No," Maureen said. "But two of them took off running as soon as they could, without looking too obvious. They could've called from out of sight. Easy."

"So what we need to be asking," Atkinson said, "is why that car needed watching over. Wright knew something was in there, and he wanted it."

"That would explain," Maureen said, "repeatedly breaking into the same car."

How had she not thought of that? Maureen wondered. The possibility that something more valuable than a car battery or spark plugs had been hidden under that hood: a drug stash, a gun, something. A broken dish-washer, a broken-down car, was there that big a difference? The thought had never occurred to her. It probably never would have without this conversation. She'd swallowed the big name and been distracted from the car. She let the thought of a big fish get her so hot and bothered that she lost her focus. Slow. Fucking. Learner. That's what she was.

"It wasn't one of the kids who got killed, was it?" Maureen asked. "Tell me that, at least."

"No. No, it was not."

Maureen stood there in the street, looking over at the dwindling crowd by the corner store, disgusted with herself over the wrong assumptions she had made that day: about the innocence of the kids, and because of his stumblebum appearance and obsequious patter with her, about Wright's weakness and stupidity. What had one of those boys told her? *Don't hate the playas, hate the game.* Congratulations, Maureen, you got played. All day.

Atkinson grinned with no humor in her eyes. She stepped to the edge of the flares, gestured for Maureen to join her. Together, they stared into the figure outlined in the cracked street, the chalk turned pink in the glow of the flares.

"It's Wright who's dead," Atkinson said. "He's the homicide vic."

Maureen ran her fingers through her hair. Relief dominated her emotions, namely relief that the man she'd decided not to arrest hadn't killed anyone. She also recognized right away that it was better for her that Wright was the victim and not the killer. She wondered, the thought distant and weak, what that recognition said about her. It was just a fact. Seeing the facts wasn't cause for guilt, it was her job, but guilt floated inside her just the same.

Had she busted Wright, she thought, he might not be dead.

And had he stayed away from the car like he'd been fucking told, she thought, he wouldn't be dead. She wasn't wearing the blame for this. Wright's death was not her fault.

"With the empty space," Atkinson said, "the fresh oil stains, and the location of the body, I'm figuring Mr. Wright went back to the well again after dark. Whatever was in there, he sure wanted it bad."

"Maybe he owed a favor or money to someone else who wanted it," Maureen said. "Maybe he was stealing on behalf of someone else."

"Another possibility," Atkinson said.

People milled around on the sidewalk and in the street, ignoring the police, who ignored them right back. Maureen looked for the kids from that afternoon. She didn't see them.

"So I guess the fact that Wright was murdered," she said, "proves your theory about something of value hidden in the car and the need for lookouts."

"Maybe. People get shot for all kinds of reasons, complicated ones and not so much. Could be that something worthwhile was stashed in that car. Could be that whoever owns the car simply got sick of Wright fucking with it and figured no one would miss him." She shrugged. "Could be the car owner didn't think anything and started pulling the trigger for target practice. Also could be that someone else was the shooter, someone who figured the owner of the Plymouth would be grateful for the favor. Could be someone else entirely hid something in that car and the owner never knew it was there. Our options are multiple, unfortunately."

Atkinson dug into the front pocket of her jeans, producing a crumpled soft pack of cigarettes. She shook out two, offering one to Maureen. "The bottom line is he got caught, then killed for it, and whoever killed him probably took the car, too."

Maureen took the offer and a light from Atkinson's brass Zippo. "So we need that car and we need to find those kids. I can knock on some doors, start asking questions."

"Let's not get ahead of ourselves," Atkinson said. "First, I need you to write up for me everything that happened with Wright this afternoon, exactly as you remember it. Put it all in. Let me decide what's important." She took a drag on her smoke. "Tonight, before your day shift, would be a good time for that."

"Yes, ma'am."

Maureen hadn't given returning to bed a thought. She'd known leaving the apartment that she wouldn't get back to sleep that night. Not a problem. Working all night was easy; she'd been doing it since she was eighteen. Atkinson excused herself and stepped away to talk with a crime-scene tech. Maureen smoked her cigarette, wondering if she'd been wordlessly dismissed from the scene. She couldn't take her eyes off the chalk-drawn figure.

Had Wright really been that small a man? She remembered him as bigger. Taller, at least, than the outline suggested. The figure on the street was halfway curled up, as if Wright had seen his shooter at the last moment and thrown his arms over his head in surrender or a futile gesture of self-defense. He'd hit the street in the fetal position. He'd died that way. When Maureen had put him in the back of the patrol car the day she'd arrested him, his upper arm had felt so thin in her grip. Not an arm that was going to stop a bullet.

Over her shoulder, Maureen heard the crackle of the fire at the end of Atkinson's cigarette as she took a drag.

"You never forget your first time," Atkinson said.

8

"Sit down, Coughlin," Preacher said.

Grunting, he shifted his weight in his too-small chair, the only kind available in the front courtyard of a cigar shop called the Mayan. He sat at a metal patio table, a heavy glass ashtray in front of him. The fanlike deep green leaves of a trio of potted palms shaded Preacher from the early-afternoon sun. With the foliage behind him, he reminded Maureen of a lazy gorilla relaxing in the underbrush, waiting out the heat.

"You're making me nervous," he said.

Maureen stood in the sun a few feet away from him, at the waist-high wrought-iron fence separating the courtyard from the busy Magazine Street sidewalk. She had her thumbs hitched in her gun belt, her sunglasses on. Bag-toting pedestrians, most of them college-age young women from Tulane or Loyola, meandered in and out of the shops across the street. Must be nice, Maureen thought, having that kind of money and that kind of time. In front of her, traffic eased to a standstill. Most of the drivers, middle-aged versions of the wandering browsers, sat sealed into their air-conditioned SUVs, talking on the phone or texting as they crept along. The fact that they weren't paying much attention to their surroundings, Maureen thought, probably accounted for their patience. These women were the same sex as her, but a different breed entirely.

"Coughlin, for chrissakes, I'm trying to relax," Preacher said. "Over here, at the table."

"We're working. I feel bad, sitting outside with a cup of coffee. It looks bad." She looked at Preacher over her shoulder. "Maybe I'll go sit in the car and try to look busy."

Preacher had a short, fat cigar in his mouth. He was rolling it between his teeth, sucking on it, trying to assure an even burn on the lit tip. His task accomplished, he studied the cigar with pride. He frowned at Maureen, as if disappointed he hadn't been as successful with her.

"It doesn't look like anything. Relax." He gestured with his cigar toward the traffic. "You think anyone cares what we're doing? They hardly give a fuck about what *they're* doing. Trust me, you're not gonna change anyone's opinion of the NOPD for the worse by having a coffee in the shade for twenty minutes. And not having it won't raise us up in the public eye. We're background, like this here palm tree."

He puffed on his cigar, raising a cloud of acrid smoke. He looked at Maureen wide-eyed, eyebrows buoyed by the obvious truth of his statement. Preacher's cloud drifted over to her. Maureen wrinkled her nose and marveled at her training officer's ability to find a brand of cigar that *had* to be horseshit rolled in banana peels. And he probably paid a fortune for them.

"If it makes you feel any better," Preacher said, "I radioed in. They know where we are, and that we're out of the car." He held up their radio. "I brought the handheld. Should civilization collapse without you on patrol, we'll hear about it."

"I'd rather stand for a while," Maureen said. "We sat in the car all morning."

Preacher pointed with his radio antenna at the other chair. "Sit, rookie. That's an order. Your coffee's getting cold."

Maureen walked over to the table and sat. She lifted the plastic lid from her coffee cup with too much force, sloshing coffee onto the table-top. It ran off the table, dripping onto her uniform pants. Well, at least it was still hot. Preacher laughed, as he always did whenever Maureen spilled coffee on herself, which was every time she had a cup.

"You ever have a dog, Coughlin?"

Maureen mopped at the runaway coffee with paper napkins. Again with the dogs. She had a feeling Preacher watched a lot of Animal Planet. Preacher Boyd, the Rookie Whisperer. "No, sir. Never had any pets."

"Amazing creatures, dogs." Preacher moved his hands around his head as if it were a bowling ball he was polishing. "Pack animals, very complex social structure. Makes them very sensitive to moods and emotions. Almost telepathic. Seeing as they can't talk and such." He made a sweeping gesture toward the street with his hand. "You think I'm trying to boss you around, but there's wisdom to be gleaned here. These people on the street, they're like dogs, and I mean that in a purely observational way, no insult intended.

"A cop pacing the fence, eyeballing the stores, the traffic, the pass-ersby, it makes them nervous. They might not even know they're doing it, but they pick up your vibe. They start looking for whatever it is they think you're looking for." He dabbed some sweat off his forehead. "But if you're mellow, it keeps them mellow."

"So, actually," Maureen said, "we're performing a public service by taking a public break."

"Exactly," Preacher said, drawing out the word. "Protect and serve. It's what I'm about. You're finally learning." He honked his nose into his hankie. He admired his deposit there and then his cigar as if the first affirmed the quality of the second. "So smoke 'em if you got 'em."

Maureen raised her hips and dug a new pack of cigarettes from her pocket. She tossed the pack on the table. "I shouldn't be smoking."

"No, you shouldn't." Preacher pushed his lighter across the table in her direction. "But don't let that stop you."

Maureen tore the cellophane from the pack, crumpled the foil, and pulled out a cigarette. She wasn't sure how much she even wanted one, but the debate in her head over whether to have one would end the moment she touched the lighter flame to the tip and inhaled.

A high-end cigar store and tobacconist melded into a block-long, ocher-colored, brick-faced condo building that had been converted from a long-abandoned orphanage, the Mayan functioned as a de facto social club for veteran uptown police. Whenever she and Preacher stopped by, half a dozen cops, mostly plainclothes and detectives with the occasional older uniform like Preacher peppered in, stood around the tall cocktail tables by the front door or sat in the courtyard, smoking cigarettes and cigars, sipping at a coffee from the CC's or a brandy from the top-shelf selection the tobacconist kept in stock. Some of the men Maureen recognized from around the district station. Some were strangers. None of them ever gave her so much as a nod.

Her throat tickled and she coughed. "It doesn't help that Spirits are five bucks a pack down here. Way less than half of what they cost me up north."

Maureen stopped, clearing her throat to buy time, regretting mentioning New York, even in cigarette terms. Preacher had demonstrated only mild interest in her past. She wanted to keep it that way.

Preacher reached across the table, picked up the bright orange cigarette pack. "These're new to me."

"All-natural tobacco," Maureen said. "These're the super ultralights or whatever. They're not bad, though I think I might smoke more now because they're so light."

"You'll quit for good someday. You're the type."

Maureen took another long drag. "And what type is that?"

"The type that can't tolerate failure. Now that you've tried to quit and failed, you'll never let that go. If you'd never tried to quit, you could go on smoking with a clear conscience. But now you've soiled it by trying to improve yourself." He turned his cigar in his mouth, puffing smoke like a cartoon train. "Put money on it."

"Speaking of failure," Maureen said. "You think we'll have better luck with those kids this afternoon?"

Preacher growled. "You do know how to ruin a good break."

"You're my training officer," Maureen said, grinning. "How are you not proud of me for getting this assignment?"

"Proud of you? Because I get to cruise Central City in this fucking heat all day, eyeballing schoolchildren, looking for three punks that'll lie to us and everyone else with a badge easy as breathing air, when instead I could be sitting here supervising the arrivals at the two o'clock Pilates class?" He puffed at his cigar. "You do that stuff? That pie-lates? Probably, the shape you're in. I see the Garden District housewives going up and down the stairs to that gym over the CC's. Seems to be something to it, the look of them." He resettled himself in his seat. "At least you quit nagging me about Mother Mayor."

"Oh, I still wanna talk to her, too. Now more than ever, with Wright getting shot."

"Sweet Jesus."

"You're killing me," Maureen said. "This is how you teach someone to be a cop? I can't stand it."

"Atkinson seems to think you're turning out okay," Preacher said. "Take that for what it's worth. Of course, I don't have to tell you what they say about her around the department."

"Really? That dyke shit is so tired."

"You know what they say, you are what you eat."

"I'm gonna need another one of those harassment forms."

Preacher smiled. "You know where they are."

"You tell me they're in your pocket," Maureen said, "and I will shoot you."

"The only thing in my pocket," Preacher said, "is my pen."

"Keep it there." She couldn't stop herself from laughing. "And keep your hands where I can see them."

Preacher stood, hiking up his pants and adjusting his gun belt. "Well played, rook. You're gonna do superlative once you leave my care and protection. And now I gotta sneak Sally through the alley before we go anywhere. I'll meet you at the car."

Maureen waited on the sidewalk outside the courtyard, leaning against the warm hood of their patrol car, watching the neighborhood, her neighborhood, go by.

Around town, she'd run into a few people she would have sworn were New Yorkers who had turned out to be New Orleans born and bred. The Irish Channel accent of New Orleans sounded a hell of a lot like New York Irish-American, Brooklyn, especially. One more thing left out of the Lonely Planet guide. One thing the guide had included, though, was how traditional directions didn't apply in New Orleans. No witness was going to tell you the perp ran east or west. On the police radio, dispatchers used the compass points, but to everyone else, nothing was north or south; it was lake side or river side. Nothing was east or west; it was downtown or uptown. At least from where she stood at the moment.

She turned, watching three detectives in dark glasses and expensive suits laughing with one another as they stood around the cigar store Indian. God, there was a lot to learn. The cop stuff, she'd anticipated, but New Orleans was like a foreign country. The place was full of tribes. Each tribe had a code and a dialect. No one had a key to it all, either. She had to learn on the fly. Waiting for Preacher, she practiced. The Mayan was on the river side of Magazine, uptown from the intersection with Seventh. The corner grocery she liked was on the river side of St. Charles, on the uptown corner of Sixth. She lit another cigarette. Norman Wright's body had been chalked up on the downtown side of Washington, on the lake side of the intersection with Dryades. She checked her watch. Almost two thirty. She wanted to get moving.

Preacher appeared atop the Mayan's stone steps, a fat minor god emerging from a stone temple. He shook hands and chatted with the guys beside the door. He tilted his chin at the car. Everyone laughed. Coming down the stairs, he patted the fresh cigar in his pocket.

He stopped to adjust his belt after he passed through the gate and onto the sidewalk, then continued over to the car. "All right then," he said, getting in the driver's seat. "I don't have all day."

Maureen took her seat beside him. Don't ask, she thought. Don't ask what the men were laughing at. "Where're we headed?"

"Mother Mayor's place," Preacher said. "You did well with Atkinson, you've got me down to a science, let's see how you handle a true hard-ass." Grinning, he slipped his sunglasses on and eased the car into the slow-moving traffic. "Let's find out how tough you really are."

9

Approaching Mother Mayor's front steps, Maureen recognized the older woman's small house as new construction intended to imitate a shotgun double, though the tacky vinyl siding undermined the effort. Built post-storm on the fly and on the cheap, Mother Mayor's place was one of four long, narrow, and charmless boxes right up against the sidewalk with two shared concrete stoops where their respective steps met in front. It was obvious that Mother had relocated there after Katrina.

Maureen wondered where Mother Mayor had lived before the storm. Had she lived in an authentic Creole cottage or a century-old shotgun on this same spot, maybe, or had she lived someplace else that she'd lost in the flood? On another block, or in another neighborhood. The way this neighborhood's people treated her, though, and the way the cops treated her, for that matter, Mother Mayor had probably supervised her small section of Central City for quite some time.

Everyone returned from the storm to something different from what they had left, Maureen had learned. Not a lot of people, not most people.

Everyone. Even if it was just a part-time job or the way the light came through the trees in the evening, everyone had seen something change for good. Over the course of a morning, an entire city of people had lost their present lives. The sense of immediate loss she could relate to, the idea that one day your life is this way and the next it's not. The head you lift off the pillow isn't the same one you laid there the night before. She'd been through that kind of thing, when she was a kid and her father left for good, while standing on the roof of her mother's house, watching the smoke billow from the Twin Towers, in her personal nightmare with Sebastian from a little over a year ago.

The scale of what had happened in New Orleans, though, a loss like that hitting a whole city at once, a city bleeding out like a murder victim with her throat cut, going empty of people first in a flood and then in a trickle, that was a hard thing for Maureen to get her mind around. Even those times her life had changed overnight, she'd at least awoken in the same bed in the same city the next morning, with her people, few in number as they may have been, surrounding her.

By now, a lot of the people helping to refill and revive New Orleans were transplants like Maureen who hadn't had a life to lose here before the storm. She knew that some of her fellow reinforcements, maybe most, had lost their lives wherever they were from. Like her, they had arrived here in search of something new, in their way washed ashore in New Orleans by the flood.

Maureen knocked on Mother Mayor's storm door and waited for an answer. She realized she hadn't slept but three hours out of the past thirty. She knocked again. Rose-patterned white curtains covered the small front window. Maureen leaned close to the door, listening for a radio or a television, anything to indicate somebody was home. She thought she heard voices inside, maybe a television.

She banged again, harder this time.

"Police, ma'am. NOPD. Please open up."

The voices stopped. Someone had muted the TV. Maureen heard rapid footsteps headed her way. Recalling what had happened at the

Garvey Apartments, she braced her feet and set her hand on her weapon. She wouldn't get caught making assumptions this time. She heard two toots of a car horn behind her. She turned to see Preacher in the driver's seat, shaking his head. Maureen dropped her hand from her gun. She did remember, at the last moment, to step to the side of the doorway, out of the path of anything that might exit that door in a hurry. The side step would buy her a few seconds of reaction time if she needed it.

The inside door flew open and there stood Mother Mayor. She wore a red-and-white caftan with a rose pattern on it, a matching scarf tied over her hair, which was up in multicolored plastic curlers. She looked at Maureen and her bottom lip rolled over in disgust.

"I knew it'd be you. I knew it."

"If I could, Mother Mayor, I'd appreciate coming in and talking to you."

"About?"

"About the murder of Norman Wright."

"I didn't see nothing," Mother Mayor said. "I don't know nothing. I can't help you."

When she moved to close the door, Maureen stuck her foot in the way. Mother Mayor, using the door, let Maureen know she didn't like it.

"Excuse me," Mother Mayor said. "I didn't see your foot."

"And I'm sure you didn't see who shot Mr. Wright, either," Maureen said. "But if I could ask you a few questions about some other people we think might be involved? Some people, young people, we need to find and we think might be in danger."

She'd added that last part, the danger part, thinking it up on the spot. Could be true. Maybe Scales had heard they'd been dropping his name in front of the cops. Maybe he was looking for them, too. Her embellishment did nothing to soften Mother Mayor's hard stare.

"You're really going to do this, aren't you?" Mother Mayor said.

"Yes, ma'am. I really am."

"You may as well come in, then. I can't afford to be air-conditioning the entire neighborhood."

"Thank you, ma'am," Maureen said. "I appreciate your time."

She glanced over her shoulder, hoping Preacher was noticing her having won over Mother Mayor, but he was hidden behind the newspaper.

"The fat one's just gonna sit in the car like that, ain't he?" Mother Mayor said.

Maureen followed Mother Mayor into the house. "We're better off with him right where he is. Is anyone else at home?"

"No," Mother Mayor said. "It's just me."

She threw a wary glance at the shelves on the wall. On them sat several versions of the Bible and about a dozen framed photos. She knew Maureen had caught her looking. "My daughter's away."

Maureen wished Preacher had told her about the daughter. No, she corrected, this conversation was her idea. She should have asked for background information on Mother Mayor. She hadn't even asked Preacher for Mother Mayor's real name. "What should I call you, ma'am? I'm afraid I haven't even asked your name."

"Ma'am will do. Or Mother."

"Okay, then," Maureen said. "Thank you."

Mother patted at the bouquet of curlers on her head. "And, by the way, it's impolite to talk to another adult wearing sunglasses indoors."

Maureen slipped off her shades and hung them on her shirt pocket. She stood blinking a moment, as her eyes adjusted to the dim interior of the house. The window shades were lowered, protection from the late-afternoon sun. An AC unit rattled away somewhere deeper in the house. The machine strained, but it did the job better than the one Maureen had at her place.

She stepped closer to the bookshelves for a better look at the photos, not waiting for Mother's permission or invitation to look. May as well learn what she could.

The photos showed a young woman in military uniform, desert fatigues, Army it looked like. A younger, thinner Mother Mayor, definitely a daughter. The standard posed head shots in dress uniform with the American flag stood alongside several pictures printed from a computer,

Mother Mayor's daughter standing beside different types of idle helicopters. In each picture, she smiled like the choppers were well-trained pets or kids of which she was especially proud. A mechanic, Maureen guessed.

One photo was set off to the side. The daughter, in civilian dress, younger and heavier than she was in the Army photos. Late high school, probably, early college age, tops. Baby fat still rounded out her face. Instead of standing before a large helicopter in a desert hangar, the young woman sat in front of a dull gray portrait-studio sky. It was a classic high school yearbook photo, except for the young boy three or four years old sitting on her lap. He had the same huge smile as his mother and his grandmother. A teen pregnancy. The Army photos made even more sense. No sight or sign of the girl's father in the pictures. No sign of her baby's father. Maureen realized she was talking to a single mother. The proud single mother of a grown daughter. That was a person she could relate to. Keep her talking about the daughter, she thought. Maybe she could get a genuine conversation going instead of getting a performance or a lecture.

"When does she get out?" Maureen asked. "I'm sure you're anxious for her to get home."

"She's back from Kabul in six months." Mother Mayor blessed herself. "God willing, this is her last tour. Kuwait first for a few weeks, then back home for leave."

"Only for leave?"

Mother Mayor smiled, revealing beautiful white teeth, a perfect match of the smile in the photos. "She's career military, my daughter. She likes the work, and the uniform. Waking up every day with a job, knowing what needs doing. Eight years in the service this fall."

No mention of the grandson, Maureen noticed. "I can relate."

"Oh, you can?"

"Sure. I like my job and my uniform. Can't say I know my way around a helicopter, though. Never been overseas, either." She tapped her finger on her badge. "They don't even let me fill up the tires on the cruiser. Yet. You have to start somewhere, I guess."

She turned back to the shelves. "He's beautiful, your grandson. Looks happy. I bet he misses his momma."

"Mmm-hmm. Or his auntie."

"So you have another daughter?" Maureen asked. And no pictures of her?

"Any of your own?"

Maureen laughed. Mother was getting short with her. So much for her whip-smart detective work. There were women in this world, Maureen thought, with more than one daughter. Time for another angle. "No, ma'am. No kids or aunties."

Looking around the cluttered living room, Maureen saw that rose-colored and rose-themed knickknacks arrayed every flat surface. Needle-points, doilies, two dozen ceramic ornaments and boxes. Maureen hadn't realized Precious Moments made black cherubs. Made sense. There was not a single live flower, Maureen noticed, no roses or any other kind of flower anywhere in the room. She hadn't seen any out front, just a patch of half-dead weeds by the steps. The house smelled of cheap air freshener, something Maureen figured came in a pretty box and promised to smell like roses. She let Mother Mayor watch her look around.

"My mother loves roses," Maureen said. "She grows them in her backyard."

"Storm took my garden," Mother said, not looking at Maureen, instead watching the silent soap opera on a large flat-screen TV. "Floodwater killed every last rose. Over by where I used to stay got four feet. I haven't got the space here to start over. The last place, I'd taken over for my momma when she passed, the house and the garden. That garden was old. New one'll never be like the old one was. Roses grow so slow. And I don't know that Deandra is the type for slow-growing things. She won't be home to tend anything, anyway. So I did it different."

She grinned at something on the television, but her eyes stayed sad. "And if another storm comes along, this one I can pack up and take with."

"I'm sorry to hear that," Maureen said, her standard answer for storm stories; she never tried to commiserate. She let people assume what they wanted about her story from her silence.

"But all that's not what you're here for, is it?" Mother Mayor said.

"We're concerned," Maureen said, "that the shooting of Mr. Wright connects to the green Plymouth he had an interest in. That vehicle, which hadn't moved for quite some time, is now missing. It's a coincidence that caught our attention. We're also concerned, primarily concerned, about three young boys around twelve years of age who were on the scene when I talked to Mr. Wright yesterday afternoon. We think they may have knowledge of the car's owner."

She paused, leaving room for Mother Mayor to jump in. The older woman didn't.

"Naturally, we'd like to talk to the car's owner about Mr. Wright, any history that was there, and the current whereabouts of the car."

Maureen paused again.

"Do you know who owns that car? Do you know anyone else in the neighborhood that might know the owner of that car?"

Mother Mayor remained silent. Maureen ran her tongue over her teeth. She counted to ten. C'mon, Mother, she thought, give me a break. Lie to me. Even a lie gives something away. On the street, with an audience, you couldn't get the woman to shut up about who was doing what to whom. "Do you know any of those boys?"

"I don't know which boys you're talking about."

"The three boys who were by the car when I went to talk to Mr. Wright yesterday. Those boys."

"I didn't see no boys out there. Just you and Mr. Wright. That's all I saw."

"Do you know any boys in the neighborhood that age?"

"Only about twenty or thirty or so."

"What about an older boy," Maureen asked, "eighteen, nineteen. Wears Rasta gear and big sunglasses?"

"I stay away from them teenagers, and they stay away from me." Mother

Mayor shook her head, looking away from Maureen. "I have a question for you."

"By all means," Maureen said, happy to keep the conversation alive. Questions could tell as much as lies. "I'm here to help."

"Do you know why they sent you?"

"We're looking for witnesses and information concerning a homicide. A killing that took place yards from your front door, if I'm not mistaken."

"They're sending a message," Mother Mayor said.

"I'm not sure who 'they' are and why they matter."

"Your people. Your bosses. You're a message. They're using you."

"I have a recent history with the victim," Maureen said. "I spoke with him yesterday. I arrested him last week. You witnessed both yesterday's conversation and the arrest. I work in this district and the lead detective on the case needs a hand. I'm sorry, I don't see the conspiracy."

"You're a smart woman," Mother Mayor said. "Young, but smart. Where's this lead detective, then, if we're all so important to the police? If it's so important to talk to and to *protect* those boys? Your partner won't even get out of the car."

"That's got nothing to do with you, or those boys, and everything to do with him. Detective Sergeant Atkinson is working night shift this week. I'm here so she doesn't have to bother you after dark." Maureen straightened her shoulders. "Ma'am, I have to say I resent the implication that I'm somehow substandard material here."

"A good man, a neighborhood man," Mother Mayor began, "a veteran, a black man who lived in this neighborhood his whole life gets shot down in the street over an abandoned car and who do we get at our door? A white rookie female and a lazy fat man. You're not even a real police officer yet, are you? You hearing a message now? Don't worry, honey, you ain't the only thing substandard that's going on here. I don't blame you. This ain't nothing new."

"Look, lady, I'm not in charge of who gets sent where," Maureen said. "I just do what I'm told. You want me to drag my partner out of the car so you can deal with a senior officer, I'll go get him. You want me to call my sergeant and ask for a black cop to come out here, I will. I got no problem with that. My feelings won't get hurt. I'm here to help you. It's your neighborhood that people are getting shot in." She took a step toward the door. "Right now. I'll do it right now. You got a favorite black cop? You wanna make a request?"

Mother Mayor went ice-cold. "You got some attitude on you, young lady. I should call your supervisor." Mother Mayor crossed her arms over her chest, triumphant.

Maureen could tell that in Mother's mind young white people feared nothing more than having their supervisor told of bad behavior. Before she could say anything, and she had plenty to say, Maureen felt a distant memory pass through her like a ghost. In it, she wore a tight skirt and a tuxedo shirt and an apron. She had a tray in one hand, her legs hurt, and some fat bitch at a small table was demanding to see her manager. In the present, she took a deep breath of rose-scented air freshener and gathered herself. She wasn't that girl anymore. What was the point of getting older if you weren't gonna get smarter along the way?

"You call who you wanna call," Maureen said, "but I'm surprised at you. You think your daughter tolerates eye-rolling over the 'girl mechanic' showing up to fix things?" She pointed at the pictures on the bookshelves. "You think those guys in Afghanistan care who fixes their chopper, as long as it gets fixed right? Half this neighborhood is always complaining the cops never listen, that we never do anything. I'm here now, trying to fix things. Work with me. Do you know those three boys or not? Do you know their names? Have you heard anything about them around the neighborhood? Where can I catch up to them, even one of them?"

She waited again for an answer. Mother Mayor was weakening. Maureen decided to turn up the pressure.

"One of those boys was present at the incident over in the Garvey Apartments the day before yesterday. Two days in a row he's around a crime scene. Drugs, guns, and now murder."

Just one name, Maureen thought. And then, before she could catch herself, because she was greedy and in a hurry, the question popped out. "Have you ever heard the name Bobby Scales?"

Damn it, Maureen. Patience, woman, patience. But the damage was done.

Mother Mayor's mind locked up, as if a hand from inside her head reached out and snatched what the older woman was going to say right out of her eyes. It was as much an answer as Wright offering his wrists for the handcuffs. Scales was a name that people knew, and it frightened them. Maureen wanted to find him, whether Preacher was on board or not.

"Thank you, Officer, but you got to go." Mother Mayor gestured toward the front door. "I got company coming. I apologize if I disrespected you. I can't help you."

Someone from Homicide, Maureen thought, probably Atkinson, had Mother Mayor on their interview list. Maureen prayed she hadn't blown a potential lead. She needed to salvage something from the interview, even if it was only enough good feeling, or guilt, to make sure Mother Mayor opened her door to the next cop. She stopped at the pictures.

"Your grandson," she said. "How old is he now? He in school?"

"He lives in Baton Rouge with his father," Mother Mayor said. "I haven't seen him since the storm. Please, Officer, you need to go. I have things to do."

Maureen dug out a business card from her shirt pocket, placed it on the arm of the sofa. Mother Mayor looked at the card as if Maureen had wiped snot on her furniture.

"Please think about contacting me if you think of anything," Maureen said, opening the door. "I do want to help. If you don't want to talk to me, call the Sixth District, or call Homicide. Ask for Detective Sergeant Christine Atkinson."

Mother Mayor said nothing, slamming the door shut and locking it up after Maureen had stepped outside.

"Fuck me," Maureen said. "Brilliant work, Coughlin. Way to alienate the one person in the neighborhood who knows everyone's business. That's fine, fine police work."

She put her sunglasses on, looked around, and that was when she saw him—the orange-drink kid from yesterday. He stared at her from the sidewalk, as shocked to see Maureen as she was to see him. He held another container of orange drink to his mouth. When he froze, Maureen wasted a glance at the cruiser. Preacher was hidden behind the sports pages. Asleep at the wheel, literally.

"Hey!" Maureen yelled, maybe at Preacher, maybe at the kid. "Hey!"

Either way, only the kid reacted. He dropped his drink and bolted across the street.

"Stop!"

10

Maureen leaped down the steps. She wasted one more millisecond over how to rouse Preacher. She went with two hard slaps on the hood of the cruiser and a good and loud "Goddamn it, Preacher!"

She took off after the kid at a dead sprint. He had a solid head start.

He cut left and darted through the open gate of LaSalle Park, taking a quick look back as he broke across the playing field, a wide-open square of grass as long as a football field and twice as wide. Maureen was across the street in a blue flash. On her way through the gate she checked for anyone who might help the kid escape. The tennis courts and playground were empty. The three-on-three at one of the basketball courts stopped so the players could watch the chase. They didn't make a move to join in.

One of them, muscular and shirtless, ball tucked under his arm, hollered, "Run, shorty, run."

Maureen wasn't entirely sure he was yelling at the kid.

Racing across a grassy field in a bulletproof vest was about as easy as doing it wearing a life jacket full of nickels. She felt like the Tin Man running the hundred-yard dash. She worried her gun belt would explode, leaving a Gretel trail of handcuffs, pepper spray, flashlight, bullets, baton, and who knew what else across the field. Not a report she wanted to write.

But as she ran, her wind was good, deep breaths pumping through her nose, and the magnificent adrenaline surge of the chase didn't hurt, either. The pain in her foot from Mother Mayor's door was gone.

The kid ran with that electric jackrabbit speed that's nature's special gift to young kids. His arms and legs churned, his head rocking from side to side with the effort. But he had to keep clutching at his drooping, over-sized shorts with one hand. It slowed him enough that he wasn't opening greater distance between them. Maureen thought she might even be closing on him. She tried to decide how to corral him without a flying tackle. God forbid the kid came out of the chase bruised or bleeding. She'd never hear the end of it. And people were watching, more than just the guys on the basketball court, even if she couldn't see them. There were eyes around her in windows and cars. She and this kid were racing at full speed in broad daylight across a wide-open ball field in view of half the neighborhood. Appearances were everything these days.

Maybe only five yards separated them, but Maureen needed more field than she had left to catch up. The kid would beat her to the opposite gate. Once they got out of the park, they'd hit a maze of side streets that he knew way better than she did. There were alleys, yards, and aban-doned vacants that he could cut through or disappear into. And then, wouldn't you know it, here comes Preacher squealing around the corner in the cruiser, lights flashing and sirens screaming. The sight of it only gave the kid a burst of speed. And then Preacher was slowing down. What the fuck was he doing?

Maureen tried to match the kid's surge. She guessed Preacher's plan. Bad idea.

Preacher wanted to intercept the kid as he hit the street, using the car. That way, the kid couldn't dodge; he wouldn't have time. Maureen put her head down. Just beat him to the spot, Preach. Slow him down for two seconds and I can bag him. Just beat him to the spot and haul ass out of the fucking car. And for chrissakes, don't run the poor kid over. But Preacher had his mind made up and stuck with his plan. And like Maureen feared, he arrived too late.

The kid blew through the gate and through the invisible collision point while the cruiser was fifteen feet away. Instead of blocking the kid, Preacher executed a perfectly timed interception of Maureen. She went sprawling across the hood of her own patrol car, slamming at half speed into the front quarter panel with a jangle of equipment and an audible *oof.*

She could hear Preacher shout "Holy shit" from inside the car.

She wanted to pull out her baton and beat Preacher's head in.

She did the only thing she could, which was recover her footing and storm away from the car. Preacher climbed out of the driver's seat and called her name, asking if she was okay. She couldn't be sure, but she thought she heard a touch of laughter in his voice. She didn't even bother looking behind her for the kid's choice of direction; he was gone. Preacher called her name again, a sharp *Coughlin!* But Coughlin was winded, sweat-soaked, empty-handed, and pissed. She was going to need a minute. Either out of sheer laziness or because he had, like his beloved dogs, picked up on her mood, Preacher stayed at the car. Somewhere in the back of her mind, way, way back, Maureen was grateful. Then the ground shifted and she lost her balance. Her head went light. She saw spots.

She doubled over, hands on her knees. She tried to focus on spreading her toes and rooting the four corners of each of her feet on the sidewalk through the soles of her boots. She felt the growing pulses of a headache at the base of her skull. She tried to let it pass right by her, like a shooting star. She focused on feeling steady on the earth, first through her feet, then her ankles, then her calves and her knees. She breathed through her nose, forcing it to be deep and slow, trying everything her yoga teacher in New York had taught her.

Don't. *Inhale.* Panic. *Exhale.*

She repeated the pattern again, then a third time, a fourth. Her pulse relented. How long was this taking? she wondered. Not long enough for

Preacher to suspect anything other than her being winded from the chase and pissed that her quarry had escaped.

She stood upright, waited for the world to tilt. It didn't. Okay. All right. She was definitely getting better if she could fight off an anxiety attack that quickly. Good to know going forward. She turned to find Preacher leaning on the hood of the cruiser. The light bar flashed blue, but he'd silenced the siren.

"Holy shit, Coughlin," he said. "I am impressed."

His amazement seemed genuine. The look on his face reminded Maureen of her old high school track coach, at least the look he used to get before he realized she could fall out of bed and run like a mustang and so stopped being impressed with her speed.

"You almost *caught* that kid. You are *fast*. No joke."

She knew the answer, but she asked the question anyway. "You didn't see which way he went, did you?"

"Fuck, no," Preacher said. "I was trying to not run you over. You were supposed to get in the car so we could go after him."

Maureen had a hard time believing that had been the plan. She suspected Preacher had come wailing around the corner with no plan other than saving himself from the total embarrassment of sleeping through the chase. CYA, that was the prime directive.

"Let's get to looking, then," Maureen said. "We've got plenty of shift left."

Preacher hauled himself off the hood. "What we need to do is go up the supermarket on Claiborne and get you a Gatorade. Let you cool down."

"Then we can look?"

"Then we'll see what happens, see how we feel."

"We?"

"Rook, you want a cold drink or not? I'm buying." He opened the driver's side door, talked to Maureen from behind it. "You can tell me about your get-together with Mother Mayor. Then we can talk about what to do next. We got two other kids to go after. Maybe one of them'll be easier to catch. Who knows, maybe Atkinson solved the case already and we just haven't got the memo."

A cold drink sounded like a good idea. She felt a cramp in her bruised arch and another threat in her left hamstring. Hundred-yard sprints in ninety-five-degree heat in full gear could do that to a person. Especially a person running on two pots of coffee and no sleep.

She walked toward the car, remembering, finally, that keeping Preacher happy was as important as impressing Atkinson. If she was smart, and patient, she could figure out a way to do both.

11

"Six feet deep," Maureen said, repeating in disbelief what Preacher had told her.

They stood by the cruiser at the far end of the shopping-center parking lot near the corner of Washington and South Claiborne.

Maureen, clutching a half-full ice-cold quart of Gatorade, watched car after car turn off Washington and into the lot through the driveway marked EXIT ONLY.

"Six feet, give or take," Preacher said. "Six here, two or three down by Mother Mayor's place." He made a stirring motion in the air with his index finger. "You saw the television footage of the two guys floating around in the pickup bed?"

"Not that I remember."

"They went spinning right down Claiborne, right past here," Preacher said, "like a canoe caught in the current. Crazy. Big truck, too. Anyways, that footage was shot down at the next light."

Hard to imagine, Maureen thought, that the place they stood at that moment, smoking cigarettes and drinking Gatorade, the soles of their boots sinking into the heat-softened asphalt of the supermarket parking lot, had been at one point essentially an extension of the bottom of Lake Pontchartrain.

"Used to be a Walgreens there at the light," Preacher said, frowning, "though maybe it was a Rite Aid, I forget. Gets harder every year to re- member what was where before. Anyway, whatever drugstore it was, that's where they were headed." He laughed. "You ever try to paddle a pickup truck? With your hands?"

"Can't say that I have."

Maureen unscrewed the cap of her Gatorade bottle, taking smaller sips this time, restraining herself from gulping the second half of the bottle like she had the first. Pounding a pint of ice-cold Gatorade had left her eyes watering, a sharp pain blooming through her chest. Learning to function in this heat, learning how to expend and recover, was proving a challenge.

For miles in every direction, Maureen thought, people had drowned in the middle of a city. As best as she could figure, the nearest levee breach had been miles away from where she now stood. All day people had drowned. In parking lots, in their backyards, in their cars, in second-floor bedrooms, in first-floor pantries, in every household hiding place imagin- able, and in the middle of wide-open, empty streets. Who drowns in a house? Or staring up at streetlights and billboards through six feet of hot, dirty water? Who drowns while straining to reach for their own rooftop, leaving torn fingernails behind in the eaves as the water carries them away? Who drowns trapped in the fucking *attic*, the family photo albums and the old cookware they were saving for their daughter's wedding floating by above their heads?

Dragging on her cigarette, Maureen imagined bodies floating down South Claiborne in the days after the levees broke, drifting under the dead traffic lights and treetops, spinning in the current like empty plastic bottles. Bodies adrift under a clear blue sky, or under a starry dome, car- ried on the floodwaters toward the lightless downtown skyline. She thought again of 9/11. Bodies falling, towers falling under a clear blue sky. 9/11. Katrina. Weren't these supposed to be once-in-a-generation, not two-per-decade events? And what the fuck was it with American tragedies and beautiful days?

She remembered the damp, moldy air of the car trunk where Sebastian had held her, bruised, bleeding, and trapped. It had smelled like a wet rug in that trunk, a wet rug left in the dark for days, weeks. She'd been told pockets of New Orleans smelled like that even months after the water had gone. In some places, she'd heard, it smelled like a corpse had been rolled up in the carpet. She took a deep breath, fluttered her eyelids behind her dark glasses, trying to chase away the pictures, to chase away the scent. Her musings always left her messing with the same question, her brain poking at the mystery the way her tongue worried at a sore or a burn inside her cheek: How do you come back from that?

Yet there it was—Claiborne Avenue, normal and busy on a weekday afternoon. Three lanes racing in each direction divided by a wide grassy neutral ground where old men kicked away the windblown trash as they played dominoes on folding tables set up in the shade of short, fat palm trees. Unreal. How did anyone who lived here put it together, hold it in their heads? Or did they not organize anything, did they let the facts and the memories drift around in their skulls till they snagged on something and hung in place, like bodies in the trees, like flies in a web?

New Orleans was like some bizarre cross between the third world and an enlightened civilization that had advanced beyond ordinary American worries, Maureen thought. And here she was in the middle of it, gun on her belt, badge on her chest. Sweating her ass off.

"Fucking retards," Preacher said. "Out in an epic flood in a pickup truck, for what? A case of Heineken and some Vicodin?"

"What happened to them?"

Preacher's head snapped around. "I give a fuck? Somebody probably saved them, then someone else probably gave 'em a house somewhere."

Maureen raised her hands in surrender. "Sorry I asked. My bad. Just curious."

Preacher sniffed, wiping under his nose with his knuckles. "You and these questions."

"I feel like I oughtta know what I can," Maureen said. "Seems disrespectful to ride around, working here, living here, *being* here and not knowing."

"You can't know," Preacher said. "You weren't here. That's not an insult. It's just a fact."

He looked away, shaking his head. They stood silent for a long moment.

"You want stories, read a book, get a local boyfriend or girlfriend or both or whatever. Write a letter to Anderson Cooper. Or Brad Pitt. Get HBO. Get on the Internet. But after we part ways, don't go around asking questions, not at the other cops. Makes people uncomfortable. They may act like they're cool about it, but they're not. You'll be disappointed and they'll be embarrassed. It's like asking to see their dicks."

"I'll remember that," Maureen said.

"Besides the fact that these days everyone who worked a day after that fucking storm is worried about getting some federal indictment shoved up their ass. Believe."

"Okay, then," Maureen said. "Thanks for the advice."

"You know me. That's what I'm here for. You'll learn what you'll need to about the aftermath. Osmotically. I mean, it's not like you can get away from it. It's not like it goes away. History. It stays when it happens to a place. Or a person."

Preacher turned, opening his arms at the shopping center: a supermarket, a dollar store, and a discount sneaker-and-athletic-wear store that Maureen hadn't noticed before. She made a mental note of the place. She'd come back later, pick up some inexpensive workout gear.

"It's the same kind of stores as before," Preacher said, "just with different names. Coming here makes me feel better. I don't know why."

"So everything's different," Maureen said, "and the same all at the same time."

"See that? You've pretty much got it figured out. Whaddaya need me for?" Preacher finished his Gatorade. He tossed the empty plastic bottle in the grass by the side of the parking lot. "I'll be in the car."

"I want to pass by Mother Mayor's again," Maureen said, bending down and picking up Preacher's empty, "and that playground one more time. I want to talk to the basketball players. Maybe they know the kid I chased. A name, at least."

"Maybe you should give Mother a rest for the day," Preacher said. "Let her cool off."

"The basketball players, then. I at least want to talk to them."

"I can save you the trouble. They don't know nothing, if they're even still there."

"Indulge me, please," Maureen said. "I'm naïve and ambitious and wet behind the ears. I wanna keep the promise I made to a superior officer."

"Then let's get going," Preacher said, sliding into place behind the wheel, "unless your pal Atkinson is signing off on OT for this bullshit."

12

Preacher rolled the car slowly down Third Street, crunching gravel in the gutter, close to the curb on the backside of the park, near where Maureen lost that young boy among the side streets. Maureen rolled down her window, eyeballing the park, the surrounding stoops and porches. In the field she'd sprinted through earlier, someone tossed a tennis ball for a brindled pit bull mix trailing a hunk of thick rope for a leash. Either because of the dog or because of the day's heat, the pit and her owner had the field to themselves. The new basketball courts with their netless hoops stood empty, as did the new tennis courts. The summer heat, Maureen thought, it drove people indoors down here the way the cold did up north.

But in the playground, alone atop the arch of a jungle gym, sat the drummer, the kid who'd lingered the other day to taunt Maureen.

"Stop the car," she said. "I see one of them, the one who mentioned Scales."

"Who?"

"Bobby Scales, who owned the green car?"

"What car?" Preacher couldn't help himself this time; he started laughing. He threw the car into park. He hit the lights, left the sirens off. "See the thing is, I have to make sure you can handle every different kind of asshole cop there is before I let you go off on your own. You have no idea how taxing it is."

"I know how taxing you are," Maureen said, struggling with her sense of humor. "Fucking very. I can tell you about that."

"Save it for your memoir, English major," Preacher said. "Let's get this done."

Maureen opened her door, climbed out onto the sidewalk. To her surprise, Preacher turned off the lights and got out of the car. She heard him come up behind her as she headed for the playground gate. "Preach, I got this, he's twelve."

"The kid?" Preacher said, hitching up his pants. "He's all yours."

Preacher lifted his chin at the field, at the panting dog and her owner. The dog reared back on its haunches, squinty-eyed, barking for the ball its owner waved overhead. "This heat, no shade, that motherfucker better have water for that dog. Some of them—the dogs, that is—don't know any better and run till they drop. They drop dead sometimes. Call me if you need help with the kid, unless he rabbits. That happens, you're on your own. You got the legs for it."

Maureen and Preacher parted ways at the playground entrance. She approached the jungle gym. The entrance behind her was also the playground's only exit. She stayed between the kid and the gate, adding up the angles like a soccer goalie. The kid showed no urge to run. He stayed on his perch, checking her out while shading his eyes with one hand, clutching his drumsticks in his other. On the ground beneath him sat a bulging backpack. He wore long black basketball shorts that ended way below his knees and a dark polo shirt two sizes too large for him. In his baggy clothes, he seemed smaller than he had yesterday. The shirt had an emblem Maureen didn't recognize on the right side of the chest, like a private- or charter-school uniform. He looked like a kid fresh out of school, which was weird, because school didn't start for two more weeks.

Summer camp? Maybe. But with collared shirts and bulging book bags?

With his drumsticks he tapped out an up-tempo stutter-step rhythm on the jungle gym. He held the sticks palms up, like a jazz drummer or a snare player in a marching band. Deep notes rang off the frame, as if the kid sat atop the bass end of a giant xylophone. His hands were quick. His gaze stayed fixed straight ahead, his eyebrows knitted in concentration as if he were trying to visualize the next sequence of beats and the motions needed to make them.

Middle school age or not, Maureen knew male posturing when she saw it. She let him have his space. She stopped her approach a few feet away, slipped her hands into her back pockets.

"You're pretty good."

"And you would know."

"Not really," Maureen said. "What song were you playing?"

"That wasn't a song," the boy said, "it was a cadence, like for a marching band. They're not the same thing."

"I wasn't in the band in school. I was an athlete. A runner. Where I'm from, it wasn't cool to be in the band, like it is here."

The kid grinned, not looking at her. He moved his sticks to his thighs, let them roll loose in his palms, as if savoring the smoothness of the wood. "Mike-Mike says you got speed."

"Not enough, apparently." Nice, she thought. That's one name without even trying.

"Heard that."

"So you know my name," Maureen said. "And now I know Mike-Mike's. Care to tell me yours? First name, at least?"

"Marques. Say it like with a 'c' but spell it with a 'q,' like Marques Colston." He sat up straighter on his perch, waited one more beat for her to say something. "You know about him, right?"

"Wide receiver, number twelve. Enormous hands." She smiled. "Gimme a little credit." She took a step closer. "Listen, Marques. You know why I'm here, why the police have been around a lot."

"Mr. Norman got shot," Marques said. "Somebody killed him." His hands picked up a slow rhythm. "I don't know nothin' 'bout that. I wasn't around."

"I know that. I know. But there are other questions we'd like to ask you. About the neighborhood. About that green car. The detective in charge would really like to talk to you, and to Mike-Mike. And to your other friend."

Marques looked past Maureen to the cruiser. He pursed his lips and moved them around, like he had a mouthful of mouthwash. He blew out his breath. Maureen feared she was making him nervous. She wanted to bring Marques's attention back to her, to ease his mind.

"She'll come to your house. You won't have to go to the district or anything. No one else will know. Tell me where you live, so I can tell her."

"Ain't no police coming to my house. I can tell you that."

Maureen felt her pulse pick up; she was blowing it with this kid. "The other day at the Garvey Apartments, you looked like you wanted to tell me something. What was it?"

"I don't remember that," Marques said. "Prob'ly nothing."

"That's not true," Maureen said. "That guy across the street scared you before you could talk to me. He's not here now. You don't have to worry about him."

Marques dropped through a space in the bars, his sneakers thumping on the rubber mat covering the ground. "I got to go."

Maureen watched Marques pack his sticks into his backpack, leaving the tips visible, to show the neighborhood he played. If he walked away, she'd have to let him go. She didn't have orders to detain him, nor did she have cause to take him in if he hadn't seen the killing. She didn't think he had. She could haul him in anyway, on some excuse, and make him wait for Atkinson. But that would bring his family into it, maybe a lawyer, and the hassle would only make him more resistant than he was already.

A first name and a nickname were what Maureen had gotten, what she'd have for Atkinson. Not much. Nothing impressive, that was for sure. Shit, actually.

And here to rub it in was Preacher, folding his arms over the top of the chest-high fence separating the playground and the ball field. He held a gooey tennis ball in one hand. At his feet sat the adoring pit, panting away like a blast furnace. The man who the dog had been playing with wasn't around anymore.

"Hey, kid," Preacher said, talking to Marques. He touched his badge. "How long you been with Roots?"

"Been with who?" Maureen asked.

Marques stretched the emblem on his polo in Maureen's direction. "The Roots of Music. It's a marching band."

"Kids from all over town," Preacher said. "Best marching band in New Orleans."

"After St. Aug," Marques corrected.

"Heard that," Preacher said. "Bobby Scales play with y'all?"

"Mr. Bobby a grown man," Marques said. "He can't play with Roots. It's kids only, yo."

Preacher raised his hands in apology, exciting the dog. He wiggled the fingers on his free hand, imitating fingering notes on a horn. "A name like Scales, I thought maybe he played a horn or something." Preacher turned and threw the ball. The dog exploded after it. "He at least help you guys out any? Drive you downtown to practice?"

Marques shrugged. "He ain't like that."

"Then what's he like?" Preacher asked.

Marques shrugged again. "Busy."

"How about Mike-Mike?" Maureen asked. "Is he in the band?"

Marques shook his head at Preacher, as if expressing silent sympathy for suffering such a dimwitted partner. "Mike-Mike can't even play *checkers*, yo. He too dumb."

"What about your other boy?" Preacher asked.

"Goody used to play," Marques said, "but then he got to fighting and Mr. Elvin kicked him out. In the spring." Marques shook his head again. "Mr. Elvin don't mess around. I slapped a kid last year, right, for spilling his grape soda on my homework? I had to do a thousand push-ups so I could stay in the band."

"A thousand?" Preacher asked. "One thousand."

Marques nodded with pride. "Not in a row, but I did 'em. We added 'em up day-to-day. We kept count on a blackboard. I did 'em all, yo."

Preacher smiled, genuinely impressed. He turned to Maureen. "Can you do a thousand push-ups, Coughlin?"

"Don't know," Maureen said. "Never tried."

"Give it a shot," Preacher said. "Let me know how it goes."

The dog trotted over to them with the ball. Preacher pulled it from her jaws, held it before the pit's face. "Last time." The dog didn't look like she believed it.

Preacher threw the ball. The dog bolted. Maureen followed the arc of the ball. Where was the dog's owner? Preacher's voice brought her back to the playground.

"You know where I can find Goody?" Preacher asked. "We're trying to help find Mr. Bobby's car."

"I ain't seen him since yesterday. Last time you saw him was the last time I saw him. I ain't nobody's babysitter."

"But you saw Mike-Mike," Maureen said. "You saw him not long ago if you talked about me chasing him."

"You didn't ask about no Mike-Mike."

"I'm asking now," Maureen said. "Is he in the neighborhood?"

"Where else he gonna be?"

"Keep it up," Maureen said. "You think Mr. Elvin is scary?"

"Enough," Preacher said. Reaching over the fence, he handed Marques a business card. "You see Goody, you tell him to call the Sixth. Ask for me, Officer Boyd, or my partner, Officer Coughlin. Mike-Mike, too. If we're not in, people can find us. We want to talk about the car, maybe Mr. Bobby. What the hell, tell him to call us, too. No big deal, but we'd like to do it soon. Before there's any more trouble."

The dog returned. She dropped the ball between her paws and

flopped in the grass, panting like a locomotive, her squinty smile fixed on Preacher. Marques took the card, buried it deep in his shorts. From the way he watched the dog, and despite the fact that the pit paid him no mind, Maureen could tell that Marques was glad for the fence.

"I can go, right?"

"Roll out, soldier," Preacher said.

Marques waddled away under the weight of his backpack, out of the playground and across the basketball courts. Maureen waited until Marques was half a block away before she spoke. "The guy with the ball? What happened to him?"

"That rope this dog is trailing," Preacher said, "is from a rape post." The calm benevolence he'd shown Marques had dissipated. "You know what that is? What it's for?"

Maureen looked down at the dog, snoozing now, its big square head resting on its paws. "It's a dog-fighting tool," she said. "It's for forced breeding."

"Mr. Etienne couldn't seem to remember where he found her," Preacher said, looking down at the sleeping animal. "A dog like this, considering the rope, probably has a history. Not a good one. The teats on her, she's had some pups. See those scars on her head? I'm gonna pretend those are birthmarks for the sake of my own sanity. I encouraged the gentleman to forget he ever found her, and that he ever saw me today." He reached into his pocket and pulled out a crack pipe that he twiddled between his fingers. "And I told him I'd forget about this. And maybe forget to decide whether or not to violate his ass back to fucking Rayburn Correctional."

He dropped the pipe into his pocket, looked down at the dog. "I got someone from pit rescue coming to get her. To clean her up and check her out."

Preacher snapped his fingers. "Let's go, girl."

The dog, exhausted, struggled to her feet, obedient.

Maureen walked with Preacher and the dog back along the fence toward the police car. If the dog had taken notice of Maureen, she wasn't showing it. She only had eyes for Preacher.

"So you know this guy who had the dog," Maureen said.

"From around the neighborhood, yeah. Howard Etienne, Junior. Little E. His dad was Big E, owned part of the Fox Den lounge up by Broad Street, was a Wild Man for years for the Wild Tchoupitoulas. Died in Houston after the storm. Heart or something. Anyways, it's been a while since I've seen Little E. He took a gun charge three years ago, went to the state lockup. Always claimed he was holding the weapon for someone else and I believed him. He woulda killed himself carrying a gun before he hurt anyone else with it. Who's he gonna rob? He's a crackhead. Everyone he knows has less than nothing. Besides, guys like E have been cycled through the system so many times, he probably never believed he'd really do time until they put him on the bus to Rayburn. A friend of a friend probably offered him a hundred bucks and a pack of lies to take the charge. So, to his credit, he did do a three-year bit for someone else in the state pen."

"Could that someone else be Bobby Scales?" Maureen asked. "If Etienne was gonna do time for someone, it would be someone who mattered, who scared him."

Preacher shook his head. "E never heard of Scales, that's what he told me when I asked."

"You believe him?"

"Undecided. E is on the streets only a couple of weeks. Just 'cause he's back on the rock doesn't mean he's back in the game, if he was ever really in it."

Preacher slid his cigar from his shirt pocket. Maureen hoped he wouldn't light up. When he was in especially good spirits, he'd smoke in the car. Unbearable. He rolled the cigar around under his nose, sniffing it, and put it back in his shirt pocket.

"Pop quiz, hotshot. If Etienne has a record and had a crack pipe in his possession, why isn't he under arrest?"

Maureen suppressed a smile. She had the answers. Her first one, that the crack pipe belonged to Preacher and was a plant—she suppressed that, too.

"You wanna haul him in," she said, "and put charges on him, you wouldn't be wrong. Good luck getting him to show up for court, though, or you, for that matter, for a Mickey Mouse paraphernalia rap. But, on the other hand, maybe we get a stat that makes us look good. He is a recidivist."

"Not bad so far." The dog mooned up at him, her stump of a tail twitching. "What else you got?"

"We leave Etienne out and about," Maureen said, the gears clicking like they had at Wright's murder scene with Atkinson, "and we see if Scales's name reaches him. Fresh out of the pen, he's a clean slate. We roll up on E again in a couple of days and see what the news is. On the street he might hear something about the Wright murder, and now he owes us a favor. In lockup, he's worth nothing to us."

"We might make a cop outta you yet," Preacher said, smiling. The smile vanished. "It's good, Coughlin, that what happened to Wright hasn't made you scared."

"What happened to Wright wasn't my fault."

"And people never blame themselves for things that ain't their fault? I've seen plenty who can't live with not saving the world. You're doing good, that's what I'm saying. You can't play this game scared. You can't play it not to lose."

It was times like these Maureen thought Preacher might actually care how she turned out.

They'd reached the end of the fence dividing the field and the playground. They exited through their respective gates and reconvened on the sidewalk.

"Listen, Coughlin, after you write up everything Marques told you for Atkinson, let me see it before you send it over. Write it before you go home for the day. Make sure Atkinson has it for her shift tonight. She'll need to know what got done today, and what didn't."

Maureen stopped on the sidewalk before they got to the cruiser. "I've got one request."

Preacher squeezed his forehead in his hand. "Why am I suddenly overcome with dread?"

"This Mr. Elvin guy, the band director, can we go downtown and talk to him? He knows these boys."

Preacher shook his head. "I don't think so."

"He's got info we need, Preach. Stuff that Atkinson wants."

"She can get it from him," Preacher said.

Maureen puffed out her cheeks, holding her breath. Don't call him lazy, she thought. Don't accuse him of anything. "It just seems like the natural next step. That's all I'm saying."

"It is the next step," Preacher said, "for the detective in charge of the case. Chain of command, Coughlin. Your information gets passed upwards. If this guy is important, who do you think Atkinson wants talking to him? You? Me? Or you think she wants to handle it herself?"

Maureen held up her hands. "Okay, I get it."

"Do you?"

"Yeah."

"So that means I won't hear about you venturing outside the radius of your ken and suchlike activity."

Maureen saluted him.

"Tell me you understand me, smart-ass."

"Yes, sir," Maureen said.

They continued toward the car.

"I would've made notes back there," Maureen said, "but you had Marques going. I figured, why remind him he's talking to the police?"

"And that was the right move."

"Well, at least I made one of them."

"Give yourself a break, Coughlin. I've got a few more miles on me. If you leave the dog out of your report, that'll make two right moves today."

"You got that information from Marques," Maureen said, "and saved this dog without even breaking a sweat or raising your voice. I hafta bow down."

"Let this be a lesson to you, rookie," Preacher said. It cost him some effort, but he bent down and scratched the pit behind her ears. "When I do get out the car, I make it fucking count."

13

Maureen parked a block up Third Street from her apartment, under a streetlight nimbused with moths and mosquitoes, in front of a sprawling Greek Revival mansion with curbside tie-up posts left over from the days of carriage horses. Gas lamps flickered at the front door, their flames refracted in a kaleidoscopic stained-glass window like a palmful of gemstones held under a candle. The mansion was one of many in her neighborhood. She lived in a mansion, as a matter of fact, one with its own enormous stained-glass window looming over the lobby and the winding staircase to the second floor. Of course, her mansion had been cut up into twenty rental apartments decades ago. Still, on the outside, it was a grand and impressive building.

She climbed from the Honda on tired legs, the backs of her thighs damp from sweating on the seat. She pinched the wet collar of her sleeveless T away from her collarbone. Her eyes burned from sleeplessness. Parking a block from her place really wasn't a problem. She felt safe and she liked any excuse, really, to stroll around the neighborhood. The strange beauty of it was why, despite joining a gym she could walk to and that boasted a whole room of top-flight cardio equipment, and despite the rainforest heat of summertime New Orleans, she took most of her runs outdoors.

She grabbed her gym bag from the backseat. Her arms sang with pumping blood after her postshift workout in the district weight room. On her phone, she checked the time. Nearly eleven. Christ, between the paperwork and the workout, she'd lost most of the night. She threw her bag over her shoulder, took a deep breath of the damp, perfumed air.

A greenhouse, she thought. A greenhouse attached to a castle where the owners had died and the plants had grown out of control. Some of what she inhaled was sweet olive, some of it was jasmine; she'd learned that much, though she couldn't remember which was which when she saw it. And somewhere in there, way in the back of the bouquet, was a neighbor's garbage can in need of a rinse, probably out in the street to save a parking space.

She would run in the streets tonight, up to the park and back, her usual six-mile route.

As she crossed Camp Street and walked along Third, frogs and cicadas going full-throat in the darkness around her, Maureen let her fingers play through the stems and vines overhanging the wrought-iron fences of her neighbors. The slightest contact doubled the strength of the scent of the night-blooming flowers. She wanted to snap off a bloom and take it home with her, but she knew watching it die in coffee-mug captivity, alone atop her refrigerator, would only depress her. Leaving the bloom intact meant she could visit it again and again as it thrived. At least until it dropped its petals to the bricks below.

Sometimes she couldn't believe she lived in a place where she walked under palm trees. She wanted a palm tree of her own one day. Even if she had to grow it in a pot on her porch. And parakeets would come and live in it, too. Because you could do that here, she thought, grow your own palm tree. All you had to do was pick which kind you wanted. The Garden District and the Sixth District. They were her life now.

She raised her hands to drum a few notes on a low-hanging crepe myrtle branch. Pink petals knocked loose by the vibration, the glory days of July behind them, landed in her hair and on her shoulders. They smelled sweet and rotten at the same time. She brushed the petals off her sweaty T-shirt and crossed the street. She stopped short when she reached the curb by her house.

There, sitting on the front steps, was Patrick. Really? Right now? She wasn't happy to see him. They hadn't made plans. They hadn't hit the stage where surprises were okay. They probably never would. She hoped he couldn't read the irritation on her face as she came through the gate. Patrick was her first New Orleans diversion. She'd enjoyed him. Now she feared he teetered on the edge of becoming her first New Orleans mistake.

Dark-haired, blue-eyed, and sleepily handsome, Patrick was all limbs, a bit apelike, with his long, sinewy arms and powerful legs hitched to a set of narrow shoulders and narrower hips. He had a forward slouch that Maureen recognized as coming from long hours leaning over a cutting table and a grill. He had nimble, rough-skinned, beautiful hands with surprisingly few knife nicks, considering his trade. Only one burn on them that she could see, a faint one on the back of his left hand. Not bad for a guy who'd spent years keeping close company with a burbling deep fryer. He cooked at the bar and po'boy shop, the Irish Garden, across Magazine Street from her apartment.

The night she'd met him at the bar, she'd strolled over in cut-off sweats, an NOPD T-shirt, and flip-flops, looking about as "cranky old lady" as she could look, to complain about the noise pumping out of the place. The Irish Garden had tall, narrow French doors that folded open, letting the noise inside pour into the street, along with the smells from the grill. The food was tempting, pretty much any time of day. The drunken cackling and screaming arguments over pool games and LSU were not. They had a good jukebox, but played it too loud and too late. Loud music, Maureen knew, kept the clientele from using their indoor voices. The obnoxiousness snowballed from there.

Maureen had marched into the bar, elbowing customers out of the way, badge in her waistband, unable to decide which identity to lead with—her new one as a New Orleans cop or her old one from New York, where she'd walked a thousand miles in the bartender's damp shoes. When the chubby, bitchy bartender answered Maureen's complaints about the noise with her own snarling commentary about old bitch-ass neighbors looking to ruin everyone else's good time, Maureen nearly went over the bar after her. Before things got worse, Patrick intervened.

He stepped behind the bar and lowered the stereo. With a wave he beckoned Maureen down to the far end of the bar, away from Ms. Surly. While she made her way over to him, the boy opened two Harps. The boy was cute. Enough so that Maureen decided that he'd make a better anti-dote to the aggravation than a fistfight with the neighborhood barkeep. He was the easy and lazy choice. Maureen knew it and she didn't care.

She polished off that first Harp fast, then nursed another while beating Patrick two out of three games at the pool table. She'd caught him letting her win the first game, calling him out on it in front of his friends. He came back and won that game straight up. She beat him the next two. His friends jeered him loudly; she recognized some of their voices from hearing them in her apartment. He took the losing and the joking well. Points in his favor. He didn't ask her where she was from, though she figured later her accent had answered the question. And it didn't hurt that he didn't once tell her she looked good. She didn't. She looked like what she was, a neighborhood girl who couldn't sleep, blowing off some steam. That seemed fine to him, and she liked that, too.

They traded numbers that night. She took him home three nights later. That was two months ago. She'd never let him sleep over.

It worried her some, but not enough to scare her off, that Patrick could see her apartment from where he worked. He could watch her walk home at night. He could see if her lights were on. On the other hand, in a box under her bed, she had blue ribbons in both hand-to-hand combat and target shooting from the NOPD academy. On her nightstand, she had a loaded gun she knew how to use. Patrick learned these things the first night he came over. He didn't take any of it personally. He had, until showing up that evening on her front steps, respected her space.

He wore his checkered chef's pants and his black rubber no-slip shoes, which meant he hadn't showered, which meant he'd come straight from work across the street, which meant he'd smell like fried catfish. Did look like he'd thrown on a clean T-shirt. Thank the Lord for small favors, Maureen thought. And who was she to complain, anyway? Anticipating a long run in the humid evening, she hadn't showered after her workout at the Sixth. Just the combined funk they'd be bringing into her tiny apartment was reason enough not to let Patrick any closer than the front steps. In this humidity, she thought, the smell of everything is intensified. And it hangs around.

Maureen passed through the front gate. Patrick raised the brown paper bag at his hip. A po'boy. "I made you dinner."

Despite herself, Maureen grimaced. "I can't eat that, Pat. I gotta run tonight."

"You can save it, I guess. For after." Patrick set the sandwich back on the step. "You're moving up in the world. Congrats."

Maureen put her bag down on the walk, sat a couple of steps below Patrick. "What for?"

"I hear you're helping a detective work a murder. That poor bastard in the paper this morning. That's a step up for you, right?"

Maureen wondered how in hell Patrick had heard about her involvement in the Wright case. Atkinson's name would be in the article as lead investigator, but her name wouldn't appear. "I haven't even seen you since then. How do you know about that?"

"You know Goo? He buses the place sometimes on busy nights? Hangs over by the pool table with a crew when we're not busy?"

"I guess." She couldn't put a face to the name, even a name like that. "I mean, I think I've heard you talk about him."

"Anyway, he knows who *you* are," Patrick said. "And he's got a cousin that lives in the apartment complex where you kicked that guy's ass the other day. The cousin saw you talking to Wright on the street, and saw you again at the murder scene last night. It's not like everyone at the bar doesn't know you're a cop."

Maureen wasn't sure what to say, if she should say anything. She felt even more invaded by Patrick's knowledge of her job than she did by his surprise visit. There didn't seem to be any point in denying the truth. Seems the NOPD weren't the only ones putting in some detective work overnight. She wondered what else the neighborhood was saying about her.

"So the cousin," Patrick said, "told Goo, who told me." He smiled. "New Orleans is a really small town sometimes."

"I'm finding that out," Maureen said.

"Y'all getting anywhere?" Patrick asked, grinning. "Any leads? Any suspects?"

"Who's asking? You or Goo or the cousin?"

Patrick leaned away from her, trying to figure, Maureen could tell, whether she was serious or kidding. She wasn't sure herself.

"Okay, hey, just me," Patrick said. "Just curious. You're one of those cops who doesn't bring it home, I get it. I watch TV."

Maureen tried to smile. "The only kind of cop I am right now is tired." She reached out and grabbed his knee. "Look, I forgot we were getting together tonight. I'm sorry. You been waiting long?"

"I shoulda called, I know. But I got news." Patrick raised his chin at the bar across the street. "This here po'boy is the last one I'm ever going to make for you."

Maureen took her hand from Patrick's knee and set it on the step below her. She leaned back into her shoulder for a better look up at him. Was she getting dumped? As minor as she considered what they had, she'd assumed the end of it would be her call. Maybe not. Again, she wasn't so sure she wanted him gone, though she knew it was her ego, not her heart or her body, telling her that. An acidic humiliation simmered under her ribs. Had this boy gotten tired of sleeping with her? Gotten bored with her body, her company? Already?

She knew she'd been pretty cavalier toward Patrick; it shouldn't sting like it did when the feelings, or lack thereof, went the other way. But she was stung. Some lessons, it seemed, she had to keep on learning.

"That sounds like a threat," she said.

Patrick laughed. The sound made her want to punch him. "I'm done across the street. Worked my last shift this afternoon."

Okay, not what she'd feared, but Maureen was surprised anyway. "Back to law school, then?"

Patrick laughed again. He did that; he didn't laugh loud or long, but he did laugh often. "I'm done with that, too. I told you, way, way done with that, no matter what my folks pray for every night." He reached for Maureen's shoulder, brushed stray strands of hair off her skin with his fingers. "I got a new gig. I got on the line at Lilette."

Maureen shook her head. It certainly sounded more serious, more upscale than the Irish Garden. But names could be deceiving. "I'm sorry. I haven't found that place yet. That's a good thing?"

"John Harris's place? Up Magazine, just this side of Napoleon?" He waited. "On a corner, painted yellow. The name of the place is painted in gold in the front window."

Suddenly, Maureen could see it. "Oh, I got it. Pat, that place is beautiful."

It was beautiful. She could see it. She didn't have to fake it. Never did with Patrick, for that matter. Looked like a very elegant establishment, she thought, if only through the windows of the place while cruising by in a patrol car, or jogging by at night. Fine dining, servers in long white aprons and ties. French.

She'd never worked fine dining. She had never worked back of the house like Patrick, hadn't lived in New Orleans long enough to learn who John Harris was. The way Patrick beamed at her, though, she knew he'd scored a serious promotion. He wanted her to be proud of him. She was.

Maureen thought of Detective Sergeant Atkinson. Maybe getting a spot on John Harris's line matched getting an assignment from Christine Atkinson. Maybe Patrick looked at Harris the way Maureen looked at Atkinson. She was proud of Patrick, and hopeful for him. And she liked the way he looked at her right then. Okay, she thought, standing, one more time. His hand in hers, she used his fingers to trace a line on the slick inside of her thigh. One more time. A celebration. For both of them catching the right set of eyes at the right time. Patrick stood, grinning, a telltale bulge rising in the front of his cook's pants. A good sweaty fuck, then, she thought, for *new* times' sake. Maybe she'd even let him get behind her, like he was always asking and she was always refusing. Why not, just this once?

They left the po'boy on the step.

14

Maureen strolled naked and triumphant through her tiny excuse for a kitchen, leaving Patrick catching his breath in the middle of the floor, tangled in the comforter with his arm draped over his eyes. She dropped the used condom in the trash. The water pressure in her place sucked. She didn't need the prophylactic bobbing back up at her later like a dead jellyfish.

She was on the pill, maybe the only regimen she followed with equal dedication to her workouts. So, no real risk of babies. Patrick swore he got regular AIDS tests, and she believed him. She'd been in the bar business too long, though, not to know her bar boys. Just 'cause he didn't know he had something didn't mean he didn't have it, so protection was paramount.

In a minor miracle, she'd made it through eleven years in the service industry, the last eight or nine involving some truly horrendous sexual choices, without picking up a single STD. Maybe sticking to older and more often than not married men those last couple of years, while no proof of advancement in her emotional decision making, had helped at least preserve her sexual health. Now that she was out of the business, she wasn't about to break the clean streak. Patrick had complained once about using a condom. Once. She'd thrown him out for it, his quivering hard-on stuffed hurriedly and uncomfortably into his jeans. He had nothing to complain about, really. She only made him wear a rubber for intercourse.

She turned on the tap in the tub and stepped in, stooping to rinse between her legs once the water warmed. Tonight, especially, he had nothing to complain about. They'd started with her on top, her prefer-ence, but right before he finished, she'd lifted her hips and slid him out. Then she'd turned around on all fours, flicked her hair over her back like she was sure he wanted and had fantasized about, and let him inside her from behind—where, and this was the big, big deal about it to Maureen, though Patrick didn't know it—she couldn't see him or what he was do-ing. He'd gripped one of her hips in each hand, so she hadn't had to worry about where they were, and, since he was on the brink before she'd made her move, he came, shuddering, in no time. Ending it quickly had been crucial to the plan. In his grunting excitement, Patrick hadn't no-ticed that she hadn't come, and, this particular time, that miss was okay with her. She could sacrifice an orgasm during the act if also not having a panic attack in the middle of sex was part of the deal.

With her fingers, she congratulated herself on the quiet victory she'd won on all fours in the middle of the living room floor.

Relieved, she rinsed herself again and sat on the edge of the tub to catch her breath.

Before everything had gone to shit in New York and done her head in, she'd liked fucking with the boy behind her. She'd never found the posi-tion submissive, like she always thought she was supposed to, like they showed in movies and on TV, slave women and whores and women meant to be taken as whores always getting it from behind like it couldn't be a woman's idea to do it that way. Men were the ones turned into knee-quaking, drooling, begging buffoons by doing it from behind. Her? She'd liked having her weight off her hips, her arms and legs remaining free and useful for bracing herself and for pushing back.

But ever since Sebastian, who hadn't raped her, had only tried to kill her, she couldn't fuck a man she couldn't see.

Maureen passed her hand over her smooth, flat belly. She touched the close-trimmed auburn hair with her fingertips. That bastard Sebastian had put fear deeper inside her than his cock or any other cock could've reached. He'd left that fear and a hot fury like its twin lingering inside her like a disease. Sometimes she forgot she carried them. Sometimes they flared unprovoked. She'd done some penetrating of her own on him, with immediate, not lingering, results. And sometimes she felt like her police uniform acted like a poultice, drawing out of her the poison that Sebastian had put into her. She worried sometimes about what she did with that poison when it broke the surface, a bubble of noxious gas up from the seafloor, or was it the swampfloor now, bursting invisible and dangerous and spreading into the atmosphere around her like a contagion.

She thought of Patrick's hard thighs against the backs of hers, of him moving slick and easy inside her. Her idea, her choice. Her brain, her body. She made a fist with her right hand, her gun hand, the hand she'd used to lay out Arthur Jackson. She studied her fist. She was reclaiming herself, one small decision, one small move, one small piece at a time. The only thing she couldn't stop doing was moving forward.

Patrick called out from the living room. "You all right in there?"

Maureen checked the tub. Whoops. Had the condom split? She hadn't checked before ditching it. Looked like it—a sticky, clingy somethin'-somethin' had collected in the drain screen.

"Be right out," she said.

She hit the hot water tap again, washing the last remnants, the last evidence, of her last time with sweet Patrick down the drain. She snatched her robe off the wall hook and pulled it on, tying a snug knot in the belt. She needed to run. She needed to wash her hair; she needed sleep. But none of that till Patrick was gone.

Back in the living room, she found him wearing only his boxers and sitting at her desk. Now the room smelled like sex and sweat and fried shrimp, a combo that left Maureen vaguely nauseated. She opened a kitchen window. Patrick reached over from his seat and turned off the AC.

"Leave it on." Crossing the room, Maureen pulled the cord on the ceiling fan to start the blades. She beat Patrick to the air-conditioner dial, cranked it to HIGH. "This place needs some air."

Patrick stood, scratching at his right buttock. "You got a cigarette?"

Maureen sat on her bed. "Around here somewhere."

She didn't move to get them from her bag.

Patrick didn't move, either, waiting for Maureen to provide a smoke. She knew he was respecting her space, not wanting to go through her drawers or her clothes or her bag, but she resented the expectation that she'd wait on him. Poor guy couldn't win for losing. She waited for the snit to pass. Patrick sensed something and knew not to ask again. He picked up his chef's pants from the floor, stepped into them. "I'll get a pack at the Spur on my way." He looked at her, running his thumbs along the elastic waistband of his checkered pants. "You need?"

"I got some," Maureen said, "around here somewhere."

"How you could lose anything," Patrick said, pulling his T-shirt over his head, "in a place this small is beyond me. You should upgrade."

"I'm thinking about it," Maureen said. She closed her robe over her thighs. She was so tired her eyes were tearing, blurring Patrick for a moment. She blinked them clear. "I'm looking around, kind of half-assing it, to tell the truth."

Patrick smiled. "We're talking about apartments, right?"

Maureen had to chuckle. "I need to make sure I'm gonna keep my job, before I can really start thinking about a more serious place."

"So, like I was saying about that job at Lilette," he said, smiling again.

He couldn't help himself, Maureen thought. Even the way he said the name of the restaurant, like it was the name of a new great girl he'd just met. It was so cute.

"It's a nice bump in pay from the bar," Patrick said, "even without a tip jar in the window, and it's only a start. I'll be kind of like you for a while, on probation, so to speak, I'll have to prove I can cut it, but if I can make it in Harris's kitchen, even if there's no room to move up, I can walk into pretty much any kitchen in the city that has an opening."

He held his hands out flat in front of him, side by side, elbows on his knees. "I think it's kind of neat how, all of a sudden, you and me are on parallel paths. You with that detective, me with John Harris."

Maureen went cold in the pit of her stomach. It was dawning on her where this was going; Patrick wanted to merge their parallel paths. He was at best starting the "let's get serious about this" conversation, and at worst he was about to ask her to move in with him. Why this? she wondered. Why now? Well, at least he'd steamrolled dead any temptation she had about keeping him on the hook.

"Listen, Patrick," she said, sliding to the edge of the bed, "I think I know where you're going here, and I have to say, I'm not sure I feel the same way." She tucked her hair behind her ears and leaned forward toward him, her hands folded between her knees. "And I don't know if I can talk about this right now."

"I know you're beat," Patrick said, "but I don't want to let this hang around. I don't have the time." He shrugged, and blushed. "And I have a lot of respect for you. With this new gig, well, the first thing I thought of was you."

Maureen stood. "Pat, I really gotta make a call. For work. Can we have coffee over this at the Rue tomorrow?"

"It's not that complicated," Patrick said, rubbing his palms on his thighs, "though I hoped it was gonna be easier than this to talk about." He wasn't looking at her now. "Anyway, I guess I wasn't a hundred percent right about how you felt. I thought I had it figured." He looked up at her. "Maureen, with this new job, it's gonna be so much to do, I can't see you anymore."

He stood, rolling his shoulders. "This thing we have, it's cool, it really is, but right now I gotta give everything to my career."

He paused, giving her a moment to speak. Maureen was too stunned to fill in the blank.

"You understand, right?"

"Yeah," Maureen said. She looked at her hands. "Yeah, I understand. Believe me, I understand." No, those were not tears pushing at the edges of her eyes. For this guy? Of course not. She was just so tired. "And I'm cool with this, just a little surprised, I guess."

"I knew you'd understand," Patrick said, smiling, and itching, Maureen could tell, to get away from her now that the deed was done. "You're not the type for a lot of drama."

"I guess not," Maureen said. "So, anyway, I'm not trying to kick you out or anything, but I have to make a call for work before it gets too late."

Patrick checked his pockets for his possessions before making his escape. He bent his thumb over his shoulder. "So, over in the bar, if we're both in there?"

"We're cool," Maureen said. "You owe me a shot for dumping me right when you're about to become this famous chef, but other than that, we're good. And I'm not holding back around the pool table anymore."

Patrick approached her. He held his hand out as if they'd finalized some long negotiation. She shook it.

"You're good people, Coughlin," Patrick said, heading for the door. "New Orleans is lucky to have you."

Maureen came to the door, ready to slide it closed as soon as Patrick left. "Gimme a shout when you're settled at Lilette. I'll come in for something to eat."

"You do that," Patrick said. "Don't you dare come in there without telling me. I mean it."

"All right, Patrick."

She slid the pocket door halfway closed, but stopped. She stepped out into the lobby and called Patrick's name. He let the front door close and turned to her, waiting for her to speak.

"This cousin of Goo's," Maureen said. "You ever met him?"

"Couple of times, I guess," Patrick said. "He passes by the bar every now and again. I think he's Goo's weed connect." He laughed. "Shit, I guess I shouldn't tell you that."

"What's he look like?"

"It's just hearsay, I've never seen anything," Patrick said.

"Can you answer me, please?"

Patrick's shoulders slumped. "Maureen, c'mon, don't be like that. You're gonna hassle somebody 'cause I dumped you, hassle me. Don't hassle my boy."

"It's not about that," Maureen said. "I'm not like that. I promise. Can you just tell me what the guy looks like?"

Patrick sighed. "He's a younger dude, twists in his hair. Dark skin. One of those Rasta wannabe kids, always decked out in Marley gear. Wears that corny shell jewelry all the time." He rolled his eyes. "I forget his name. He's got some goofy nickname he goes by." He shrugged. "Go figure, right, with a cousin named Goo."

"His name isn't Scales?"

"That wasn't it. It was something else." He pulled open the door, letting in the sounds of the bar and the nighttime traffic. "Am I free to go now, Officer? I'm not really thrilled with this conversation."

"Yeah, of course. Thank you. Sorry. Not the guy I was thinking of, anyway."

"Glad to help, or not, or whatever. See you around."

"Just one more thing," Maureen said. "Do me a favor and don't talk about me to people I don't know." She shrugged, gave a small grin. "It's just a thing with me, but it's important."

"Sure. Will do, or not, or whatever." Patrick walked out the door shaking his head.

Maureen slid closed the pocket door and locked it. She stood there with her forehead pressed against the hard wood. She heard the heavy front door slam closed behind Patrick. If he'd had any doubts about letting her go, she thought, she'd certainly killed them with that parting inquisition. She heard him gather up the po'boy from the front stairs, walk around the building, and toss the food in a trash can beneath her window. She thought hard about crawling into bed and pulling the covers over her head. She wanted to hide out, let the world turn without her until her shift in the morning. She could forget about Patrick, and even forget about the job long enough to fall asleep, but the smell of her own skin, of the sex and the sweat—she had to get rid of that before she could rest.

She tossed her gym bag on the bed and unzipped the side pocket, where she found her cigarettes and her phone. She slid a smoke from the pack, lit it, and flipped open the phone. She thumbed her way to Atkinson's number and called it. She had to talk to someone about this kid with the shell necklace. The way he kept surfacing, he was into more than selling dime bags to the local part-time help. He was somebody, or he was somebody's soldier. He wouldn't be so interested in me, Maureen thought, if I wasn't close to something he wanted to hide.

As the phone rang on the other end, Maureen wondered if the detective sergeant had read her report. Maureen knew she'd gotten some worthwhile info, even if it wasn't as good or as much as she'd hoped. She'd written a good report. At the very least, she'd earned another day on the case. But that was the thing about getting dumped, even by guys you were planning on dumping. The rejection left you feeling like nobody wanted you, and like everyone you knew had been laughing at you behind your back. It wasn't the breakup that stung, that humiliated her, to be honest, as much as it was her failure to see it coming. What else was there in her life that she'd decided worked one way and really worked another?

"Atkinson."

Only everything, probably. "Officer Coughlin, Detective Sergeant, following up on my report from today."

"You available tonight? Right now?"

You have no idea, Maureen thought. "Absolutely."

"Meet me at Cleveland and Claiborne. Under the overpass."

Maureen wasn't sure where that was. Ask, she told herself, ask and get it right. Don't end up driving around looking for it and keeping her waiting. "Central City?"

"CBD," Atkinson said. "By the old Charity Hospital." A pause. When Maureen didn't fill it, she said, "There's a bar close by called Handsome Willy's. Park there. You'll see us. We've got lots of lights." She hung up.

The old Charity, Maureen thought. She knew the place, knew the stretch of Claiborne Avenue that Atkinson meant. Not much around that part of downtown but a bunch of parking garages and the massive empty shell of the old hospital complex. There was a bar there? Why would anybody put a bar in the middle of those ruins? She put on a pot of coffee. It would be ready to grab and go by the time she got out of the shower. She was going to need it.

Fuck it, she thought, stripping off her robe. I didn't move here to sleep.

Graduation weekend, before the ink was even dry on her academy diploma, Waters advised her to keep on the lookout for a rabbi, for an older, wiser cop with good connections and a broad, sheltering wing. Despite everything she'd seen in the news, Waters assured her, there would be good cops left in that department. They'd be eager to find other good ones. They'd raise them up from fluffy fucking chicks if they had to. Even if there's only one left, he told her, make sure you find them. For a very brief while, Maureen had thought maybe Preacher was her rabbi. But while he certainly had plenty to teach her, and had more street skills than he let on, Preacher had his eyes firmly fixed on the sunset of his career and was intent on riding into it on the back of a very slow horse. Maureen needed a broad wing, preferably a female one, and one attached to a bird on the rise.

15

Midafternoon on the day of Maureen's academy graduation in June, Maureen, her mom, and Waters were down in the Quarter, over by the river, sitting around a table under the big green-and-white striped awning of Café du Monde. Maureen was learning that the Mississippi, like her, like every other part of the city, had its good days and its bad. Some days, its bad days, the river stank like rotted fruit or even flesh, or wet rust. Some days the smell was industrial like smog, and smoke, and slicks of spilled oil. But on Maureen's graduation day, the sun was bright and the river was having a good day. It smelled like summer rainwater with a hint of salt.

Amber fanned herself with a swamp-tour brochure that had been left on the table. She wore big dark knock-off Ray-Bans that they'd bought at the French Market. She'd laughed out loud at the idea of a swamp tour. Who would ever?

Amber's cheeks and neck were flushed with the heat. The time in the sun during her walking tours of the French Quarter, chosen because it was historical, and the Garden District, important because it was her daughter's new neighborhood, had brought up her freckles.

Strands of reddish hair sprayed from Amber's bun. Maureen kept waiting for her mom, now fifty-five, to start going gray, but so far it hadn't happened. She had less red and more blondish, maybe, but no gray. And she wasn't using any dye, either. Amber had kept her red hair, and she had kept her slim shape, which was the late-arriving upside, Amber had told her daughter once, to being underwhelming in the bust and back-side departments. Her mom looked healthy. She looked happy. Not something Maureen could've said about her mom a year ago, or at any point over the preceding twenty years. The change in Amber gave Maureen hope, and not only for her mom.

Maureen turned in her chair toward the river and into the breeze. Atop the big white riverboat, on a small riser behind the smokestacks, a woman merrily murdered "Yankee Doodle Dandy" on the boat's steam-powered calliope.

"Does that thing ever stop?" Amber asked.

"The tourists love that calliope, Ma. It's one of those unique things. You can't hear it just anywhere."

"You can hear it everywhere," Amber said, brochure fan pumping, "and I'm a tourist and I hate it."

"You're more than a tourist, Ma," Maureen said. "You've got family here now. Family in New Orleans. Exciting, right?"

Amber said nothing, but she laced her fingers into her daughter's and they held hands as they watched Waters guide his bulk, reduced by diet and exercise after his retirement, but still considerable, among the hap-hazard arrangement of tables in the Café du Monde courtyard. Most of the tables were two-tops inhabited by groups of four or six. Silent, ex-hausted families dutifully munched their beignets. Teens in perpetual motion, the last people in the world, Maureen figured, who needed strong coffee, tumbled in and out of one another's arms and laps, coffee cup or a pastry in one hand, smart phone in the other.

Waters had gone to the railing, where he'd passed a couple of bucks to the three-man horn section stationed on the sidewalk.

"Liza Jane," he said, hitching up his cargo shorts and settling into his seat. He held a green bandana in his hand, patted his sweaty forehead with it.

"Who?" Amber asked.

"The name of the song they were playing," Waters said. He whistled the song's chorus. "It's called 'Little Liza Jane.'"

Maureen could tell that Amber's boyfriend enjoyed New Orleans more than Amber did. Then again, he'd supported this move from the beginning. Maureen sometimes forgot that her mother had supported her becoming a cop, too. It wasn't the job that Amber didn't care for, Maureen reminded herself, it was New Orleans, or, more specifically, its considerable distance from Staten Island.

"I wish they'd coordinate shifts or something with the organ-grinder," Amber said. "Isn't anyone in charge of these things? World's most musical city, I'm sure. I don't think they're very good."

"Compared to what, Ma?"

"I should've been in the band when I was in school," Waters said. "I would've played the tuba, like that guy over there."

He wasn't changing the subject, Maureen knew, as much as he was dropping her a hint not to start a sparring match with her mother. Waters threw a glance at Amber, then looked back at Maureen, who realized that her mother labored in genuine emotional distress. This was how Amber handled stress, releasing her tension in short, powerful bursts of snide and sarcastic complaint, like belts of smoke from a locomotive, with as steady a rhythm.

Maureen hadn't realized until those moments at Café du Monde, the first of their last evening together in New Orleans before Amber and Nat returned to New York, how very hard her mom took her daughter's new-found success. Maureen had done everything she could to make New Orleans look good to Amber, and had been very open about how quickly and freely she was falling in love with the city. Now she feared her plan had backfired. Amber had not given up hope until that evening that New Orleans, the city, its police department, the whole thing, had been a re-bound fling inspired by a desire for rebellion after being hurt and thwarted by New York. Amber would never admit it, but she'd hoped since the day that Maureen arrived in New Orleans that the city would betray her, sending her home into the consoling arms of her mother. But Maureen had gone and completed the academy as valedictorian. She'd been as-signed to her district and her first field-training officer. Amber was real-izing that she and Waters had not come to collect Maureen and bring her back to her old home, but that they had come to do what they had been invited to do—see her off and wish her luck in her new home.

A server approached the table, a stout, short-haired Vietnamese woman in an obvious hurry, her white button-down shirt clouded with faded cof-fee stains, her black clip-on bow tie and her white paper hat askew at op-posite angles. She set three small waters on the table hard, the fast-melting ice chips clinking in the short glasses, water sloshing over the rims. She tucked her tray under her arm. "Your order?"

Amber rose in her seat and opened her mouth to speak, but Maureen cut her off. "Two large au lait," she said, "both frozen."

"Frozen?" Waters asked.

"Trust me on this," Maureen said. She turned back to the server. "And a small decaf and two orders."

The server repeated everything back. Maureen agreed with a nod and the woman was off on her way.

"You understood that?" Amber asked.

"Her accent's not that thick," Maureen said. "She just talks fast."

"I'm a New Yorker," Amber said. "Don't tell me about fast talk. Two thousand miles to hear a Chinese accent. What for? This is what you moved for?"

Maybe it was better, Maureen thought, that her mom and Waters weren't staying longer. So far the three of them had skirted Amber's ap-prehensions about her daughter moving to a poor city that was more black than white, ammunition she'd employed in desperation during one of their final and most pitched battles about the move. Maureen knew Amber's temperament would degrade as she grew more and more upset about leaving her daughter behind. The bigotry would surface, and it wouldn't be pretty.

The three of them sat together in silence for a while, the serene picture of the family they almost were, watching the tourists and street performers on the sidewalk and across the street in Jackson Square. Maureen wondered briefly what it might be like to work down here in the Eighth District instead of uptown in the Sixth. That was another exciting thing about Homicide; it was a citywide department. She'd see it all from there—if and when she got that shield. Get ahead of yourself much? she thought, grinning. You're only hours out of the academy.

Their server bustled back to the table, the three coffees in foam cups and two plates of three beignets balanced on a plastic tray. The woman set everything down and named the price. Maureen had her wallet at the ready, but Waters was faster. He handed the server a twenty, saying, "No change."

The server tucked the bill in her apron, gave a short, curt bow, and walked away.

"You're welcome," Amber said.

"Nicely done," Maureen said to Waters.

He plucked a beignet from the stack, powdered sugar falling on the table. He tore it in half, steam rising from its soft, honey-colored insides. "I'm learning."

"Does smell good," Amber said. Using her fingertips, she turned a beignet by its corners on the plate, trying to avoid creating the same splash of powdered sugar that now adorned the front of Waters's Hawaiian shirt.

"You can't fight it, Ma," Maureen said. "It's part of the fun."

She grabbed a beignet, shook it once, then tore off half in her mouth, spraying her face and the front of her uniform shirt with bright white sugar.

"All over your nice new uniform," Amber said.

"I didn't become a cop to stay clean."

Waters chuckled as Maureen chewed her mouthful of hot pastry. Amber couldn't help herself and smiled. "Even as a little girl, you always were half a mess."

Maureen warmed up inside, as if she had a big bellyful of beignet; the casual insult from her mom was worth the smile that came with it. Considering what they'd been through together, and apart, sharing this table was no small miracle. Maureen took what she could get and was grateful when it came to her mother. The sugar tickled the inside of her nose and she thought she might sneeze. With the back of her hand under her nose to temper the itch, Maureen rose from her seat. A memory from not as long ago as it felt rose to her mind, a time when a different white powder tickled her nose. She felt glad and relieved those days were behind her in both miles and time. Right now was much, much better.

"I'll be back in a sec," Maureen said. "Lemme clean up a bit. I'll show you the Moonwalk along the river."

"It's broad daylight," Amber said.

"No, the guy who's mayor now," Maureen said, "his father, Moon Landrieu, used to be mayor. It's named after him."

"New Orleans had a mayor," Amber said, "named Moon." She looked at Waters, who chewed a mouthful of beignet.

Maureen realized her mom, though it was unintentional, did a quite respectable version of an incredulous middle-aged black woman. Maybe it was a universal mother thing, Maureen thought, or a middle-aged-woman look of knowing disdain that she herself would do well to master, considering her new line of work.

Waters finally got his mouthful down. "New York had a mayor named Lindsay," he said, struggling to suppress a grin.

"Lindsay was his *last* name," Amber said, nostrils flaring, her voice rising. She caught her breath when she realized she'd been baited. "The two of you. God give me strength."

This sharp playfulness between Nat and her mother was new to

Maureen. They'd always been sweet to each other, but there was an edge now, a charge. Maureen knew what it meant; they'd finally started sleeping together. She was relieved and proud and nervous and a little uncomfortable. Probably what Amber would feel, Maureen thought, if her daughter ever landed a decent partner and shared a bed with him on a regular basis. Amber grabbed her purse and moved to get up. Maureen set a light hand on her mother's shoulder, keeping her in her seat.

"Ma, earlier this afternoon I was declared fit to police the mean streets of New Orleans. I don't need my mother coming with me to the restroom."

Purse on her lap, Amber raised her hands in surrender, slumping her shoulders. "Fine, fine. God forbid I have to go to the bathroom myself."

"Do you?" Maureen asked.

"No."

"Okay, then." Maureen leaned down and kissed her mom on the head. "I'll be back in a minute. Save me one, at least."

"I'm not making any promises," Waters said. "This is a tough city."

Maureen wove her way through the tourists and the tables and out the back entrance of the patio, over by the to-go window. She headed along the cobblestone path toward the restroom. The line for the women's room stretched out of the building. Maureen took her place on the end, behind a tall woman in a wide sun hat. The woman gave Maureen a polite grin as she looked her up and down, noting the uniform. Maureen straightened her shoulders, puffed out her chest.

"Military school?" the woman asked.

Maureen leaned forward a few inches, forcing her lips into a smile. She tapped the blue-and-gold patch on her sleeve. "Police academy, ma'am. I graduated today."

"Congratulations, dear," the woman said. "Though I have to say, I'd have thought you needed to be bigger to be a police officer."

Before Maureen could answer, a sharp, high-pitched scream echoed inside the bathroom, followed by gasps and the sounds of a struggle. No one in line moved, but several ladies glanced at one another and leaned forward, trying to peek into the building. Maureen stepped out of line and moved for the doorway. For a moment, she thought some drunken dope had wandered into the wrong bathroom. Instead, a stick figure of a young woman in torn-up black clothes stumbled out, a big black purse wrapped in her tattooed arms. She collided with two women in the line.

The young woman regained her balance and turned to run into an alley behind the nearby shops, watching the bathroom doorway over her shoulder. Before she could get up to speed, Maureen stepped into her path, her left arm tight to her side. She bent her knees, lowered her shoulder, and threw a block on the purse snatcher that would've brought the Superdome crowd to their feet. The air she'd knocked from the thief's lungs hit her face. It stank like bad wine. The other woman hit the ground hard, the back of her head striking the cobblestones with an audible thud, her buzz cut not cushioning the impact. The purse flew from her arms, contents spilling in every direction.

At the sound of her name from behind her, Maureen turned and saw Waters trotting in her direction. People from Café du Monde gathered by the fountain and the take-out window. Like zombies, people wandered out of the trinket and T-shirt shops, blinking in the sunlight. Some took pictures.

Peering over Waters's shoulders, she couldn't find her mother in the crowd. Street crime, Maureen thought, live and in living color. Absolutely the last thing she wanted her mother to see before heading back to New York. Maureen knew her mom had cultivated careful illusions about her daughter's career, despite the fact that she'd been the one to pin badge number 1412 on Maureen's uniform at graduation. She looked down.

"Thanks for fucking nothin'."

She rolled her shoulders and took a deep breath, trying to calm down before anyone in a uniform, anyone *else* in a uniform, showed up to commandeer the situation. The purse snatcher groaned, rolling onto her side. Maureen squatted, placing her hand firmly on the back of the woman's neck, squeezing.

"I think I'm gonna puke," the skinny woman said.

"You should stay where you are, miss," Maureen said. "You fell and you may have suffered an injury. Someone will be along shortly to assist you."

Waters arrived at her side, breathing hard. Sugar coated his fingertips. He was trying not to laugh. "You gotta be kidding me. Already?"

"She ran right at me," Maureen said. "What was I supposed to do?"

The wild-eyed owner of the purse, holding it tight to her chest, ran up to Waters. "Thank you so much. That scumbag scared the hell out of me. He jumped out of the stall like a crazy person."

"It's a woman," Maureen said. "And it was me that caught her."

The thief made to sit up. Maureen set her hand on the small of the woman's back and held her down. The thief uncorked a barely discernible rant about fascism and oppression into the pavement. The victim, confused, looked at Maureen, then back at Waters.

"Aren't you the crossing guard?" she asked.

"This isn't even my district," Maureen said.

An enormous coal-black cop in uniform emerged from the crowd and approached Maureen and Waters. The big cop smiled while shaking his head at the woman lying at Maureen's feet.

"Dice," the cop said. "Another day, another dollar, huh? How did I know it'd be you on the other end of this? What would I do with myself without you and your junkie bullshit to clean up after? Where are all your junkie friends at now? Waiting for you to show up with your score?"

From the ground, Dice said something Maureen couldn't hear. The big cop didn't hear it, either. He ordered Dice, whom he addressed more like an unruly child than a criminal, to get up and take a seat on the edge of the nearby fountain and not move. The woman continued grumbling but complied with the big cop's orders, straightening her tattered clothes and her pocket chains, muttering to no one, finally sitting on the fountain's edge with her hands between her knees and her head down.

Two more officers, a short white man and a rotund black woman with a blond crew cut, came around the back of Café du Monde, shouldering their way through the crowd, which had now thinned at the officers' loud insistence that the cameras disappear or be confiscated, or end up in the river. Not far away, loud hip-hop music announced the start of another acrobat performance up the street. On to the next attraction, Maureen thought.

None of the three cops, Maureen noticed, was in any kind of hurry to apprehend Dice. The cops resembled office workers gathering early for a notoriously boring weekly meeting. Maureen had the strange feeling they were mad at her for mucking up their afternoon. One of them was going to get stuck with the paperwork. If they arrested anyone. Maureen had yet to see a set of handcuffs.

The giant cop finally noticed her uniform. He frowned at her, noticed the silver numbers pinned to her lapels.

"You're from the Sixth?" he asked. "I know you?"

"Starting on Monday," Maureen said. "Maureen Coughlin. Just graduated today."

"You saw what happened, Coughlin of the Sixth?"

"Dice snatched a purse in the ladies' room," Maureen said. "The vic, this lady over here, said she'd been hiding in a stall. God only knows how long she was in there. I knocked her over when she came running out."

"You knocked her over?"

"Yo, she lit that dirty bitch *up*, yo."

A white kid, gym-buff and maybe twenty years old, in low-slung plaid shorts and a white tank, his white LA Dodgers hat turned to one side, bounced out of the crowd. "That shit was fire, yo. Pow!"

The big cop raised his hand. "Dial it down, Kid Rock."

The kid rolled back-and-forth-back-and-forth, heel-to-toe-heel-to-toe in his big white sneakers, his steady motion almost hypnotic. Maureen recognized that particular stimulant-driven rhythm. "I'm just sayin'. I saw it. I can give a statement and shit, if I can give it to her."

Maureen was ready to knock the kid down and search his pockets and his socks and sneakers. Her palms itched. They were damp. She'd find something on him: coke, meth, any number of expensive pills. The kid was that fearless kind of wired. The kind that made you not only feel too strong, but too smart, too slick, as well. She'd probably be doing him a favor, she thought. The way he was hopped up, he was going to end the night in an ambulance or a squad car anyway, depending on whether he was on the giving end or the receiving end of a beating.

"I got you," the cop said to the kid. "Thanks for your input."

"I got *you*," the kid said to Maureen, backing away, one hand tucked under his chin, his other arm outstretched, index finger pointing in her direction. "I'm over at Coyote Ugly, when you're ready to take that statement."

Didn't this punk see her uniform? Maureen wondered. Wasn't she wearing the same uniform as the three other cops? A hundred profane retorts tumbled around in her head. But even if this joker didn't seem aware of her dress blues, she had to remember who she was now. She could express herself, but she couldn't let it fly like she had in the bars. "Tell it walking, Vanilla Ice. We got the witnesses we need. Thanks for your help and have a good day."

Her sharp dismissal caught the kid by surprise, piercing and deflating his drug-induced illusion that he was charming. The insult and the mood shift it had produced flickered in his eyes. He palmed his crotch, leaned maybe four inches in Maureen's direction, his chin stuck forward. It was enough. That lean caught the big cop's attention. He loomed over Maureen's shoulder like a rising wave.

"Have a good day," he said, calm and kind as could be. "Sir."

The kid said nothing, the strut blasted out of him. He backed away into the alley between the shops and was gone. That reaction, Maureen thought, that is real authority. It was worth more than any number of TV-ready wisecracks. She stepped out of the big cop's shadow. It was then that Maureen finally spied her mother.

Amber stood at the back of the crowd, on the fringe of the scene, in the shadow of the striped awning, her dark glasses hiding her face, her hand covering her mouth. Maureen's heart sank. This episode in the alley was the last thing she wanted her mother to witness before leaving New Orleans. Crime and criminals. This was Maureen's life now. That's what her mother was thinking. Maureen looked away from Amber, watching as the big cop turned to Waters.

"And you, sir?"

Waters put out his hand. The cop shook it.

"Nat Waters. NYPD, retired. I'm a friend of the officer's here. Just down with her mother for the graduation. I got here after the perp had been subdued. With appropriate force, I would say."

"Damn, probie," the cop said. "This has got to be some kind of record. Graduated this afternoon, you said?"

"First in her class," Waters said.

"Congratulations and welcome to the job."

"Thanks. So you'll call me if you need me?" Maureen said, drawing her shoulders back. "Coughlin, over at the Sixth."

The big cop noticed the powdered sugar on her shirt. "Go back to your beignets and your nice family, Coughlin of the Sixth. We got this."

16

Heading downtown over the Claiborne Avenue high-rise on her way to meet
Atkinson, Maureen drove past the Superdome. Lit up with spotlights to
show off its new metallic skin, the Dome looked like a brass-jacketed bullet that had flattened against a wall. Driving with the windows open, she
smelled the crime scene before she saw it. Acrid smoke, burned plastic,
like a trash fire. The source of the smell had to be her destination, unless
the Central Business District was having an especially bad night and she
was passing a fire on her way to a murder.

She closed in on the scene, taking the ramp back down to street level.
Something organic and sour hung in the air, underneath the chemical
smells. The odor was familiar, but Maureen couldn't place it. She hoped
the first idea that popped into her head, that someone had burned a body,
was wrong. She hadn't expected fire. Leaving her apartment, she'd assumed the call involved another shooting. Poor investigative technique,
she knew, to make assumptions, but the gun was far and away the city's
most popular lethal weapon. Wherever she went, whatever the call, it was

smart to anticipate a gun in the mix one way or another. She had hers in its leather holster, tucked in the back of her jeans.

She breathed in the tainted air again and wondered if crime scenes became like wines, each with their own smells and flavors—top notes, grace notes, and finishes. Girl, she thought, her own ideas making her queasy, you did not get out of the cocktail business quite fast enough.

As she descended the exit ramp, the crime scene materialized ahead on her left. The city used much of the long, narrow space under the overpass as an impound yard, the run of concrete slab intersected by narrow cross streets connecting the business district on one side of the highway to Mid-City on the other side. High fences topped with curving spikes boxed off and guarded the impound lots. A dark car parked in the middle of the scene, its four doors thrown open, was the focus of everyone's attention.

Half a dozen cops in uniform, along with a handful of crime-scene techs in their NOPD windbreakers and plainclothes in shirtsleeves, milled about. Maureen cruised past. A couple of the uniforms threw blank glances her way. There was an ambulance, but no coroner's van. She couldn't tell whether the coroner had already left or hadn't yet arrived.

Maureen made the right, turning off Claiborne onto Cleveland. She turned right again onto South Robertson, passing an island of buildings in a sea of empty parking lots: a small fire station, the bar called Handsome Willy's, the one Atkinson had mentioned in her phone call, a pizza place, and an abandoned Vietnamese restaurant, its windows filthy and cracked. She parked on the street outside the bar. She killed the lights and the engine and got out of the car. She secured her gun at the small of her back.

Brass-band music blasted out into the night from the open door of the bar, carrying loud voices and laughter with it. The life in the music, the cheer in the voices, struck Maureen as incongruous with the desolate surrounding neighborhood.

At the end of the street, across Tulane Avenue, looming over a smaller, newer medical building, was the dark, empty hulk of the old Charity Hospital, a sprawling, bone-colored Art Deco complex that had flooded in the days after Katrina and had been left to rot in the years since the storm. Coming from her green and noisy neighborhood, Maureen felt like she'd walked onto a Gotham City movie set. Taking in the enormity of the Charity complex, she understood the serious acreage around her devoted to parking. Before the storm, the neighborhood had probably teemed with doctors and nurses and staff, with patients and visitors. Now the area reminded Maureen of a neglected graveyard surrounding the ruins of a giant spectral cathedral, maybe one like the abandoned church where she caught her breath on her runs.

But then again, she thought, the Superdome was only a Superman leap over the ruins of Charity. Of course, the Dome had itself been a desolate wreck at one point, the broken heart of New Orleans. Now, though, the Superdome was, from what she'd heard, also the beating heart of the city for the six months of the year it was football season. Sometimes her new city made her dizzy, the way so many things could be true about it at once. Maybe it was the bends in the Mississippi River, but sometimes New Orleans felt to her more like a fun-house-mirror reflection of a city than any real city people had come up with on purpose.

Her arrival caught the attention of the two uniforms across the street charged with keeping the traffic moving along Claiborne, exactly what she'd be doing were this her shift. She wondered if they knew looking at her that she was a cop. She wondered if she had the look about her yet, the one that let cops distinguish their ilk from civilians at a glance like vampires could. Whatever their thoughts, they didn't stop traffic for her.

Waiting to cross the street, she reminded herself of her place. She was an officer in training called out to assist an experienced homicide detective. If she got asked to direct traffic, she'd ask for a whistle. If she got sent for coffee, she'd ask how everybody took it. But it was hard not to imagine herself as a detective, as *the* detective, arriving at the scene and taking charge of the investigation. Someday, maybe, Maureen told herself, but not tonight.

When the traffic backed up at the red light, Maureen grabbed her chance to cross. She weaved her way among the chrome bumpers and headlights, throwing a huge moving shadow on the concrete pillars of the highway overpass. Atkinson saw her coming, and met her at the edge of the scene, lifting the caution tape high to let Maureen bend and pass underneath it. She said nothing—no greeting, no gratitude or apology for Maureen coming out again in the middle of the night. She let the tape snap into place and turned her back, walking away.

The detective was again clad in an untucked man's dress shirt, blue-and-white check with a button-down collar this time, and the same old dirty jeans and cracked cowboy boots. Her curly hair was pinned up with no particular purpose other than to keep it out of the way. Maureen got the impression she was looking at Atkinson's nonuniform uniform. She liked it; it was a wardrobe designed for ease of use and comfort, easy to wash, easy to put on right out of the dryer. Atkinson's clothes were for work; she wasn't out to impress anyone. It was an attitude that Maureen aspired to. All business.

Atkinson took long strides, and Maureen followed along behind her, trying very hard not to look like the bumbling puppy on the heels of the bigger dog. They walked toward the car, which Maureen now saw had partially burned. The windows and windshield had been smashed. Crumbs of glass sparkled in the street. All four tires had burst. The front end, exterior and interior, was charred black. The dash, the steering wheel, the seats had melted. Despite the damage, Maureen could make out its dark green color. She had a bad feeling. She knew why Atkinson had asked her out to the scene. She was looking at Bobby Scales's Plymouth from Central City.

The front had burned much worse than the back end, which looked smoke-stained but intact. Shouldn't it be the other way around, Maureen thought, since the gas tank was in the back? Obviously, then, her second thought said, someone set this car on fire in the front on purpose. The next question was why. It didn't take an expert arsonist to know the fuel was in the back. Maybe the fire starters feared an explosion and wanted time to get away? Like if they, or he, were making their escape on foot.

As Maureen and Atkinson approached the vehicle, the rubber-gloved crime-scene techs backed away. Above everyone's heads, ghosts of black smoke rolled and roiled, trapped against the steel-girdered underside of the overpass. Maureen could feel in her belly the rumbling echoes of the cars passing overhead.

"This is it," Maureen said, not even waiting for Atkinson's question. "This is the car that Wright was breaking into when I stopped him yesterday."

She touched the back of her hand to her nose. The smell was stronger right here by the car, the burnt-flesh smell, especially. Maureen's eyes watered as she walked in a slow circle around the car.

"I had a feeling," Atkinson said.

"The plates are gone," Maureen said. "Couldn't we pull the VIN from the chassis, if we're lucky and it hasn't melted away? Maybe that's why the front end was torched, to melt those numbers off the dash and the front door."

"Maybe," Atkinson said. "Though that information's useless, in truth. We don't even know if Bobby Scales is a real name or a street name. The car could belong to anyone and Scales could've been using it, or fixing it, for whatever reason. Who knows? He could've bought it without paperwork changing hands, a neighborhood thing. There's no real chain of ownership we can use to prove anything. Most of our info does come from middle school boys."

"This burning does mean, though," Maureen said, "that the car's owner, or user, or whatever, shot Wright. He wanted to get rid of the car before we got our hands on it. That's what we're working on so far, right? That Wright got shot for messing with the car and so the owner, Scales or not-Scales or whoever, destroyed the car so we couldn't trace it to him and put Wright's murder on him."

Maureen waited for affirmation, but Atkinson said nothing.

"That flies, right?" Maureen said. "That's what you're thinking? Something about this car tells us who shot Wright. It's the connection between the shooter and the victim. It's the motive for the murder. That's why burning it makes sense. Destroy that connection."

Atkinson wrinkled her nose, as if Maureen's ideas smelled like spoiled milk. She scratched at her forehead, brushed some loose curls away. An idea, something Maureen couldn't read, floated across Atkinson's face. The detective looked back in the direction of the fire station and the bar. "There's something else I want you to see."

"Sure," Maureen said. "Whatever you've got."

Atkinson moved around to the back of the car, gesturing for Maureen to follow her.

Maureen noticed the trunk was closed but not locked, as if someone had shut it with the intention of returning to get something from it later. Atkinson glanced once over her shoulder to make sure Maureen was close. Maureen noticed that the techs surrounding them stood still, their hands at their sides, their rubber gloves on, watching and waiting. They didn't talk. Maureen felt shaky. Perspiration popped along her brow. Someone was in the trunk. She had possible candidates. She tried to push their faces from her imagination.

"You smoke," Atkinson said.

"What?" Maureen asked. "Yeah, yeah, I do."

"Light one."

"I left them in my car." She looked around, sheepish. "It's a crime scene."

Atkinson dug something from one of her back pockets. A black bandana. She handed it to Maureen. "Cover your nose."

Maureen took the bandana but only squeezed it in her fist. "Shit."

"Come closer. Deep breath."

Atkinson put out her hand. One of the techs approached and placed a flashlight in the detective's open hand. Atkinson clicked the light on, raised it high over her head, the beam pointed down. As soon as the trunk was opened, the light would land on whatever lay inside it. Or, Maureen thought, whoever.

"No chalk this time," Maureen said. "Is there?"

"Not this time," Atkinson said. "This is the real thing, officer."

Maureen half expected an offer to back out, but the offer didn't come. She wasn't a civilian anymore. Atkinson opened the trunk.

The burnt-flesh smell, the sharp rot hit Maureen like hot coffee thrown in her face. Flies swirled out of the trunk. Maureen ducked under a big one that buzzed by her ear. Christ, already? She slapped at the air with her hands. She caught herself and stopped. Real professional, Maureen. In the trunk, a rubber sheet covered the body. A small person. No bigger than her. Smaller, in fact. What the fuck?

"Bandana," Atkinson instructed.

Maureen covered her mouth and nose, as eager to hide her face as she was to block off the smell. It was going to get worse when Atkinson pulled back the sheet. This is gonna hurt, Maureen thought.

"Officer Coughlin, I need to know if you recognize the person under the sheet. I need a name if you know it." She gave Maureen a moment. "Ready?"

Maureen nodded. Atkinson pulled back the sheet.

Lying on his side, curled in a ball, was Mike-Mike, the young kid she'd chased across the park. His arms were crossed over his chest. His hands were balled into fists. His eyes were squeezed shut like a kid's, shit, he *was* a little fucking kid, trying and failing to tough his way through a scary scene in a movie. He looked like a kid overacting, pretending to be asleep because he knew his folks stood checking on him at the bedroom door. Maureen got the feeling Mike-Mike had never been watched over like that. Not as he died, not ever. He'd died hard, and terrified. Maureen's hands started twitching at her sides. Rage hit the back of her eyes in a hot wave, like a snake spitting poison from deep inside her skull. Her vision blurred.

"Mother. Fucker."

Mike-Mike had been fast. Someone else had been faster. There was always someone faster.

"We could smell him as soon as we got here," Atkinson said. "So we popped the trunk right away. I was hoping you could give us an ID. Is this one of the boys from your report?"

"They called him Mike-Mike, his friends," Maureen said.

She licked her lips, tasted something smoky she immediately tried to forget.

"He lived in Central City, I think. I was told he lived in the neighborhood. I tried to stop him for questioning this afternoon. He ran. I chased him. He got away. It's in my report." She turned to Atkinson. "He was there with two friends when I approached Wright about breaking into the car. This car." She could feel the rage oozing down the back of her throat, thick as paste. It was warm like snot, or blood. Better it all went down her throat than down her cheeks as tears. "This boy was"—Maureen shrugged—"I don't know, eleven, fucking twelve. Maybe. Fuck."

"That'll do for now." Atkinson clicked off the flashlight. "Daniels," she called out to one of the techs, "some water for the officer. Take your time. Take a walk."

Maureen turned away from the car, took a few slow steps. She heard Atkinson call the techs back to the car. She wanted to breathe deep, but the stench made it impossible. She had the absurd fear of inhaling a fly. Her back to the burned-up car, she leaned forward, her hands on her thighs. A hand passed her a plastic bottle of water. She rinsed her mouth and spat the water in the street. She was afraid to drink, afraid to wash into her belly the rest of what clung to her throat. She drank anyway, the whole bottle in breathless gulps. Then she closed her eyes as tight as Mike-Mike's and threw up the water into the street. It burned on its way back up. Visions of flies in tiny NOPD windbreakers danced in her head.

17

After the coroner had come for Mike-Mike and the car had been towed away, Maureen sat with Atkinson at a gray plastic picnic table outside Handsome Willy's. They were alone. The brass-band music and dancing had ended.

Inside the bar, the houselights were up. Through the open door, Maureen watched the young staff cleaning the tables and the floors, cigarettes tucked into the corners of their mouths, tendrils of smoke rising into their eyes. A couple of listing and ragged regulars played the video poker machines. Maureen had no idea of the time. The sky remained dark, but she expected the daylight to stain it at any moment. She hated hanging around a bar at closing time, but the owner had assured them it was fine.

Worse things, he said, than having a couple of cops around at this time of night.

Atkinson had bought cocktails, each sixteen ounces' worth of something Hawaiian Punch–colored that Atkinson called Handsome Juice.

"It's a rum punch," Atkinson said, sitting on the opposite bench and setting Maureen's drink down in front of her. "A good one. Good enough that you can have just this one or I can't in good conscience let you drive home."

"Not really my kind of thing," Maureen said, lighting a cigarette. She'd drink it, though, because Atkinson had bought it for her.

"You want something sweet on your palate after that," Atkinson said. "Trust me."

Maureen thought of wine again. White with fish, red with beef. Were there liquor pairings for homicides? Rum with burnings, bourbon with strangulations, vodka with shootings? Not a question to ask out loud. She set her smoke in the plastic ashtray and settled her face in her hands. Was Atkinson going to want another report? Just not tonight. Please.

"This a regular haunt of yours?" she asked. Genius. So much better, Maureen thought, than 'Come here often?' Christ, she needed some sleep.

"It's a great place to hang before and after on game days," Atkinson said. "Short walk to the Dome from here."

"I haven't been here in the city for football season yet," Maureen said. "I'm a little nervous. People seem pretty crazy just over the start of training camp. I'm not much into sports."

"There's sports," Atkinson said, "and then there's the Saints. You'll see. You'll get sucked in. I never gave two shits until after the storm. Then I worked, inside, for that Monday Night game in '06. The sound. Unbelievable. Unreal, nothing like it in my life. Now I have season tickets with a couple of other cops and a Steve Gleason jersey." Atkinson paused. "I don't like it, putting a body like that in front of you so soon. It was special circumstances." She shook her head. "Your FTO is gonna love me."

"I knew the car," Maureen said. "And you were right, I knew the kid. I know who his friends are. You made the right call. Where else would you get a starting point for him tonight?"

"I knew he was one of them, those three," Atkinson said, "but I had never met them. I had no name. There was no ID in the car."

"I know why you needed me," Maureen said. "I'm up for it, Detective Sergeant. I am."

"You did pretty good with it," Atkinson said. "I'll give you that, but you'll wanna show less emotion. You'll get that down. Not so much for the other cops, but for the civilian spectators, and there are always spectators."

Atkinson took a long sip of her drink. She set her elbows on the table-top, leaned closer to Maureen. "But it should always hurt when they're that young. It should never make sense. It should never be okay. Not the young ones. There will be bodies, I promise you, where you collect the cas-ings and think 'good riddance' and you'll probably be right, and that par-ticular file will always be on the bottom of the pile, and your feelings about that are between you and the mirror, or wherever you look when you want to see yourself. But not the young ones."

"I don't see how that could ever happen to me," Maureen said.

"That's why I'm telling you," Atkinson said. "Because it can happen and it will, if you're not careful. It's easier than you think. Becoming heartless and apathetic is the easiest way to last at this job. And it gets tempting to start blaming the victims. Especially when you start to see how many of the people you have to deal with are already the walking dead. The ones with badges and the ones without. Doesn't make you any better at it, but it makes it easier."

Atkinson sipped her drink again. She swirled her straw around in it, stabbing at the cherries on the bottom of the cup, the crushed ice crackling.

"He didn't look that badly burned," Maureen said.

"No, he didn't. Not on the outside, at least. I didn't see any obvious trauma. There wasn't a blow to the head, or a stab wound, gunshot, some-thing like that. The coroner's got him. We'll try to pinpoint cause of death, the time. Was he dead when he went in the trunk? Did he die in there? All of it matters. Some of it's quick to figure out. Some information could take a while."

Atkinson slipped a cigarette from Maureen's pack between them on the table. She lit it with a match and watched the flame burn down the cardboard toward her finger, finally shaking it out and tossing it in the ashtray. She watched the last of the smoke rise.

"He's kind of a dope, our arsonist."

"How's that?" Maureen asked.

"We're not exactly a world away from Central City. Half of New Orleans East is still empty, and the farther east you go toward the Mississippi border, the more empty it gets. There's lots of better places all over the parish to ditch this car."

"Well, then our suspect is dumb," Maureen said. "Good to know."

Over Atkinson's shoulder, she could see a couple of firefighters unfolding and sitting in lawn chairs, out on the concrete apron in front of their house. They were hard to check out in the dark, but one of them looked pretty cute. Okay, the rum and exhaustion had gone to her head.

"I mean, who sets a fire two blocks away from a fire station?"

"Dumb is the one shared quality," Atkinson said, "of ninety percent of the people we bust. Nothing new. And nothing that helps much."

"Or he was in a hurry." Maureen waited a beat for a response. She was perking up again, almost against her will. What wind was this? Fifth? Sixth? "Right? Just get the car somewhere he can set the fire and scram before he's seen."

Atkinson took a deep breath, let it out slowly. "Did you just use the word *scram*?"

"The front of the car is trashed," Maureen said, "but we may score a print or some DNA from the trunk, right?"

"That car sat on Washington Avenue for who knows how long," Atkinson said. "The whole neighborhood's DNA is probably on there." She shook her head, but a grin played on her lips. "Everyone with the fucking DNA. Fucking TV." She pointed a finger at Maureen. "You oughtta know better."

"But we'll look?"

"Yes," Atkinson said. "We'll look."

"So, what, a day? Two days with the coroner?"

Atkinson stared at Maureen for a long time. "Do they teach you anything about real-world police at the academy anymore? Anything about, you know, being a working police officer in New Orleans?"

"More like a week?"

"I have no idea when the good doctor will get back to us. In his own good time, I'm guessing."

"What about this kid's people?" Maureen asked. "They're gonna want to bury him."

Atkinson said nothing.

"Tell me he's got people," Maureen said. She felt a strange panic rising inside her. "Jesus. Tell me someone will claim him. Someone noticed he didn't come home tonight."

"I can't promise you any of that," Atkinson said. "But it's likely, though, that he had people, and that they'll come for him. They'll put his face on a big white T-shirt and they'll blame us for him being dead. And then one of them, an uncle, a second cousin, will go looking to kill someone, or at least get to talking about it." She swallowed the last of her punch. "And 'round and 'round we go in the unbreakable cycle of life and death."

18

Later that morning, at six fifteen, before roll call, Maureen stood at the coffeepot. She felt a hand at her elbow. Preacher. She'd heard his heavy breathing as he approached.

"Morning, Preach," she said, turning, faking a smile. She hoped the pressed uniform and extra makeup would fool him into thinking she'd gotten at least a partial night's sleep. She hoped he didn't notice the tremor in her hands. She wrapped both of them tight around her coffee cup. "Ready for another day of protect and serve?"

"Christ, Coughlin. You look positively malarial." Preacher set his empty mug on the counter. "What's wrong with you? What're you doing here?"

"Working," Maureen said. "Only one more shift. After today, you get to make me a real police officer."

"If you live that long."

Preacher took her mug from her hands, set it beside his on the counter. He led her by the arm a few steps away from the coffeepot, the busiest place in the district right before roll call. "You need to go home. I'm send-ing you home."

This can't be good, Maureen thought. This can't be anything but bad. This can't be how your last day of training is supposed to go. "I'm fine. I'm a little short on sleep."

"You're lying," Preacher said. "What happened? What did you do last night?"

"Atkinson," Maureen said. "She had me out at another scene last night, late." She reclaimed her coffee off the counter, slurped it. "I got an hour. In the locker room."

Preacher really did look pretty furious. "What she needs is to let me finish training you before she starts."

"It's not like that," Maureen said. "She needed me. Somebody killed one of those kids last night. One of the three from the Wright shooting. We found him in the trunk of a burned-out car. That same car Wright was breaking into. Over by Charity."

The information gave Preacher pause. "Which one? Which kid?"

"Mike-Mike. The one I chased. Not Marques from the playground. As far as I know he's fine. Atkinson's trying to trace the car's owner and figure out how Mike-Mike died. And why, I guess."

Preacher frowned at the floor, thinking. Maureen hoped he might forget about her condition and let her put in a day's work. She needed it, and not just to finish her training.

"Two things," Preacher said, finally. "One, I'm not driving the car all day, and you're in no shape, so there's that. The second, I got a reputation. Everyone's gonna look at you and wonder what the fuck I'm doing to you. They're gonna wonder why my cute little trainee suddenly looks like she climbed out of a grave to get to work. So you're going home. Go home."

He turned away, headed for the stairs down to roll call.

Maureen trotted after him, begging him in a harsh whisper to wait, drawing looks from the other cops preparing for the day shift. She felt like she had back in high school, when the track coach told her, his best runner, that he was leaving her home for the weekend's meet. What had been the reason? Mono? Flu? Hangover? Or was that when she'd been suspended?

She reached out for Preacher's arm, spilling his coffee.

"How do we know they're gonna stop at Mike-Mike?" she asked. "We gotta find his people so they can come get him. We gotta find the other kids. We got work to do."

They were halfway down the stairs. Preacher stopped, turned to her. "Do not make a scene, Coughlin. You wanna undermine what little respect your work has gotten you, throw some teary-eyed fit. You're not the only cop in New Orleans. You're not even the only one in the Sixth. What happened last night will be in the morning report. The entire day shift will hear about it in about three minutes. We'll go looking for the kids. I'll go looking for the kids."

"Promise me," Maureen said.

"Relax with the drama," Preacher said. "There are better cops than you in this district. We can do the job."

Ahead of them down the hall, Maureen saw the rest of the shift taking their seats for roll call. She ached to be there. For a moment, she resented Atkinson. It was hard enough doing what she was trying to do, a new job, a new city, so much to learn, so much to forget from back home.

Preacher checked his watch. "Coughlin, follow orders. Go home. Don't make me rethink how ready you are to move on. If you can't get a good night's sleep with the bad guys still out there, you need to get into another line of work. Your pal Atkinson gets her sleep, I promise you that."

He turned and lumbered down to the foot of the stairs. He stopped, hitched up his pants, and turned to Maureen. "And that don't make her a bad cop. Or a bad person, neither."

In her eleven years of waiting tables, no matter how beat-down, coked-up, or hungover she'd been, Maureen had never been sent home from a shift. As a cop, it had taken five weeks and change for that to happen. It was the difference in the jobs, she told herself, not a difference in her. She hadn't gotten older and weaker on her way to taking up a harder job.

She wouldn't believe that. Older maybe, but she had only to look in the mirror to know she wasn't any weaker.

On her way home, Maureen stopped at the Buffalo Exchange, a secondhand clothing shop on Magazine. She bought three button-down men's shirts.

19

"Forgive me, Father," Maureen whispered, sitting on the floor of the confessional, "for I have sinned." There was no priest on the other side of the rusty screen. There was no one else in the church.

She took a deep breath, held it till her chest ached and she saw spots. Between the run through the Channel and the hotbox interior of the old church, Maureen was as wet and sticky as if she'd been caught in a downpour. Her tank top, her sports bra, and her shorts stuck to her skin everywhere they made contact.

"When we were getting close to the end, Sebastian called me a little redheaded angel of death. He was fucking with me, trying to get inside my head. I knew it then and I know it now. I told him to go to hell or something at the time. But I've been hearing him inside my head again lately. And I think I might have accidentally helped kill a little boy. I wonder if I didn't put a target on him when I chased him through that field. But I don't know what else I should have done. He shouldn't have run. He shouldn't have been afraid of me."

How had she not brought any water on her run, she wondered, or anything even to wipe away the sweat? Because, a voice in the back of her head told her, then this wouldn't be appropriate penance, would it? Without the discomfort, her run would be an indulgence, the luxury of exercise and youth and health. The suffering made it a sacrifice. She was putting herself through some weirdo Catholic version of the no-pain-no-gain posters she used to see at the gym. Get some sackcloth running clothes, she thought, and take it all the way back to the Dark Ages, why don't you?

Before her run, she'd grabbed a troubled four hours of sleep after being sent home from work. She dreamed over and over of Mike-Mike in the trunk of the old Plymouth. She dreamed that she put him in there, cradling him in her arms like a small child being lowered into a bassinet, his T-shirt stained with orange drink that turned to blood and back to sugar water again. His big eyes opened up at her, pliant and afraid, which was ridiculous. The last time she'd seen Mike-Mike's eyes, in the seconds before the foot chase began, they'd been wild with surprise and panic. She slammed the trunk closed. Under the palms of her hands she felt the thumping as Mike-Mike tried to punch and kick his way out. She heard his muffled shouts and screams as she pressed down on the trunk lid until the metal grew scorching hot to the touch and the sour, sickening odor of broiling human flesh made her nose run and her eyes water.

And then, still asleep, she dreamed that she was awake in the pitch dark, the stink of mold and exhaust in her nose, her brain lying to itself and looping in on itself, putting her back in the trunk of a car on the empty roads of Staten Island. For a horrifying half second the last year and a half of her real life became the dream and she was bumping along on her way to where Sebastian was going to kill her.

She'd finally awoken for real, clutching a pillow that smelled like the hard rubber of a spare tire. She hurled the pillow across the apartment with a grunt.

On her nightstand, she found her lighter. She needed confirmation she was awake for real this time, and not being fooled again by yet another layer of dream. She lit the lighter and held her palm over the flame until it hurt. Then she sucked the burn on her palm and held it over the flame again. When the world didn't flip on its axis and turn inside out, she used that flame to light a cigarette. She climbed from bed and started searching the apartment for her running clothes. She'd had these dreams before, especially when she slept at odd hours, the kind of dreams that piled one on top of another until she lost track of where the dream ended and her real life began. She taught herself the trick with the lighter as a way to manage them. The pain was telltale. She was twelve when she did it the first time. Already smoking then. Already playing with fire.

Maureen looked around the confessional chamber, a strange lightheadedness coming over her as she recalled her dreams of that morning. She saw what she swore was a tiny spider building a web in the upper corner of the confessional. Sweat rolled down her forehead and into her eyes, stinging them and blurring her vision. The box that held her seemed to be running out of air. Why was she doing this? Would it kill her to buy a notebook, she wondered, and keep a journal instead, to haunt a coffee shop like everyone else her age in her neighborhood? Why was she hiding in an empty confessional like she was some kind of fucked-up jill-in-the-box? There wasn't even a hand pushing her down into the dark. She retreated to it voluntarily and stayed until the sheer volume of the noise in her head, her devils' dark music, chased her leaping into the light. The answer, she knew, lay in the trunk of that car on Staten Island.

In what ways would she change, if she could, who had lived and who had died in those dark times? Maybe she wouldn't change a thing. And maybe that was the truth she was running from. She didn't feel guilty that she had killed two men, she felt guilty that she had lived when friends of hers had not. She was drowning in survivor's guilt, waiting for someone to absolve her for living, and yet she had kept secret so much of what had happened to her. That she had almost died, and hadn't, had been the start of her rebirth. It was undeniable. And she was ashamed of it. Ashamed of surviving and moving on with her life.

She thought of the bloody-nosed woman from the Garvey Apartments. She'd probably welcomed the man who beat her back into her apartment, into her bed, before the ink on his arrest report had even dried. What did Arthur Jackson feel? Maureen wondered. Regret? Triumph? Did he feel anything, or had he gone numb a long time ago? She thought of her mom, who until very recently would probably have taken back her runaway husband had he ever deigned to show his face. Her father, that man who did his harm with his absence instead of his presence. Did you even need, Maureen wondered, another person to have an abusive relationship with? Maybe yourself was all you needed. Plenty of people, Maureen knew, authored their own abuse, their own pain and suffering, and for them other people were simply the instruments of punishment, the cattails of the flagellant. She worried she was one of those people.

Mike-Mike and Marques and Goody, Norman Wright and Mother Mayor—did she really care about these people, or were they the day's punishments to her, thorns for her to twist in her own side? Was that why she'd become a cop, to ensure that she'd never run out of suffering? You have to know, she told herself, that this city, like any other, will keep tossing kindling on your martyr's pyre for as long as you have the strength to cry out for more. Mercy is a human quality. New Orleans is just a city.

Maureen reached out her hand, pushed open the confessional door. The air didn't move, but somehow she felt cooler, lighter. Dull orange light fell into the chamber, the bright afternoon sun muted by the stained-glass windows. She stood and stepped out into the church. This time, instead of rushing for the doors, she lingered. She looked around. Over her head, the holes in the roof shone gold like daytime stars. So quiet. So lifeless. Like a tomb, this dead cathedral. What a waste it was to let it rot. How much work had gone into this place? How many hours? How many hands? The soaring arches, the stained glass, the statues, the tile work and the life-sized Stations of the Cross painted on the walls. And that was just the interior.

How many bag lunches and after-work beers and loads of laundry had built this place? How many pairs of boots and gloves? How many blisters and calluses and backaches? And now, after all the effort and all that money, after the prayers and the funerals and the weddings and baptisms and confessions, after all that life, this corner property was worth more without the church than it was with it standing. The church was worth more in pieces than it was whole, like a body harvested for organs. Funny. She'd never known this church as anything but a dead place, a place to hide out like a feral cat among the crypts of Lafayette Cemetery, and she'd miss it when it was gone. She didn't want to see it carried away in piles and pieces in the back of a truck. She'd seen that happen once already, in New York. It was too sad a thing. A lost building took lives away with it when it fell, whether there were people inside it as it went down or whether only ghosts hovered in the high corners of the ceiling.

She headed for the door, letting her hand drift over the back of each of the old pews. She dipped her fingertips in the dry bowl of the holy water reservoir, felt the smooth marble under the dust. She had never waited for anyone else's permission or instruction to want what she wanted. She had to stop waiting to be forgiven for taking it. She'd finish her time with Preacher strong. She'd nail the animal that had put that child in that trunk, no matter who it was.

Putting that skin on her wall before she even got out of field training would turn some heads. The right heads. She liked that, and decided she was at peace with her ambition.

She pushed out the heavy doors and into the afternoon.

At the foot of the steps, she stretched her thighs one at a time, pulling each heel around to the small of her back. She felt good. Quick and light instead of heavy and waterlogged in the heat and humidity. Despite the cramped quarters of the confessional, her body had stayed loose in the warm church. She felt a twinge of regret over losing Patrick. Time with him would've made a nice distraction. She leaned forward, touching her toes, letting her head hang loose, her ponytail flopping over and touching the flagstones. Maybe she should raise her romantic sights above the level of distraction. Maybe that's what Patrick was doing for himself in letting her go. She liked him more at that moment than she ever had while they were sleeping together.

She hit the street running.

About halfway between the church and home, as Maureen ran, her chest and thighs burning, she heard a car approaching behind her on Constance. She turned and saw over her shoulder an enormous maroon Escalade rolling up the road, halogen headlights bright. The giant vehicle cleared the parked cars on either side of it by only inches. A few mirrors looked like they might be in danger. Tooth-rattling bass notes echoed off the surrounding houses, overpowering even the rough-edged bark of the rapper riding the beat, and setting off the alarm on one of the parked cars. The Escalade moved slowly enough for Maureen to know that the driver had noticed her in the street; she wasn't worried about getting run down. She looked on either side of the street for a clear spot to step out of the way.

On this block of Constance, though, the curb on both sides was jammed: cars parked bumper-to-bumper, trash cans in the street. The bass got louder. The Escalade's engine revved behind her, impatient. She glanced again over her shoulder. It had crept up on her heels. She ran a little faster. The SUV stayed close. She gestured with her arms that there wasn't room for her to move out of the street. The driver hit the air horn, the sound loud as a freight train's. Maureen nearly screamed. Okay. Now they were fucking with her.

More aggravated than frightened, she turned, backpedaling, and raised her middle fingers up high. She couldn't see the driver through the dark windshield, but she knew he could see her. She also realized, as she ran backward on a street rife with potholes, that the truck was close enough to crush her if she fell, or even stumbled. The engine revved again, as if the driver were emphasizing the same point. Maureen turned back around and sped up. She could feel the heat of the big engine on her back like hot breath. The bass vibrated her ribs.

She threw herself aside, hard to the left, crashing into a pair of plastic garbage bins before landing in the gutter, scraping her palms and an elbow.

She staggered to her feet, panting, frowning at the grit and the blood on her hands.

Instead of continuing on, the Escalade had stopped. So had the music.

This oughtta be special, Maureen thought. Wait till this prick finds out I'm a cop. If he didn't believe her now, she thought, she'd deliver some incontrovertible evidence down the road.

The truck's door didn't open, but the driver's side window rolled down. The odor of marijuana drifted from the truck and into the street like fog rolling into town off the river. A young man in aviator shades and a black ball cap turned to one side showed Maureen his profile. He wore a cowrie shell necklace. The whistler, the Bob Marley wannabe who'd corrected Marques at the Garvey Apartments. He rolled a toothpick around in his back teeth.

"Little Girl Blue," he said. "You need to let the little boys be. They're looked out for. Don't you worry none, ya heard? Write some tickets."

Maureen said nothing, instead trying to get a look at the whistler's passenger. The boss never drove; it was a point of honor borrowed from the Mafia and the Irish mobs before them. If anyone in that truck was Bobby Scales, it was the passenger, who had his face turned away. All she could see was the back of a shaved head wreathed in smoke. There he was, only a few feet away from her, and she had nothing on her, no badge, no gun, not even her phone.

"You don't know who you're fucking with," Maureen said, loud enough for both men to hear her.

"Yeah," the whistler said. "I do. Do you know who *you* fucking with?" With a faint whine, the window started back up. "Have a nice day, Officer."

The SUV drove away, the bass pumping, as loud and steady as artillery fire.

20

By the time Maureen got back to her apartment, she was rubber-legged and dizzy.

As soon as she was through the door, she stripped off her shirt, tossing it on the floor. She pounded down two tall glasses of room-temperature tap water while leaning a hip against the kitchen counter. She put on a pot of coffee and smoked a cigarette in front of the air conditioner, which now made a new noise. That couldn't be a good thing. She looked at her cigarette. One day soon, her lungs were gonna start making new noises.

She checked her phone for messages. Nothing from Atkinson, though Maureen wasn't sure what she'd been expecting. Preacher had called half an hour before she'd returned home. Nice of him, Maureen thought, to be checking up on her. She called him back. He answered after a few rings.

"Feeling better?" he asked. "I take it you were catching up on that much-needed sleep and that's why you didn't answer when I called."

"I am," Maureen said. "I was."

She knew she should, but she couldn't tell him about the run-in with the Escalade. She was supposed to be staying out of trouble. Plus, as long as the Escalade was her secret, she had options for the next time she saw it, whether she was in or out of uniform. Her elbow throbbed like a warning. "Thanks. Good looking out, Preach. I'm grateful."

"Not a problem," Preacher said. "Though I am getting sick of explaining to everyone that you didn't quit. I didn't know anyone else had even noticed you being around." She could hear him drag on his cigar. "That's more on me than on you, by the way, that rumor about you quitting. So how soon can you get here?"

Get here? Shit. She bent forward and started pulling at the laces of her running shoes. Wherever she was now going, she'd need a shower before she left. She needed to destroy the evidence that she hadn't been home like she'd said. "Um, where is that?"

A sigh. "Did my message not go through? I hate fucking voice mail. Push this, beep that."

"I didn't even listen."

"Not a new thing for you, I'm guessing. I'm at the Mayan. Spry young thing like you, you've had enough sleep for now. You need to get here before I get a call. I'm sitting here with a couple things of interest to you." He paused. "Look a little ill, in case anyone spots us."

"I'll be there in ten," Maureen said.

"Make it seven," Preacher said. "I'm a busy cop in a dirty town. Believe."

Wearing jeans, her boots, and a tight black tank top, Maureen walked to the Mayan, having decided fighting for parking would take up as much time as walking. The sun felt good on her bare shoulders. After a couple of blocks she was glistening again, of course. She was starting to accept perspiration as a permanent condition of being outdoors in the summer. She dabbed at her throat and forehead with a bandana she had brought. She sipped from her water bottle. She was learning to handle the heat. Moving in it without the weight of the Kevlar or the equipment belt was pleasure enough to set her dreaming again of plainclothes work.

She found Preacher in the tobacco shop courtyard, seated alone at a table, an extra button undone on his uniform. He had the day's *Times-Picayune* spread out in front of him. His cruiser was parked in front of a fire hydrant. A lone Sixth District detective, his badge clipped on his belt, stood at one of the cocktail tables by the shop door. He puffed an enormous stogie while talking on a cell phone. If he noticed or recognized Maureen, he gave no sign.

"Tight clothes look good on you," Preacher said. "I thought I told you to look ill?"

"Couldn't live a day without me?" Maureen said, coming through the gate. She joined Preacher at the table.

"Don't know what the fuck to do with myself," Preacher said. "I'm rudderless without you, Coughlin."

She gestured at the newspaper, the crossword half finished. "You seem to be managing."

"Despite everything you've done," Preacher said, "to redefine what it means to be a trainee in this department, I do have a few tricks of my own."

He slid two files out from under the newspaper. Maureen wasn't sure if he'd been hiding them or if he was being dramatic with his presentation. "Your boy Mike-Mike, the prints came back from his corpse. He was in the juvie system."

"He had a record?"

"Brief and unspectacular. On the other hand, he was thirteen years old." He reached the file across the table. "The particulars on the late Michael Travis Pilgrim."

Maureen took the file. She lit a cigarette, opened the file, scanned it.

Shoplifting, truancy, trespassing. Everything from the past eighteen months. So Michael had started fucking up recently and had tumbled downhill fast. Shit, she thought, my file wouldn't be any different if I'd been put through the system at his age instead of given slaps on the wrist and rides home to my mother. She didn't know it then, but being a little lost white girl had its advantages. She read on. As the charges on Mike-Mike got more recent, they got more serious. Accessory after the fact in an armed robbery. A weapons charge from a separate incident, possession of a stolen gun.

She closed the file, trying to piece some things together. The pattern wasn't hard to see. After a few misadventures he should have outgrown, Mike-Mike had hooked up with more serious criminals who had led him, used him, and she was sure, finally, had killed him, discarding him under the overpass. Mike-Mike had watched someone wield a gun and liked what he saw. He'd then gone out and got a gun for himself. Who was it, she wondered, that he'd first watched on the accessory charge? Someone older. Someone intimidating and dominant. An alpha. Had that same person put him up to murdering Norman Wright, only to throw him away like an empty shell casing when the job was done?

"It says here he was living in Baton Rouge," Maureen said.

"Probably where his people landed after the storm. I think they got flushed out of the Magnolia and never made it back." He shrugged. "And then that project and three others like it got torn down, of course. Maybe they're on the waiting list for the new development. Maybe not. Maybe they stopped trying to get back."

"So he's a runaway?"

"Oh, they probably sent him back here, to the old neighborhood. They knew he was here. Bought his bus ticket. Maybe got him a ride with a friend of a friend."

"He was here alone? At his age? To live on the streets?"

"That's the story with a lot of these young knuckleheads," Preacher said. "They're living in exile with grandparents or cousins or whatever, cutting up in Atlanta or Houston or Baton Rouge. The other kids at school hate them 'cause they're black, or they're poor, or just 'cause they're different and kids are cruel, and that's if they even go to school.

"Who knows who or where the fuck their real parents are, if the kids ever knew to begin with. The people they're staying with get sick of the trouble, maybe they got real problems of their own—health, their own kids, money—so they send their Mike-Mikes back to New Orleans, to some other cousin or aunt or friend. To go to school, of course." He put "go to school" in air quotes. "Most of 'em get an education, but it ain't in school."

"I'm guessing he got sent here about a year and a half ago."

"You noticed that," Preacher said. "No troubles till he got sent home. We're reaching out to Baton Rouge PD, see if they got anything on him."

Maureen closed the file. "So who was Mike-Mike living with here?"

Preacher handed over the other file. "He was living with one Todd Goodwin Curtis, as far as we can tell. Known to friends, family, the Sixth District, the Eighth District, the Second District, and several officers and judges of the New Orleans juvenile justice system as Goody."

Maureen opened the file. Another mug shot clipped to another criminal record. He looked familiar enough. It was the taller, older kid from when she'd accosted Norman Wright. The bossy one, to go with Marques, the quiet one, and Mike-Mike, the dumb one. Goody was nearly fifteen. His record was considerably more violent than Mike-Mike's: numerous assaults with and without weapons, armed robbery, other weapons charges, drugs. Maureen felt she was looking at the future Mike-Mike would've had, and the one Marques was approaching, should he survive his entanglements with Bobby Scales.

"So Goody and Mike-Mike are related?" Maureen asked.

"In some distant and meaningless way, probably. The definition of family gets stretched in this town, especially in the tougher neighborhoods. They might've known each other, been friends before the storm."

"I feel like I'm looking at things I shouldn't be seeing. How did you get this file, these names?"

"Like I said, Michael's prints came up in the system. That gave us his name. And then I asked for any other file with a name that came up more than twice alongside Michael's. Kids are creatures of habit, maybe even more than adults. They got busted together three times, Goody and Mike, the last time for riding around on bikes, sticking up tourists right here in Uptown, over by the B and Bs on Marengo. They were using a stolen gun."

Preacher tried relighting the stub of his cigar, but it wouldn't take. "I wouldn't say Mike-Mike was harmless. He might be one to pull a trigger out of fear, but Goody, a record like that, he's got the meanness in him. I don't know how many people they stuck up before we caught 'em, but every one of those victims is lucky they didn't eat a bullet."

Preacher stubbed out his cigar. He picked a fleck of tobacco off his tongue. "What you're looking at, right there, with Mr. Curtis is a ring leader in training. And a time bomb, if you ask me. That's one pissed-off little boy. He's an alpha dog looking for a pack. He's destined for the business end of a gun. That's where his life is gonna end. It's just a question of whether he's doing the shooting or getting shot. I don't need no child psychologist to tell me that. Believe."

Maureen slowly closed Goody's file and placed it side by side with Michael's, their full names written in block letters in black ink. Some cop's careful handwriting that didn't look much better than what she figured the young boys would produce.

"What's it take to go to jail in this town?" Maureen asked.

"If you're a juvenile," Preacher said, with a shrug, "murder one is a sure thing, but killing someone in any ol' way is a good place to start. Anything that can get you tried as an adult, really."

"And for the kids who do everything but kill someone?"

"Diversion programs."

"Diversion from what?" Maureen asked.

"School, gainful employment, productive futures," Preacher said. "At least that seems to be the end result, if not the desired effect. We got no place to put these kids. No room, no money. They stay on the street, where they can keep tearing apart their lives. Why do you think we've got twenty-year-old drug lords with twelve-year-old soldiers? The kids take the rap for everything."

Maureen wanted to slip the files back under Preacher's newspaper, to hide them. From herself, and from everyone else. She wanted the boys in the files to be the boys that she'd first taken them to be on the street. It would be safer for them and a lot of other people to hear Preacher tell it. She would feel a lot less naïve and a lot less unprepared for her new career.

A third file seemed inevitable. May as well get it over with. What crimes awaited them? Car theft? Bank robbery? Capital murder?

"Marques?" Maureen asked.

"No sign of him. Not in our records, anyway. That's a very good thing. He's either better behaved or slicker than the other two."

"I'm gonna choose to believe in better behaved," Maureen said.

"I had a feeling you might."

"And Bobby Scales? Do you see him anywhere in this? These kids had to get their guns from somebody."

Preacher shrugged and raised his hands. "Nothing on him on paper. Not a sign, not a word. I'm wondering if the guy's a myth. Or a mask."

"Like an urban legend?"

"More like a random name," Preacher said. "A name somebody heard on TV, maybe. A stranger slips those kids some cash, says, 'Tell anyone who asks that this car belongs to Bobby Scales and they better not fuck with it.' Could be a game the kids were playing, to collect a little cashish and to mess with people in the neighborhood. Who knows who really owns that car? I wouldn't count on anyone coming forward to claim it. Especially not now, not with a body in it."

"If it's games," Maureen said, "why kill Wright?"

"We don't know why Wright was killed. Remember that. And some-times, most times, even, there's not some criminal conspiracy at work." Preacher set his hands on the table, frowning at them. He laced his fingers together. "Sometimes it's just a whole bunch of stupidity going off at the same time in a real concentrated area. That happens. Especially in the summertime 'round here. Stupidity and fireworks." He raised one hand in the air, sitting back in his chair. "But that's what Atkinson gets paid the big bucks for, to find out who killed Wright."

"And who killed Mike-Mike."

Preacher nodded, hands now folded Buddha-like over his belly. "That, too."

"Speaking of Atkinson." Maureen pressed one hand flat on each of the files. "I really should take these to her."

"That's the next logical step," Preacher said.

Maureen waited for the unspoken "but" that she'd heard at the end of the sentence.

"What?" Preacher said. "You don't think I'm going to interfere with the detective sergeant's investigation, do you? You don't think I want to be associated with a trainee who can't get the job done? Didn't she ask you to find out who these kids are in the first place?"

"She did."

"But don't think I'm delivering these files over to Homicide myself. I ain't got time to go downtown. I'm a busy man. I don't get extra bonus days off, like some other people."

Maureen fought back a smile. Preacher was hooking her up, sending her over to Homicide with important information, really making her look good in front of Atkinson.

"You know what they call her, don't you?" Preacher asked, as if reading her mind. "Atkinson?"

"I can only imagine," Maureen said. "And I'm sure I don't want to know."

"The Spider," Preacher said.

"Oh, please," Maureen said, standing. She couldn't wait to call Atkinson. How could she be losing patience with Preacher, in the middle of what he was doing for her? She tucked her pack of cigarettes in her pocket. "Is it because she weaves elaborate theories about her cases, or is it something more traditionally sexist, like she devours her mates?"

"If she mates at all," Preacher said, "nobody knows who with. I never asked." He chuckled. "They call her the Spider because she's patient. She sits and she waits and she waits some more and what she's after always seems to come to her."

He lifted his chin, eyed Maureen down the bridge of his nose. "Don't forget your files."

21

Maureen walked Preacher to the cruiser, made a promise to see him bright and early and ready to go in the morning. One day left. Whatever he wanted, she would do. Everything between them needed to be super smooth. When her training ended, she was going to miss their relationship. Not that she wouldn't see him around the district, but things wouldn't be the same. She trusted him to be straight with her about important things. She certainly knew him better than she knew anyone else on the NOPD. She hoped that after her training ended she'd be able to reach out to him, for advice, for a few laughs.

From behind the steering wheel, Preacher called Maureen over to the car. She leaned in the passenger side window, forearms across the top of the door. Not getting in the car with him felt strange.

"Anything breaks around the neighborhood today," Preacher said, "and I'll let you know." He started the car. "I'll put the lean on Little E, too. I get a feeling I won't see those kids, but him I guarantee I'll see. Maybe he knows a thing or two. He will, if he knows what's good for him."

"I appreciate that, Preach, and the hookup with the files, too."

Preacher waved Maureen closer to him. She bent farther into the car. He leaned across the front seat of the cruiser. "It's not for you, Coughlin. None of this is for you, not really. If it helps you, like, residually, I'm okay with that, I might even be happy about it, but I don't like neighborhood kids dead under the I-10 overpass any more than you or Atkinson or anyone else does. I'd like to stop it from happening again. You can't think of everything in terms of how it's gonna help you." He dropped the car into gear. "At least don't let it show like it does. Get some rest tonight."

Preacher drove away, leaving Maureen to reconsider how much she was really going to miss him. But she put the sting of his words aside, and filed away his advice. Humility never killed anyone. She recalled something she'd heard from an instructor at the academy. *Your ego should be for the work,* he'd said, *always for the work first.* He'd talked about the New York Yankees, about how they were the most successful franchise in professional sports and about how they were also one of the few teams that didn't wear names on their uniforms. He insisted those two things were connected. He talked about how there was a reason the badge had a number and not a name, a number that passed along to another cop after your time with it was done. In the spirit of her lessons, Maureen made a wish that the case were solved and the other two boys were safe and Bobby Scales sat behind bars. And that she'd have nothing to do but go home and go to bed early for once. But she wasn't betting on it.

She took her phone from her pocket and walked around the corner of Sixth Street, away from the noise of Magazine. She called Atkinson's cell.

"Atkinson."

"Detective Sergeant, it's Coughlin."

"You holding up okay after last night?"

"Never better," Maureen said. "Concerning last night, I have some info about Mike-Mike and Goody. I'm free. I can bring you the files, over at Homicide."

"I'm not there." Atkinson's tone was sharp, her words clipped. Maureen wondered if she shouldn't have made the call. Was she overstepping?

Delivering the files to Homicide would've been the best, the most modest and professional move. Maureen heard traffic through the phone, construction, too, and the squeal of a bus's brakes in the background.

"I'm just getting out of court," Atkinson said.

"Criminal or juvie?"

"Divorce."

Maureen's voice caught in her throat. Dope. So much for trying to sound savvy and casual about the court system.

"Meet me back at Handsome Willy's," Atkinson said. "I'll buy you a couple of tacos and we'll take a look at the files. Maybe we can walk over the crime scene one more time."

Nothing had been solved, Maureen thought, and she hadn't been cut from the loop just yet.

Maureen found Atkinson standing on the concrete patio outside the dark doorway of Handsome Willy's, smoking a cigarette and staring up at the ruins of Charity through black Ray-Bans. Atkinson, to Maureen's surprise, wore a deep-caramel-colored pantsuit with a sleeveless white blouse, the jacket of the suit draped over her arm. Maybe it was the pose, maybe it was simply seeing Atkinson in the daylight and not lording over a nighttime murder scene, but as Maureen approached across the parking lot she noticed that the detective sergeant was actually a bit of a bombshell: tall and buxom, with the straight posture of a soldier.

She turned, startled, when Maureen called her name.

"I should be better," Atkinson said, "about letting people sneak up on me."

"I'm unobtrusive," Maureen said. She handed over the files.

Atkinson took them but didn't look at them. Maureen felt the urge to insist on the importance of finding Goody and Marques as soon as possible. She said nothing. Preacher would be looking. He'd have the other cops in the Sixth looking, continuing to carry out Atkinson's orders. Nothing needed Maureen's emphasis.

Atkinson led them inside the bar. "I'm starving."

Handsome Willy's was more compact inside than it looked from the street. The narrow barroom had deep red walls and a pressed-tin ceiling. The bar ran along the right side, three cocktail tables stood against the wall on the left. A makeshift DJ booth and a couple of video poker machines were in the back by the restrooms. The place had a seedy charm, even if it felt a little dim and desolate walking in out of the sunlight. An older black man with a Heineken in one trembling hand studied a folded newspaper. Beside him, a skinny hipster in a straw hat, a High Life on the bar in front of him, thumbed away at his phone.

Maureen tightened her ponytail, hoping for that breeze on her neck she could never seem to catch. The owners went easy on the AC, which, to her surprise, Maureen was learning she liked, even in the high heat of summer. There was only so much filtered air she could tolerate.

Atkinson walked straight to the far end of the bar and spoke to the paperback-reading bartender, who, putting her book facedown, smiled at Atkinson. They obviously knew each other. They talked in front of what Maureen figured passed for the kitchen, a complicated construction of hot plates, chafing dishes, a microwave, and a Crock-Pot; paper products were stacked amid a tangle of extension cords and wires. Their order complete, Atkinson set the files on the end of the bar. She lit another cigarette, watching the flashing images on the video poker screens. Maureen lit one of her own smokes, for something to do. She studied the bar, trying to match it with her companion. It was a hard pairing to figure.

Old album covers, classic hip-hop and soul, hung on the walls behind the bar: Biggie Smalls, Public Enemy, Isaac Hayes. Not what Maureen would've figured for Atkinson's musical tastes. A couple of rusty and dented horns were hung over the cocktail tables. The yellowed newspaper pages trumpeting headlines from the Saints' Super Bowl run made more sense. The bartender, a slight, quiet, pretty brunette with luminous white skin set off by gorgeous, colorful tattoos, built four tacos, placing two each in wax-paper-lined plastic baskets.

"What are you drinking?" Atkinson asked, the bartender setting a can of Coke and a plastic cup of crushed ice in front of her.

"An Amber," Maureen said. "Draft. Please." She reached for her wallet.

"I got this," Atkinson said. She gave Maureen a small smile. "After the morning I've had, let me do something nice for someone."

"That bad?" Maureen asked. The bartender brought her beer.

"You think murder is confusing?" Atkinson poured her Coke. "Try marriage. Twelve years into it he decides he wants a housewife. What the hell am I supposed to do about that?"

She grabbed her drink and a taco basket. "Let's eat."

Maureen followed Atkinson out the back door. In the courtyard, Maureen better understood the appeal of the place and how it could do enough business to survive in a mostly deserted neighborhood. Dried bamboo fencing masked the chain-link and wide, colorful umbrellas shaded the picnic tables. There was a modest L-shaped tiki bar, closed on a weekday afternoon, but complete with an imitation thatched roof on top and a gas grill behind it. A small plywood stage occupied the back corner of the yard. Empty beer kegs sat on it now, but there was space enough for a four- or five-piece band. Wouldn't have to worry much about bothering the neighbors out here, that was for sure. Two big fans blew a warm breeze through the yard. Old-school soul music from the stereo inside played through hidden speakers, a touch Maureen had always liked in a bar. The courtyard was, of course, surrounded by empty stretches of parking lot. It must be really weird out here at night, Maureen thought. Like dancing on the deck of a small ship in the middle of a flat, dark ocean. Handsome Willy's was a neighborhood bar without a neighborhood.

Atkinson led them to a picnic table by the stage. They sat in the umbrella's shade, in the direct line of a fan, eating in silence. After the first taco, Maureen understood the bar's appeal even better. The food was amazing. It wasn't easy, Maureen knew, to make simple fare so stunning.

Most of the places she'd worked couldn't handle it, not that the customers expected much beyond something to soak up the alcohol. Here in New Orleans the whole city seemed to excel at the basics, and most people expected excellence, especially from the unfancy, tucked-away joints that thrived in every neighborhood.

Maureen dropped her crumpled napkin in her empty basket. "Damn. I could eat six of those. Easy."

"Not bad, right?" Atkinson said. "I don't just come here for the crime. Speaking of, what'd you do before you found your one true calling with the NOPD?"

"Waited tables," Maureen said, "for a long fucking time." She decided to preempt the next question. "Then some things changed, a few things clicked in my brain, I finished school first, and now here I am."

She faked a smile. Atkinson wasn't buying her casual act, at least not the simplicity of the explanation, but the tiny curl at the corner of the other woman's mouth told Maureen that she'd received the important part of the message: that Maureen didn't want to talk about the details.

"You're a braver woman than I am," Atkinson said. "I tried waiting tables once. I don't think I lasted six weeks. Closest I ever came to getting arrested was working that job."

"I'm sorry to hear about your divorce," Maureen said. And she was sorry, but not as eager as she was to move the conversation away from her past, waiting tables, and anything else Atkinson might ask about. She moved the plastic basket aside and sipped her beer. "That sucks. He sick of you being out on the streets?"

"Yeah." A pause. "No. I don't know. His excuses change every time I talk to him."

Typical married-man bullshit, Maureen thought, lighting a cigarette. Don't commit to anything that might be used against you later: words, feelings, or anything else. Not that she knew from the married side of things, but she did know from the other-woman side.

It had always eluded her, even when involved with married men, why men went through the trouble of getting another woman only to treat her the same as they treated their wives, which is to say, poorly. Or maybe it's me, she thought. Maybe I was never any good at being the other woman. I'm not needy enough.

"It is what it is," Atkinson said. "Things haven't been the same for us since the storm. I give him credit for hanging on for six years. God, I make him sound like a car-wreck victim, like he's got brain trauma or something. He works in oil-and-gas exploration. There are a lot more glamorous places he could be working than New Orleans and South Louisiana. You know, like Houston." She shook her head. "Maybe he's the smart one. He knows I'd never leave here, and he knew better than to waste his time and mine asking if I would.

"The divorce, it's just . . ." She looked up, as if her next words floated in the smoke trapped on the underside of their umbrella. "Draining, I guess. The job is enough, and now I got this hanging over me. Lawyers, meetings, explaining myself to strangers."

"So it's New Orleans forever," Maureen said.

Atkinson raised her Coke in a toast. "For better or worse, till death do us part." She drank down her soda. She pushed aside the last half of her last taco, produced her cigarettes.

"My folks, we've been in New Orleans since yellow fever. I'm born and raised. They own an antique shop in the Quarter. My dad was a business lawyer, made his money, and the shop is kind of a retirement hobby. Anyway, at the shop they have an accountant-slash-office-manager-slash-whatever. Nice girl. A control freak who can't do much right, but a nice girl. She's good to my parents. About a year ago she went through a long divorce. Came out the other side okay, but you would not believe the drama, the agony. It was like a death in the family, the end of her marriage, it really was. And her husband was a prickly little shit. Broke, bucktoothed, and arrogant as the day is long."

"But not yours?" Maureen asked. "The marriage, I mean. Not so intense?"

"No, not so much." Atkinson winced. "Not at all. No drama, no nothing. Not the divorce, not the husband, not the wedding. None of it. And then I think about that girl from the antique shop and I get jealous. Isn't that stupid? I'm forty-five. I'm not holding out hope for the fairy tale, but I just sit there in the conference room surrounded by lawyers and thinking the whole time that this should hurt more. *That's* what hurts. That's what weighs on me, keeps me up at night. The lack. Should divorce be this"— another pause, another look up—"I dunno, boring? It makes me really depressed." She chuckled. "But then I used to look at him sleeping next to me and think the same thing about marriage. So what do I know?"

Maureen ran her finger around the lip of her plastic cup. She was having a hard time looking at Atkinson. She had a feeling Atkinson didn't have many people to talk things out with, especially other women. As long as you didn't count dead bodies, that was.

"Working in the bars," Maureen said, "I saw people at the beginning and at the end of their relationships, you know? Either on the hunt or drowning their sorrows. I didn't see much of the middle."

"You married?"

"Never even close." She hadn't seen much of the middle in her own life, come to think of it. She went from starting to over pretty quick. "Is this the part where you tell me to give up on that? Where I'm married to the job? To the city?"

Atkinson laughed. "Oh, hell, no. I don't make those kinds of pronouncements, especially not the 'do as I say, not as I do' type. You've been riding around with Preacher for too long. I'll let him have the birds-and-the-bees-of-the-job conversation with you." She moved her ashtray aside and slid the files in front of her on the table. "Let's stick to what I know."

She opened the first file, Mike-Mike's. She smoked as she scanned it, flipping pages back and forth. She did the same with Goody's file. Maureen watched carefully. Nothing in them seemed like news to Atkinson.

"It's like they photocopy the same file," Atkinson said, "and just change the pictures inside them. And even those don't change much. Young, male, black, drugs, guns. Drives me fucking crazy, the sameness of it. You'd think by now that either their side or our side would've found a better way." She got up from the table, picked up the files. "There wasn't a third?"

"Preacher said Marques is clean," Maureen said. Floating across Atkinson's face, she could see the same cynical take on the absence of a third file that Preacher had voiced at the Mayan. "He's not in the system yet, at the very least."

"Thank the Lord for small favors," Atkinson said. "May he never know the inside of the system." She pulled out her phone and checked the time. "I'm in a hurry. I gotta go home soon and change. I can't go to work dressed like this." She looked at Maureen. "Real quick, Officer Coughlin, let's go see what the crime scene has to tell us in the hot light of day."

22

Under the overpass, Maureen stood right where the green Plymouth had been recovered the night before. The afternoon heat was close and thick and the air dirty. Traffic passed in both directions on either side of Claiborne Avenue. The impound lots were half-empty and unattended. Nothing was left of the previous night's crime scene but smoke and oil stains on the pavement. Found in the car trunk, Mike-Mike didn't even leave a chalk outline behind. He was bundled up in a cooler down at the morgue. The Plymouth sat in the police impound yard. Maureen wondered if either would get the close inspection it deserved.

She slid off her shades and leaned forward, studying the entrance gate to the impound lot. Scrapes and a couple of minor dents where the paint had flecked off. The bumper of the Plymouth had hit the gate. She looked through the gate at the old beaters scattered around the yard. Had the impound yard been the car's destination? Maybe breaking into the impound lot had been the original plan. Break in and abandon the car. The way the city ran that lot, months could pass before someone noticed the car had gone unclaimed. Who would ever suspect someone of breaking a car *into* the impound yard? That plan would also explain the short journey from Central City. And when the thieves couldn't get in, Maureen thought, they burned the thing in an act of desperation. Had an accomplice inside the lot let them down, maybe?

That plan, though, pointed toward the car thieves not knowing about the body in the trunk. Only a couple of days would've passed before the smell gave the body away. If they knew about the body, they'd want it hidden for good, not for a day or two. Even the most apathetic city employee wouldn't be able to ignore a stink like that. Maureen stuck to her theory that what had happened last night had been about the car, and about its role in the murder of Norman Wright.

"Have you heard anything new about Norman Wright?" Maureen asked.

"We're checking the bullets against other recent gun-crime arrests," Atkinson said. "Maybe we can use the bullets to ID the gun, maybe it's a gun we know from other crimes and we can work backward toward an owner or a shooter from there."

"You don't sound too optimistic."

"That's because I'm not. Realistically, our best bet is to bag someone else, preferably someone with a record we can squeeze him on, who can put a finger on the shooter."

"You think you can flip someone over a dead neighborhood drug addict?"

"I can flip someone over a stolen tip jar from CC's." Atkinson shook her head, as if to assure Maureen her comment was directed at the sad state of affairs among New Orleans criminals and not her own investigative prowess. "Ninety percent of crooks are pussies."

"The other ten percent?"

"They're hard. They do a lot of damage. I'll admit it." She looked at Maureen. "But they leave enough of a mess for us to use against them. Usually, anyway. In six months, you'll be able to pick the true hard cases out of a crowd on the corner like they're standing under a spotlight."

Maureen couldn't wait to gain that talent. She'd missed it in Goody's case.

"How about Mike-Mike?" she asked, dodging falling dollops of pigeon shit. "Have you heard anything? Did he die in the fire or before?"

"Waiting to hear from the coroner," Atkinson said. "He wasn't shot, though, which is interesting. I've been thinking a lot about him." She frowned at Maureen. "I knew there was a reason I wanted you out here with me. Stay right there. Don't move."

After a quick side-to-side check for oncoming traffic, Atkinson backed a few steps away from Maureen. "Raise your right arm."

Maureen did so, as if asking a question in class. She searched her brain for what Atkinson was after; she wanted to figure it out without being told. She hoped the pigeons overhead had concluded their business. "Okay?"

"No, no, I'm sorry. Out in front of you, like you're raising your weapon."

Maureen made a pistol of her fingers then lowered her arm. Her back straight, she bent her knees slightly and rotated into a shooting stance. She settled her pretend pistol into her other hand, standing as she would at the range. She lined up Atkinson in her sights, surprised at how uncomfortable she was with pretending to shoot at another cop.

"Hold the gun with one hand," Atkinson said. "And lean away from it a bit. Really stretch your arm toward me."

Maureen started to catch on. She followed Atkinson's instructions, positioning her body as if she feared the explosion about to take place in her hand.

"Good." Atkinson tapped her finger under her left collarbone. "Here." She touched her throat. "And here."

Maureen closed one eye and raised her arm to line up the shot.

Atkinson broke into a wide, brilliant smile. "That's what I was looking for."

"I thought you said Mike-Mike wasn't shot."

"Not Mike-Mike, Norman Wright."

"The shooter," Maureen said, peering over her outstretched arm, the lightbulb going on, "was shorter than Wright. You think Mike-Mike was the shooter."

"The bullets that killed Wright," Atkinson said, "had an upward trajectory. Whoever shot him was looking up at him. And shot him from close range."

"So it was probably someone he knew."

"Or at least recognized," Atkinson said, "and had no reason to fear. Someone who could walk right up to him."

"Like a kid from the neighborhood," Maureen said. "Damn."

"It adds up," Atkinson said. "The small-caliber weapon, the upward angle, the easy access to the victim. I'll put a hold on releasing the body. We can test Mike-Mike's hands for gunfire residue. I'm pretty confident we're going to find it."

She called in her orders to the coroner's office. They stepped up onto the sidewalk as a car passed by, an old, broken-down Nissan sedan, the bass booming behind the dark-tinted windows. Maureen knew she was being paranoid, but the song, though muffled and distorted, sounded like the same one that had been playing in the Escalade. As each bass note hit, Maureen felt herself flinch. She tried to keep her face blank as she listened to the detective.

"Figuring this out doesn't give us a suspect in Mike-Mike's death," Atkinson said, raising her voice over the car as it waited to cross Claiborne, "but it gives us motive."

"A cover-up," Maureen said, her eyes on the car, "of Wright's murder. That points to a third party. Mike-Mike had orders."

The car rolled away, the volume fading. The car was a message, Maureen thought, it was a sign that she needed to tell Atkinson about the Escalade. Could she tell Atkinson without the story getting back to Preacher?

"Somebody was confident we would catch the shooter," Atkinson said, "and afraid of what he might say once we had him." She grinned. "We've been getting better at that."

"But it opens a new investigation into a new murder," Maureen said. "What's the point of that?"

"There's only an investigation because we found the body," Atkinson said. "Mike-Mike kills Wright over the car, for whatever reason, but most likely on someone else's orders. That someone else kills Mike-Mike, puts him in the trunk and gets some other yo-yos to ditch the car. Bam, all the loose ends are tied off. But—and this is a big but—the yo-yos fucked up. We weren't supposed to find the car or the body."

"The first time I saw Marques," Maureen said, "wasn't when I accosted Wright. It was at that domestic at the Garvey Apartments. He was in the area. He tried talking to me and Preacher."

"What did he say?"

Maureen shook her head. "He didn't get a chance to talk. Another kid, an older kid, whistled at him from across the street and Marques clammed up and walked away."

"This older kid, you think he's involved? Based on a warning not to hang around near the cops? That's thin."

"It's more than that," Maureen said. "I thought the guy might be Bobby Scales, until I saw him again, this afternoon, when I was out for a run. He and a buddy nearly ran me down with their Escalade."

"The guy driving the car, he knew who you were?"

Maureen nodded.

"So he knows you're a cop," Atkinson said.

"He called me Little Girl Blue," Maureen said. "Told me, warned me, to leave well enough alone."

Atkinson sighed. "We don't scare people like we used to. It's a fucking shame. What's he look like?"

"Dark skin," Maureen said. "Hair up in twists, always decked out in Marley gear and shell jewelry. The car reeked of weed."

"Shadow," Atkinson said. "I know that kid. Me and him, we go back. He's probably twenty-one by now. He called me Little Girl Blue once. He thinks he's funny. I broke his nose for him."

"He calls himself Shadow?" Maureen asked.

"He got it from us," Atkinson said. "I didn't know he was doing business uptown. I know him from trouble over in the Sixth Ward a couple years ago. Haven't heard from him in a while. I figured he'd got himself killed and we just hadn't stumbled over the body yet."

"He was the driver," Maureen said. "For another man in the car. I think that guy was Scales."

"That sounds right," Atkinson said, nodding. "We called him Shadow because he was never the main guy, never the one we really wanted. He was always off to the side, against the wall somewhere while the real business was going down. I don't know who started calling him that or how he found out about it, but he liked the name so much he kept it. You're sure the passenger was Scales?"

"It all stacks up," Maureen said. "Goody is running Mike-Mike and Marques. Scales and Shadow are running Goody."

"Gimme a second to call in about the Escalade," Atkinson said, holding up her phone. "It's a pretty conspicuous vehicle. As for Shadow, I'm gonna name him as a person of interest in these murders. Because we need him in one piece, I'm going to leave out what he did to you. We can deal with that when we get him in a box."

"If you say so. Whatever you think is best."

"Maybe we can snatch up Shadow and Scales," Atkinson said, "and put a stop to things this very afternoon."

While Atkinson was on the phone, Maureen walked a few steps away, to the other side of the overpass, Atkinson's information rolling around in her head. She listened to the pigeons cooing and the traffic thumping overhead.

She'd made assumptions about the young boys because of their age, though she'd been warned against that very mistake. An error not unlike, she thought, letting Arthur Jackson burst through his front door and land a punch. At every turn, what the boys appeared capable of only worsened. Marques had been at the scene of Jackson's arrest and subsequent drug bust. Coincidence? Or was he on assignment, keeping tabs on the cops. The next day, while looking like kids on their way to the playground, Marques and his friends were in fact acting as lookouts in a criminal enterprise. But being a spy or a lookout was a long way from being a killer. Or was it? What did she really know? In a year and a half Mike-Mike had gone from lookout to killer to corpse.

She turned and studied the intersection where the Plymouth had been found. She thought again of what a terrible choice of location it was for dumping the car. She toed the edges of the burns in the street, thinking of the amateurish fire.

The fire, it seemed to her, had been much more about destroying the car than disappearing the contents of the trunk. She wished they had the arson analysis. She knew it would show a common accelerant, something handy that could be scored at the last minute, and obtained without attracting attention: gasoline or kerosene, something easy to steal from around the neighborhood, from a car or an unlocked garage. Whatever it was, the fire starters hadn't used enough of it. Not enough to disguise the most damning piece of the scene. Mike-Mike.

His dead body, Maureen realized, was the only obstacle to her naming Marques and Goody as the car thieves and the fire starters. More precisely, her own squeamish feelings about the way the body had gotten there inhibited her conclusions. Marques and Goody *could've* killed Mike-Mike. They *could've* put him in the trunk and set the car on fire. They were physically capable of those actions. She couldn't ignore the possibilities that she didn't want to be true. What had Preacher called Goody? A time bomb. An alpha dog. He considered Goody capable of killing. And in the time they had spent together, Preacher had been wrong about very little, if anything.

She'd assumed that the three boys were close friends, though when she stopped to think about it, she had seen no real evidence of this. She hadn't, she noted, seen them together before or since that afternoon by the car. Marques had been alone in the playground when she'd talked to him. What if they were actors? Middle school business associates thrown together by a common task. Anyone watching Maureen and Atkinson have lunch at Handsome Willy's would've assumed that the women were friends. Maureen knew they weren't friends. They were two women who'd only just met, who would never have had lunch together if not for work, who might never again spend as much time in each other's company, or talk as personally as they had today. What if she saw what the boys had wanted her to see, because they intuited by her new blue uniform and her white skin what she wanted? She felt a headache hatch at the base of her skull.

"Is it possible that we're overthinking this?" Maureen said.

"How so?" Atkinson asked.

"Well, I was thinking," Maureen said, her ideas suddenly elusive, loose strands that she couldn't capture and weave. "Well, wait a minute."

"Talk."

"What if," Maureen began again, "what if instead of looking at some elaborate plan here, we're looking at a string of mistakes and misjudgments, one fuckup after another, and that's why the choices made here don't seem to make any sense. Because they don't. They're not supposed to. Maybe it's a stupidity explosion."

"Uh, okay. Keep going."

"Preacher's been teaching me about the neighborhoods, about how tight and self-contained they are. That, for a lot of folks, if it hadn't been for the storm they'd never have left New Orleans in their whole lives. That the ones who came back will probably never leave it again. That a trip to the Superdome or the Quarter is a major excursion."

She pointed back up Claiborne Avenue, toward the hospitals, back toward Central City.

"For young kids living their lives in the same eight-, ten-block radius, we're a long way down Claiborne. We're far from home." She shrugged. "Besides the fact, how far is a twelve-year-old driving a car going to get, even in the middle of the night? All the good places to dump a car, and a body, out in the east, or even down in the Ninth Ward, there's no getting out there without driving on the highway, or taking some convoluted twisty route through half the neighborhoods in the city. No kids are gonna want to do either of those things, even if they're capable. As soon as we put nervous kids behind the wheel of the Plymouth, everything starts to make sense."

"And the body in the trunk?" Atkinson asked.

"I'm holding out hope," Maureen said, "that Goody and Marques were only in charge of disposal, that they never knew it was in there."

Atkinson grinned at her. "Cling to that optimism, Coughlin. It's misguided, but it'll keep you showing up for work every day."

"You really think Goody and Marques killed him? And that they tried to dump the body?"

"It wasn't me," Atkinson said, "and I'm reasonably sure it wasn't you. Everyone else is on the list. Goody has an ugly record. He reads like a bully. Maybe he put Mike-Mike up to killing Wright."

Maureen lit a cigarette. "Middle School Murder, Incorporated. Christ Almighty."

"More than you bargained for?"

Maureen knew that no was the correct answer. It was what she wanted to say. She got close. "Maybe. A little bit."

"This is it, this is the job," Atkinson said. "You want that ugly feeling in your gut to be the tacos, but it's not."

"It goes away?"

Atkinson wrinkled her nose, as if catching a whiff of the feeling they were discussing. "Sometimes you don't feel it as much."

"That's not the same as it going away."

"No," Atkinson said. "It's not."

"But what possible motive could Mike-Mike or Goody have had? Or anyone, for that matter? Wright was a bum. Why kill him?"

"He was a bum," Atkinson said with a shrug. "Who's gonna miss him?"

"Kill him because there's no reason not to?" Maureen said. "That doesn't make any sense. Even if it's just a bum, we, the police, still show up when a body drops. That's got to be counterproductive to somebody's agenda. I don't like it."

"It's proof you can pull the trigger," Atkinson said, "and that you can take orders. It's a way to prove yourself."

"Maybe Wright was a snitch?"

"Not for Homicide," Atkinson said. "I checked. Not that there weren't plenty of other opportunities for him. Beyond him getting shot, any other reason to think snitch?"

"He got kicked through the system awful fast the last time he got busted."

"Talk to whoever busted him that time," Atkinson said. "Maybe they did him a favor."

"It was me. I arrested him last."

"And the next time you caught him fucking up?"

"I talked to him," Maureen said, "and then I let him go."

"Think about how that looks."

"No," Maureen said. "He wasn't mine. I would've told you that the night he was killed. I just got here. I don't have anyone on the street. The neighborhood knows that. I was trying to cut the guy a break."

"Since you'd kicked someone's ass the day before?"

"It's a give-and-take," Maureen said. "That's what Preacher told me. Pick when and where to be gung-ho and to look the other way. That next time I ran into Wright I was trying to give a little leeway, instead of running him off to jail."

"So you could ask for favors from him later."

"What? You don't do it?"

"All the time," Atkinson said. "Relax. I'm not accusing you of anything. That's the game."

"I can't figure out the rules in this department."

"Nothing comes for free, especially from the cops. Pay now or later, but pay you will. That's a rule of life, not the NOPD. The neighborhood knows that."

"I might have thought that later," Maureen said, "but the only thing on my mind at the time was to cut the guy a break, do *him* a favor."

"You need one of those T-shirts," Atkinson said.

Maureen didn't get it. "T-shirts? What kind of T-shirt?"

"One from the Road to Hell Paving Company." She checked her phone. "Not a bad start to a shift that hasn't officially started yet. I'm pretty confident we got Wright's killer. That's one in the black."

"I wish we didn't have him at the morgue."

"Me, too," Atkinson said. "I do. And those other two boys. We need to track them down. Word is out by now that we found Mike-Mike and the car. Scales will know. I don't want those boys paying with their lives for this mistake."

"Preacher's looking," Maureen said. "One of us would've heard had he found something."

"Maybe I'll put a call in to him anyway. Okay. I really have to go. The night shift awaits. I wish I didn't have a dozen other cases to work, but I do." Atkinson put out her hand. "Thanks for coming out here on your day off. And for your help."

"Thanks for lunch," Maureen said.

What else should she say? Good luck with that divorce? Good luck with those murders? Maureen found it hard to let Atkinson go without making plans to meet her again.

"Thanks for letting me see some of how you work."

"There will be more opportunities," Atkinson said. "I don't think we're running out of murders anytime soon. The minute you find those other boys, I want to know."

"Will do."

"Who else knows about this run-in with Shadow? You tell Preacher?"

Maureen shook her head. "You and I know. That's it."

"You got your service weapon on you?" Atkinson asked.

"Not right now," Maureen said.

"Carry it," Atkinson said. "Everywhere. Shadow or Scales gets near you again, do what you have to do to protect yourself. Come strong. No empty threats. He's not our only route to the truth about these murders."

"Okay."

"That's an order, Coughlin. Understood? And for the time being, do your running indoors."

"Yes, Detective Sergeant."

"I'd rather speak at your weapon-discharge hearing, where I can help you," Atkinson said, "than at your funeral, where I can't."

23

Outsmarting herself in pursuit of a shortcut back uptown, Maureen ended up lost and frustrated in the medical district of the CBD. The streets formed a maze of one-ways and intersections. Even with the windows open she sweated like a savage, beads of moisture trickling down her temples, the back of her tank top stuck to the seat. Not the situation, not the time of year, not the city, she thought, to be driving a piece-of-shit Honda with no AC. Not when you don't know where the hell you're going. She knew, intellectually, that the pedestrians and the other drivers around her didn't know she was lost, but she was embarrassed in front of them anyway. She felt stared at, felt watched and judged. Not a good sign when those feelings started coming on. Just breathe, she told herself. She tried to stretch her legs, but the car was too small.

Her phone rang on the passenger seat. She checked it quickly before the light turned green. Preacher calling. She hated answering the phone while driving. Letting it ring as she tried to navigate, she hoped the call wasn't too urgent, probably a generic follow-up to see how things had

gone with Atkinson. It could wait. Panic tapped its rough, eager fingertips along the edges of her eyes and her lungs, probing for a grip. Her
chest tightened and a headache burned at the base of her skull. She
could feel her heart beat against her breastbone.

She needed to get out of the traffic, out of the confusion. Out of the
car if she could.

Poydras Street, the main artery through the CBD, finally materialized before her. Relief shot through her belly and down her thighs like a
blast of cool air. The main streets she knew. She'd be fine. When the
light changed, she made an illegal left turn to put the Superdome and
the medical district at her back and drove toward St. Charles, where she
could turn uptown.

At Lee Circle, she pulled into an abandoned gas station and gave her
heartbeat a minute to settle. She turned off the car. She listened to a streetcar, its big bell clanging, roll through the Circle. She focused her vision
on the wall of an office building in front of her across a weedy lot. Two
squiggly black lines, starting to fade, were painted large across the orange
bricks. Some kind of funky art installation, Maureen recalled, from some
citywide art project a couple of years ago. Before her time. She couldn't
for the life of her figure out what the picture was supposed to be or mean.
Black hair ribbons tossed on the floor? That was what the painting most
resembled. Maybe it was a public Rorschach test. Check your psyche
against what you saw, learn about yourself on your way downtown. Or not.

Better than a plain old ugly building, she guessed. Somebody had
gotten a paycheck for painting those black ribbons. Good for them, she
thought. Take it where you can get it. She wondered what had been abandoned longer, the dirty gas station or the art looming over it.

She lit a cigarette and returned Preacher's call.

"What's your twenty?" Preacher asked.

"On my way home from meeting with Atkinson."

"You're one of those people," Preacher said—she could hear the smile
in his voice—"who has to pull over to talk on the phone, aren't you?" A

pause. "Atkinson's on day shift now? Took you quite a while to drop off a couple of files at HQ."

"We had lunch. I was in traffic. St. Charles is busy. I was being extra cautious. More people should drive like me."

"Lunch. Since you're out and about disobeying orders for the afternoon, drive over to the sno-ball stand at South Tonti and Washington. Our favorite animal rescue vigilante has had a busy afternoon. With mixed results, naturally. Ah, lament the best intentions of mice and crackheads."

"You're having a sno-ball with Little E?"

"It's a complicated story," Preacher said. "It'll make more sense when you see it with your own eyes. Believe."

"Since I'm working these murders," Maureen said, "does today count as my last training shift?"

Preacher hung up.

Maureen tossed the phone onto the passenger seat. She started the car and looked up at the painted building one more time. Whatever you say, Preach.

24

The sno-ball stand was a tilting butter-yellow shack about the size of a tool-shed, squeezed between a set of row houses and an empty lot that had been fenced off and then abandoned. A large dead oak in the center had col-lapsed, its top branches smashing through the fence. The area had become a dumping ground: tires, busted appliances, torn and dirty baby clothes, along with the usual litter caught in the tree branches. Preacher had parked the cruiser halfway up on the sidewalk by the oak. Flouting traffic laws seemed to be his preferred way of expressing his authority. Maureen had parked her Honda parallel to the police car. He's rubbing off on me, she thought, getting out.

A young mother in white short shorts and a hot-pink T-shirt, a pink cell phone pressed to her ear, dragged a sticky-faced young boy by the arm into a dramatic detour around the cars and out into the middle of Washington Avenue. Between the cars and the tree, no room to pass re-mained on the sidewalk. If the young woman cared about traffic, she didn't show it. She glared at Maureen the whole time, even over her shoulder as she walked away, talking a mile a minute into the phone—a true multitasker. Maureen returned the stare through her sunglasses, hanging her badge over her belt. The woman made a show of noticing the badge. Maureen could read her mind: *Like I give a fuck.*

Something about the boy, his unlaced sneakers, his little legs churning to keep up with his high-strung mom, picked at Maureen's brain. She thought, of course, of the boys she was looking for, but they were twice the age of that child. They hadn't always been. Somebody had once towed them around the neighborhood by the arm. Then they let go. And now the city was having trouble finding someone to claim Mike-Mike's body.

Preacher called her name. She walked his way.

He stood over by the twisted fence, a sno-ball in a paper cup in one hand, his shades on, his big blue belly hanging over his gun belt, and a smile on his face—like they were meeting for an evening stroll in Audubon Park. His lips were purple with flavored syrup. Sitting on the ground, his back against the fence, was Little E. One arm, wrapped in a white towel, hung limply across his lap. He didn't appear to be handcuffed. In his other hand he held a sno-ball that he ignored, the melted ice dripping down the sides of the paper cup and onto his dirty jeans.

A shapeless line of adults and children gathered in front of the service window at the stand. The quiet adults, outnumbered three to one by the chattering kids, threw occasional hard glances at Preacher. They watched Maureen approach, speaking only to correct unruly children, their eyes remaining on her as they did it. Maureen could feel their resentment hot and thick in the air like the humidity. They were just buying the kids a cold treat on a hot summer day, yet here were the cops, right in the middle of their afternoon for no good reason, putting the lean on a guy from the neighborhood. Making a spectacle and scaring the kids in the process.

Preacher waved to her with his free hand. *Do as I say*, Maureen heard Atkinson say, *not as I do.* She wished Preacher had picked a less public locale for his interrogation. He certainly knew what the people around them were thinking; not that he cared. He was not one for advancing the cause of "community policing," another catchphrase beaten senseless at the academy. This oughtta be good, Maureen thought. This *better* be good.

"Officer Coughlin, you look flushed," Preacher said as Maureen joined them in the high grass at the edge of the lot. He raised his sno-ball, his fingers stained with purple. "Get yourself one of these. My treat."

"No, thanks," Maureen said. She lifted her chin at Etienne. "I see you've got company."

"You, him," Preacher said. "There's nothing better than a sno-ball on a hot day, and I can't give one away."

Little E whimpered a bit. "My arm hurts."

"You're lucky you still have it," Preacher said. "You owe me that arm. That's my arm. And probably your skull, too."

Maureen noticed small bloodstains on the towel around Little E's forearm. "Uh, Preach? The arm?"

"So there I am," Preacher began, "making the rounds, actually with an eye out for my man here, 'cause he's a good man to know. And while I'm rolling down Josephine Street, about all out of hope, who should appear in my field of vision but our hero, a pack of hysterical, screaming children jumping around him and an angry twenty-pound puppy hanging from his arm."

"They bad to that dog over there," Little E said. "They don't feed him or nothing. That's what makes him mean."

"He's healthy enough to take a chunk outta you," Preacher said. "Now shut it." He turned to Maureen. "E knows how I am about the dogs, so every dog in the 'hood now he's trying to snatch up and deliver unto Caesar. There's a difference between rescue and theft that I can't seem to clarify for him." He dug at his sno-ball with a plastic spoon. "Between the two of you, I wonder why I even try."

"I understand this is important to you, Preach," Maureen said. "I do. But we have people we need to find."

"Turns out," Preacher said, "the dog wasn't his biggest problem. Because as I'm getting out of the car, out on the front porch comes an angry young brother with a baseball bat, and I'm wondering if it's for Little E or the dog." Preacher raised his cup and sucked in a mouthful of ice. Maureen could hear him crunching it in his jaws. "It wasn't for the dog."

Maureen turned to the cruiser, checking the backseat.

"Not me," Little E said. "I know them people, them kids."

"I know you know them kids," Preacher said. "That doesn't mean they know you, or aren't afraid of you." He turned to Maureen. "Because after the young man pries the puppy loose and tosses him inside, he comes down from the porch to talk to me. He tells me E's been lingering in the vacant across the street the past few days, watching them kids in that yard, ain'tcha?"

Little E shook his head so hard Maureen thought it might fly off. "No, sir, that ain't me, that ain't what I do. I was watching that dog, the way they was mistreating it. Been watching for a couple of days. I was looking for a chance to take it, I admit that. But it was for the dog's own good."

"About the kid with that bat," Maureen said.

"In a minute." Preacher crumpled the paper cup in his hand and tossed it in the long grass. He pulled a bandana from his pocket, wiped his hands, wiped his mouth. "The thing is," he said to Little E, "knowing how you feel about dogs, and knowing that your daddy would've put you on the bottom of the river a long time ago if you were that way about kids, I believe you, Little E. But that badass with the bat and the attitude doing his best to look out for them nieces and nephews of his? He thinks you came through that gate for that little girl and not that dog. And me being a cop, I don't know how much he believes anything I tell him to the contrary, try as I might to change his mind."

"Officer Boyd, you can't do me like that," Little E said, the barest hint of righteousness in his voice. "I mind my business. I do good for you when I can. I ain't like that about little kids. I'd put *myself* in the bottom of the river if I was like that."

"Let me see that arm," Preacher said.

Little E unwrapped the towel, raising his arm so Preacher could see the swollen dog bite up by the elbow. Maureen leaned in for a look. White lint from the towel stuck to the puncture wounds. The bite wasn't as bad as Maureen had feared. It looked to her like the bleeding had stopped. The wound needed a good cleaning, maybe a couple of stitches.

"You'll live," Preacher said. "I'm gonna call EMS for you, though. Make sure you get cleaned up right." He keyed the mic on his radio, called in for nonemergency first aid. He turned to Etienne. "What's the story when they get here?"

"I was trying to catch a stray," Little E said, "and it bit me. I don't know where it went."

Preacher leaned forward. "You're helping everyone out that way, E, including yourself. Remember that." He turned to Maureen. "Stay here with him. I'm gonna get the first-aid kit from the car."

Watching Preacher stroll over to the cruiser, Maureen wondered why he was bothering now with first aid. He'd already let Little E sit there for some time with nothing more than a bar towel for his wounds. Why not just leave it for EMS? Was he having second thoughts about the opinions of the spectators? No, it wasn't that. It was CYA. EMS might wonder why E hadn't received any first aid from the police department. Preacher knew that treated puncture wounds and a solid story from Little E would prevent questions. *You have to be careful*, Preacher had told her in the past. *You never know when you're gonna run into someone who actually gives a shit.* If pressed by the medics, which was doubtful anyway, E would vouch for Preacher. Because when, not if, Little E got in trouble again, EMS wouldn't help him out, but Preacher would.

Maureen squatted beside Little E, bringing herself down to eye level with him. "Who was the kid with the bat? What was his name?"

E shrugged.

"Where was this house with the dog? What block of Josephine?"

E said nothing. Had Preacher told him not to talk to her?

"The guy with the bat, does he wear twists and a shell necklace? You ever heard of a guy they call Shadow? How about Bobby Scales—what've you heard about him?"

E turned his head away. Maureen wanted to smack him.

Preacher walked up to them. He set down the big tackle box of first-aid supplies. He patted away the sweat from his face with his bandana.

"Do me a favor and do the honors, Coughlin."

Maureen opened the box. She pulled on a pair of latex gloves, then dug out a couple of peroxide pads. She extended one gloved hand. E took the cue and settled his wounded arm into her hand, his eyes watching Preacher the entire time.

"This is gonna sting," Maureen said.

E flinched as she dabbed at the punctures and swabbed around them, cleaning up the blood. She dropped one bloody pad in the grass, opened another, and went back to work. And just like that, she realized, the thought making an audible popping sound in her head, she was complicit in Preacher's minor deception of the EMS. She would have bet her whole career that he didn't even know what he was doing. It was ingrained in him that everyone fudged a little. Maureen understood. Preacher's way, everyone carried some of the weight. Everyone had something to lose. This was how Preacher kept the information flowing and the moving parts moving.

She couldn't argue with the logic. A couple of white lies did make everything better. E didn't have to explain why he went crashing into a yard full of kids. A visit with a doctor, even if it was in an assembly line of an emergency room, would do E some good. His freedom, his life back on the streets, was already wearing heavy on him. He wouldn't have to explain his new vigilante-style dognapping career. The SPCA wouldn't come and take the dog. The kids wouldn't lose their pet and, considering the animal's response to Little E, their protector. And the little dog wouldn't go to the pound and be put down for biting someone trying to steal him away from his home and his pack. There was someone at the house that Preacher thought important. And now that person might be less spooked next time someone in a uniform came to the house.

Maureen saw it all. She saw how everyone came out ahead by playing Preacher's game.

And what was so bad about it? She couldn't say, no matter who asked, either over a beer or under oath, that Preacher was a dishonest or dirty cop. Zero tolerance was the department mantra; she knew that. But was the lack of tolerance for breaking the rules or bending them? Or for getting caught?

She laid some clean gauze over Little E's injury, encouraging him to hold the bandage in place with pressure. No point in taping it with EMS on their way. She could see them coming up Washington now.

"My arm hurts," Little E said. "Worse than before. You shoulda left it alone."

"The pain's how you know the peroxide's getting where it needs to be," Maureen said. "The pain means you're getting better." She stood, massaging the small of her back. She lit a cigarette. "Don't worry, E, you're gonna be fine. We're all gonna be fine."

25

Once the EMTs had taken over Little E's treatment, Maureen joined Preacher over by the cruiser. Preacher leaned on the hood, dipping the entire front of the vehicle. Maureen stood in front of him, toeing at the gravel on the sidewalk, arms crossed, a cigarette burning between her lips. She found herself wishing that she could work without the uniform, without the vest and all the equipment. She was dying for a cup of coffee.

"Little E wouldn't tell me a thing," Maureen said. "You tell him not to?"

"What would I do that for?" Preacher asked. "That's on him. He doesn't owe you anything. He's not gonna help you because you're a cop. You hafta earn it."

"You're kidding me."

"Even snitches have some degree of self-respect, Coughlin. It's just another hustle out here, like a part-time job that pays under the table. You remember that, you'll make more friends."

"The kid at the house, who was he?" she asked Preacher.

"Nobody we're looking for," Preacher said. "But the house where he lives, where Little E was watching the kids, it's over on Josephine and Danneel."

That got Maureen's attention. She knew that corner by reputation. Everyone on the job did; it had once been the heart of a particularly bloody stretch of Josephine Street, itself a war zone. Talk around the department, and not just in the Sixth District, said that the heart had started pumping blood again.

"This thing with Wright and the kids goes to Josephine Street? That's what you're telling me?"

"Yes, indeed."

"Where the Christmas thing happened last year," Maureen said.

"Five shot, two dead," Preacher said. "Two sisters, Christmas fucking morning."

After that even the *federales* had made moves to shut down the J-Street Family, as they called themselves, taking doors up and down Josephine on Ash Wednesday, hauling eighteen suspects off to jail. Fifteen of them under thirty, every one of them with a record. Open cases, outstanding warrants. Half faced federal racketeering charges. A few were back on the streets. Three of them had been murdered since then by other criminals in what the police were sure were revenge killings. Investigations into those killings were proceeding slowly, to say the least.

The cache of weapons, Maureen recalled, was the big news. Automatic weapons, combat-ready weapons that probably should have been in Iraq or Afghanistan. An operation, she'd heard, that had tentacles stretching east to Atlanta and west to Houston, maybe even to Mexico and California. So many guns had been confiscated, rumor had it, that the feds had considered terrorism charges. The massive effort had brought about ninety days of quiet to the neighborhood. Nature does abhor a power vacuum, Maureen thought.

Josephine Street was a long, bloody, heartbreaking scar, Maureen thought, right through the Sixth, right through Central City. She couldn't wait to get there.

"Anyway, here's the kicker," Preacher said. "I ask about Goody and Marques because, fuck it, I'm there, I'm out of the car. To my sheer fucking astonishment, the kid with the bat, he can't get the words out fast enough. He don't know no Marques, he says, but we can stop looking for Goody, because the boy's hopped a bus back to his people in Baton Rouge. And that he was only headed elsewhere from there. Says he's Goody's second cousin, gave him the bus fare for Baton Rouge himself, took him down to the Greyhound station. Saw him get on the bus. Said he never heard of Bobby Scales, of course. Surprise."

Maureen shook her head. "No, no, no. Of course he knows Scales. He's telling you what Scales told him to say."

"Why would Scales tell us anything?" Preacher asked. "How would he anticipate that we'd end up on Josephine Street and plant a message there? Why not let us keep looking for Goody and wasting our time? I believe this kid. I get the feeling it's not us that Goody's running from."

"Right. Exactly. What if Scales wants us to stop looking? Makes it easier for him to go after Goody himself."

"And why does he want to do that?"

"Atkinson thinks Mike-Mike was the shooter in the Wright case," Maureen said. "She thinks it was Goody and Marques that tried getting rid of the Plymouth. Probably under orders from Scales. They fucked it up and now Scales is after them. He needs to clean up, get rid of all three of them."

"She thinks this, Atkinson does?"

"Can we go back to Josephine Street and talk to the kid with the bat?"

"And ask him what?" Preacher said. "Anything he's gonna tell us, he's already told us. You're the one that doesn't trust him."

"Do we have anything on him that we can use?" Maureen asked. "He have a record?"

"I ran his name after I talked to him. He took a shoplifting charge about three years ago, did his probation fair and square. Otherwise he came up clean."

"You ask for ID? Make sure you got his real name?"

"And let him go back in the house, where I can't see him? Try and follow him in and possibly create an incident? It's not my job, it's not *our* job, to make trouble where there isn't any. I had no reason to treat that kid like a criminal. Even on that corner."

"But you have a reason to treat Little E that way?"

"The same Little E that just got out of state prison? Everyone is different. Little E responds to a little heat, it opens him up. Like an oyster. It makes him feel dangerous." Preacher lifted himself up off the car. "I'm not entirely pleased with your tone, Coughlin, by the way. I'm glad you're eager to leave the nest, but some proper fucking respect, please."

"I don't like it, this Baton Rouge thing," Maureen said. "I don't buy it."

"You don't have to," Preacher said, "but I don't know that your delicate personal feelings change anything about any of this. When you make detective, then you can have feelings that matter. If it's any consolation, if Goody is mixed up with a Josephine Street crew, new or old, by business, by blood relation, or whatever, he's better off on a bus far outta town. He's better off anywhere but here. Believe that."

Preacher walked around the car to the driver's side door. Maureen made a move for the passenger side. She stopped, remembering she was off for the day. She knew what Preacher would say next, and she didn't want to hear it.

"Now go home," Preacher said, "and rest up. Today's been a good day. Let's have another good one tomorrow. And do whatever it takes, do whoever it takes, to shave the edge off that Irish temper before you come back to work."

He took a few steps back in Maureen's direction, pointing his finger at her.

"And do not under any circumstances, Coughlin, for any *fucking* reason, let me hear that your skinny white ass was over on Josephine Street tonight. Not if you want to be anything more than a meter maid in this town. Understood?"

"Yeah." Maureen knew better than to deny that the idea had crossed her mind.

"That is a fucking order, soldier. Do you believe it?"

"Yes, sir. I believe."

Mike-Mike was dead. Goody was gone. She thought of Marques.

And then there was one.

26

Maureen sat on a bench inside Jackson Square, near the tiered black fountain, listening to its falling water in the shade of the blooming crepe myrtles. The lost petals of their tiny pink flowers carpeted the benches and the paths through the square. Over the crepe myrtles loomed the wide, dark-leaved live oaks. Birds sang short songs in the branches overhead. A good breeze blew in off the river, rustling the leaves of the live oaks and cooling Maureen's bare shoulders, relaxing her. She watched the sparrows and the squirrels as they scavenged watchful and wary underneath the empty benches. When she stretched her arms, she felt a sting on her back, right between her shoulder blades. Running around outside all afternoon, she'd gotten a sunburn. The park smelled like sweet olive and honeysuckle, but the breeze also carried tangy whiffs of the beast-of-burden-and-urine smell of the horse-drawn carriages lining up outside the square along Decatur Street. Alas, Maureen thought, no place is perfect.

She sipped her Café du Monde frozen au lait, which was the closest thing in this world to ambrosia, she'd decided. If ever another storm came, she was taking every weapon she could find and setting up camp outside Café du Monde. She'd defend the place to the last. She set her coffee down beside her and lit a cigarette. She stretched her legs, hanging her elbows over the back of the bench. Not a bad place for a nap. A bad time for it, though. She'd go to bed tonight right after dark, sleep the sleep of the dead. She was so looking forward to it.

Outside the gates of the square, on the flagstone plaza in front of St. Louis Cathedral, the listless members of a ragtag brass band stood in a loose circle, wet towels on the backs of their necks, dented horns in hand, chatting around a plastic pickle bucket. They'd played maybe half a song since Maureen had arrived twenty minutes ago. Not a lot of people to play for. She wondered if the guys hanging around without instruments laughing and cutting up got a share of the money in the pickle bucket, what there would be of it, on a day like today. Maybe they were management, Maureen thought. The shoeshine guy left his post outside the empty, open-fronted tourist-trap restaurant and joined in the conversation. A skinny gray cat wound itself through his legs as he walked.

Yawning, Maureen watched what few brave and/or foolish tourists visited New Orleans in August as they milled about the square. Most were European. She heard British accents, some Italian, some French. Others were Americans. She didn't need to hear them talk. They had the fattest shopping bags and the biggest, whitest sneakers. Maureen knew she was far from what a native New Orleanian would consider a local, but at least she didn't look like one of these pasty, doe-eyed folks shuffling around the square.

Wherever they were from, as if preprogrammed, all the tourists took multiple pictures around the Andrew Jackson statue in the center of the square. Then they took a few more huddled together in front of the regal St. Louis Cathedral, their possessions hanging loose on their shoulders and in their hands. The big statue of the hat-waving war-hero president on horseback was the one everyone flocked to, the one on every other postcard, but Maureen preferred the newer French Market monument to Joan of Arc, the Maid of Orleans. Joan sat on horseback, too, upright and proud in glorious sun-spattering bronze. Instead of waving her hat as if trying to rally a college-football crowd, Joan manned her post at the front of the cavalry charge while holding high a weapon, a bannered lance. Maureen loved the warrior part of the story. The young-martyr part she tried not to think about. The virgin part didn't apply.

As Maureen watched, the sweating and smiling tourists couldn't hand their cameras and their phones over to passing strangers fast enough. Big handbags, big shopping bags, jewelry hanging loose from their wrists and ears and throats, wallets bursting from back pockets. She wanted to shout, could you people look any more like a bunch of victims in waiting? At least make it a challenge, make the crooks earn it.

She watched as a heavy man in khaki shorts bent forward to hand his daughter coins for the fountain. His wallet stuck halfway out of his back pocket. Talk about the Big Easy, Maureen thought, shaking her head. The man made her glad she hadn't been assigned down here to the Eighth District. Dealing with tourists would be too much like waiting tables again. She wanted to be done with supposed grown-ups who refused to listen, refused to follow, to even read, directions and simple instructions—people who refused to fend for themselves while in public.

She sipped cold coffee through the straw.

Yeah, she thought, because you're so much better equipped for dealing with Mother Mayor and the J-Street Family or whatever the hell the local killers and drug lords call themselves these days. If only her mother, Maureen thought, could see her now.

27

On her graduation day, after the purse-snatching incident behind Café du Monde, Maureen had walked with her mom and Waters in the direction of their Canal Street hotel—the large, safe, and familiar Marriott where Maureen had booked their room in advance of their visit. Not only had she reserved the hotel and picked them up at the airport, but she'd also done everything else she could to Disneyfy her mother's first New Orleans experience. She controlled what parts of the city they saw, keeping Amber and Waters corralled in the touristy parts of the French Quarter and the prettier areas of Uptown—St. Charles Avenue, Magazine Street, the Garden District, Audubon Park and Zoo. She couldn't prevent them from reading the paper, but as luck would have it, no one got shot in New Orleans for three whole days. No cops got brought up on charges. Even the weather had been unseasonably kind. Good omens all.

Maureen knew her mother would never love New Orleans. She'd never expected her to. The city was too different, too distant. Maureen knew Amber might not even visit New Orleans again after this trip. But she had wanted her mother to at least enjoy the place. She hoped that would help her mistrust it less and, most important, no longer fear the city as she did knowing it only from TV and the Internet. There was some success.

Over the long weekend, they'd approached an understanding: Maureen, Amber, and Maureen's new home. The night before the incident at the Café du Monde bathrooms, they'd had dinner on Magazine Street at a seafood place called Casamento's, not far from Maureen's apartment.

"It's world-famous," Maureen had said, leading them through the busy front room, past the white-tiled oyster bar where the thick-gloved shuckers talked a mile a minute in their musical accents. "We're lucky they're open and that we got a table. They keep odd hours."

"Sounds like someone else I know," Amber said.

As they sat, she scanned the tiled walls, ceiling, and floor. Everything was white tile. "It's like having dinner in a shower. Easy to clean, I guess. What do I know?"

Amber fought the good fight, but the hothouse charm of the city that had so besotted Maureen upon her arrival had started softening the sharp, icy edges of Amber's defenses. Over trays of chilled raw oysters, which Waters enjoyed but Amber could not even look at, never mind eat, Maureen could see her mother softening. Maureen ate oysters with horseradish, drank cold local beer, and waited.

Eventually, Amber set her fork down beside her half-eaten iceberg-lettuce salad. She picked a lemon seed from her iced tea and placed it on a corner of her paper napkin.

"I can see why you like it here," she said. "The people certainly seem pretty happy. And I can't say they're not nice. It's different, all right. It's not home. I'll give it that."

Faint praise, Maureen thought, for the place where your daughter has staked her claim. But she also knew better than to ask for more. Maureen could become the city's first female police superintendent and Amber would never concede her daughter had made the right choice in leaving New York City. So she took Amber's words for what they were: her mother's best effort. And, really, what else could a daughter ask for? Maureen thought her strategy had worked.

Her victory had been short-lived.

As they walked to the hotel from Café du Monde after the purse-snatching incident, Amber was as distressed as Maureen had seen her the whole trip. She watched her mother's eyes, wary, bright and electric. She didn't like the way they moved. Maureen, Amber, and Waters hadn't talked about what had happened, and they wouldn't discuss it, ever, once they parted ways at the hotel.

"Maybe we should have dinner at the hotel restaurant," Amber said. "I'm sure they have good food."

Okay, Maureen thought, here we go. Now she's afraid to even walk out of the hotel. She caught sight of Waters and decided to let him lead the defense of their dinner plans. He looked like a kid who'd been told on Christmas Eve that Christmas Day was canceled. Maureen almost laughed out loud. Man, he could do hangdog disappointment with the best of them, she thought.

"We were gonna do that fancy place tonight," Waters said. "I've been looking forward to it. You've been looking forward to it. I brought a tie."

"I'm sure you can wear a tie to the hotel restaurant," Amber said.

Maureen watched her mother flinch as two kids coming their way on a small bike caught her attention, two black teenage boys in baseball caps, both laughing, one pedaling away, the other balanced, barely, on the handlebars. Seemed a dangerous undertaking, Maureen thought, considering the heavy traffic flowing into the Quarter. The danger was probably the point, Maureen decided. She remembered those days.

"You picked the place, Am," Waters said. "It's that lady you like from that show. Spicy Susan. It's her place. She might even be there. You could meet a famous person. It'll be fun."

"We've had all the rich food that we, that you, can stand," Amber said. "And the woman's name is Spicer, Susan Spicer."

"Amber," Waters said, slowing to a stop so Amber had to turn and face him. "We're having a good time. I'll go back to salmon burgers and quinoa tomorrow when we get home. I promise. C'mon. It's been a great vacation and a great visit with Maureen. It's a big weekend for her."

"The biggest," Maureen said.

"Don't let that clown back there ruin it," Waters said. "Besides, you're with two cops."

The boys on the bike wobbled along in their direction. Maureen watched Amber try not to watch them. She couldn't help herself. And though people walked close by her at a regular clip in both directions, some even bumping her shoulder and her handbag, those passersby were adults, white adults, Maureen noticed, and Amber ignored them. Her gazed stayed fixed on the approaching black kids. Something small and prickly squirmed in Maureen's gut.

C'mon, Ma, she thought, don't be like that.

"Oh, that?" Amber said. "I'm not worried about that. I'm tired. We have an early flight tomorrow."

"The flight's at noon," Waters said. "The airport's twenty minutes away."

"There was a very long security line," Amber said. "I saw it when we arrived. Somebody in this family has to plan ahead."

"Ma, it's a six-thirty reservation. Even in New Orleans you can be back in your room by ten."

"Don't you two gang up on me," Amber said, fighting a grin. "I hate that."

Amber screamed. Clutching her purse to her chest, hunching over it, she twisted her back to the street. Everyone around them froze. Maureen watched the bike go by. The kid pedaling the bike turned and flipped up his middle finger, to make sure everyone knew the implications of Amber's panic.

"Fuck you, lady."

The rider kept on laughing.

Maureen took a deep breath, trying very hard not to lose it on Amber for making a scene while at the same time wanting to belt that kid for cursing at her mom. A stranger walked up to her. A white stranger. "Aren't you gonna do anything?"

It took Maureen a moment to remember she was in uniform. "Like what?"

The stranger was incredulous. "Those black kids tried to rob that lady you're with. I saw it."

"No," Maureen said. "No, they didn't. I watched them coming all the way from the corner of Canal. They didn't do a thing but ride by."

The stranger gave Maureen the up-and-down, as if checking to make sure he hadn't mistaken the uniform. "No wonder this city's a mess, cops like you."

"Then don't live here," Maureen said. The words were out of her mouth before she knew she'd thought them. Listen to me, she thought. Next thing you know I'll be calling everyone "y'all."

"I don't live here," he said. "Never would."

He walked away, a white-knuckled grip on his Hard Rock Café shopping bag, his head swiveling on the lookout for danger. Maureen turned to her mother, who was looking everywhere but at her daughter. Without a doubt, Maureen thought, New Orleans has a lot to teach me.

28

In Jackson Square, Maureen got up off the bench and stretched, wincing at the sting of her sunburn. She checked her phone. She wanted to call Waters. She had lots to tell him and ask him about the past couple of days. Before finishing his career as a homicide detective on Staten Island, he'd worked the Bronx and Brooklyn in the golden era of crack cocaine. He knew drugs and gangs. Even on the Island, drug crime had been the main source of his homicide cases.

She should call Atkinson as well, she thought, and tell her what Preacher had learned about Goody. Maureen was eager for Atkinson's opinion of the information, whether or not she believed it. Maureen found the more she thought about the story, the less skeptical she grew. Considering what had happened to Mike-Mike, Goody getting out of town made sense. She wondered if Goody and Marques could escape Bobby Scales. So many connections stretched between New Orleans and Baton Rouge, with the way the aftermath of the hurricane had divided families, whole neighborhoods even, between the two places. The connections that formed Goody's path out of town could be the same ones that led Scales right to him.

Marques had to be found. Now that Mike-Mike was dead and Goody had been flushed out of town—unless he was dead, too, something Maureen knew she had to still allow as a possibility—Marques might talk to them. Tell them things he hadn't at the playground.

Maureen watched as the music teachers, two men and a woman, exited from under the stone arches of the Cabildo, one of the three-story Spanish colonial courthouse buildings flanking St. Louis Cathedral. The young players followed close behind their instructors, a noisy cluster of maybe thirty middle schoolers, boys and girls alike chattering and laughing, wearing matching polo shirts like the one Marques had worn at the playground—the noisy kids spreading like a bag of spilled marbles across the square. The teachers moved among the kids, redirecting the students toward where they needed to be, which for most of the kids was a pair of yellow school buses parked behind Maureen on Decatur. Other kids ran straight to the cluster of Jackson Square musicians, eager to talk shop. From what Maureen had seen around the city, the kids in Roots of Music weren't more than a couple of years away from playing in sidewalk ensembles of their own. She figured it beat bottle-cap tap dancing outside the French Quarter Walgreens. Had to be more of a future in being the player than in being the dancer.

While looking for Marques, she thought of Mike-Mike and of his brief time as one of those polo-shirted kids. She wondered how many of these kids were headed back to Central City, how many would put down their horns and their drumsticks for more dangerous things as they got older. At least with an instrument in hand they had a choice to make. It was easier to pick up bad habits with empty hands. Maureen wondered which of the teachers had made the call to cut Mike-Mike loose. A hell of a thing to live with. Word of Mike-Mike's fate would have reached the instructors and the kids at Roots by now, including Marques.

She'd hoped Mike-Mike's death would have scared Marques into calling her, or anyone in the department, but she couldn't say she was surprised that it hadn't happened. What kid in a neighborhood as tight as his would turn to strangers, the cops especially, when he got in trouble? If she were in Marques's situation, Maureen thought, she wouldn't go to the police. No way.

The drummers straggled out of the building last. Sticks in hand, they beat out rhythms on whatever they could find: signposts, garbage cans, lingering horn players, and fellow drummers.

Marques appeared, blinking in the sunlight. Maureen had ruled out going to a teacher first. If she did that, she'd have to tell the teacher she was a police officer. She didn't want to get Marques in trouble. A cop looking for you was never a good thing. She didn't want him saddled with another thousand push-ups. And she didn't want to expose him in front of the other kids. Most of all, she didn't want him banned from the one place she knew he could be found. She wanted to keep this visit as quiet as possible.

Marques saw her approaching and moved away. His head turned from side to side as he searched for an escape route, maybe the alleys alongside the cathedral.

Maureen quickened her steps, not chasing but keeping tabs. She kept her badge in her back pocket.

Marques drifted in one direction, then changed his mind and considered the other. Maureen admired his savvy. The boy knew that if he straight-up cut and run, his teachers would see and would want to know why. He was trying to fade away into the background, out of their sight and out of hers at the same time. His place in this band, she thought, matters a lot to him. It was the reason he hadn't joined Goody in Baton Rouge. She told herself that was a good thing. For him and for her. She called his name. His shoulders slumped and he turned to her.

Smiling at Marques, Maureen reconvinced herself that talking to him here was best. No one had a clue where he lived, who his people were. What would be a better place to talk? His friend's funeral?

"I've been looking for you," Maureen said.

"I figured," Marques said, eyes on his shoe tops.

"We need to talk." Maureen squatted down so she was looking up at him. From that position, Marques couldn't hide his face from her. "It's important. Very, very important."

"Because of what happened to Mike-Mike."

"Because of him," Maureen said, "and because of Goody."

She watched for a reaction to the second name, a wince or a flinch, something that might tell her Goody had suffered something worse than exile to Baton Rouge. Marques revealed nothing. Maureen wasn't sure he'd heard a thing she'd said. His eyes were everywhere away from her. The kid was miserable. Terrified. Exhausted. Could she blame him? He was too young to be the Last of the Mohicans. The fear shrank him, and he wasn't a big kid to begin with. Most of his bandmates had dispersed, but a few had hung around. Heads had started to turn in their direction. She needed to get him away from the others, the kids and the teachers alike. She needed to help him relax.

There was a gelato stand behind the cathedral at the end of the alley. She thought of Preacher and Little E. Okay. She'd buy him something.

For a moment, it didn't seem right to her, what she was doing. E was an adult; he had choices. What did Marques have but a bunch of adults who kept telling him a choice was the one thing he didn't have? And the alternative to her was what? Maureen wondered. The trunk of a car? Under the floor of a flooded-out vacant house?

She stood, held out her hand to him, saw that it shook, felt stupid for offering it. One of his best friends was dead. The other was running for his life. The kid thought of himself as a man. According to Atkinson, he might already be a killer. Didn't look much like one, Maureen thought, but lots of people thought she didn't look much like a cop.

Maureen tucked her hands in her back pockets. "Take a walk with me. We'll get an ice cream around the corner."

"I'm gonna miss the bus."

Marques shuffled his feet, taking subtle leans left and right, as if trying to hide behind her and see around her at the same time. Escape was still his first choice.

"I'll drive you home," Maureen said.

And find out where you live, she thought, and who you're living with, and what they know about what you've been doing. The way she thought, the double-dealing, the way the angles appeared to her so quickly, her brain made her feel dirty and underhanded and kind of like a natural cop all at the same time. Was she ashamed because she was dealing with a child? He's hardly an innocent, she reminded herself. But, Christ Almighty, she thought, was there a worse excuse to do something to a kid than *for his own good*?

"Wanna get moving?" Maureen asked, trying to smile.

"You need to tell Mr. Elvin," Marques said. "I can't leave with nobody unless Mr. Elvin knows them first."

Good policy, Maureen thought, but she wasn't too into Mr. Elvin knowing she was a cop.

Elvin Dodds, the last of the teachers in the square, was a substantial man who stood military straight. He wore loose khakis and an oversized blue-and-white-striped polo shirt. Long braids hung down his back. Around his neck hung thick-rimmed drugstore reading glasses on a thin chain. Even from a distance, Dodds radiated an air of cool authority. Maureen could tell he wasn't a man to be messed with, and that he didn't need clothes or jewelry to get that message across to the kids he taught or anyone else. Wasn't hard to see, Maureen thought, why younger kids, especially boys of a certain age, craved his respect. He was everything a lot of fatherless young boys would want.

Marques tugged on Maureen's arm. His eyes had welled up. Fear and frustration were boiling over in him. He was doing everything possible not to be a scared little boy. He was failing. "You need to tell him I ain't in trouble. He said I'm almost ready to march. I wanna march. I been practicing like a motherf—like crazy."

"I can do that," Maureen said. "I will do that. I'll explain to him that you're only helping me. I promise."

She squatted again. She took Marques by the arms, as if to stop his shaking and hold him together. She had to do this. She had to put him through this now so someone else didn't do worse to him later.

"Can we sit and talk for a minute?" Forget the walk, she thought. Forget the ice cream. She needed to ask as little as possible from this boy. She needed to get what she could and get it fast. "We'll sit right here on a bench where Mr. Elvin can see us."

Marques gave her the tiniest shrug. She didn't see his shoulders rise, just felt the effort in her hands. She released him.

"Have you learned any new cadences?" she asked. "Any new marches?"

Marques wouldn't look at her. He flashed no bravado, did no posing. They didn't move to the bench. This is not the same boy, Maureen thought, who she and Preacher had talked to on the playground. After what had happened to his friend, how could he be? He'd never be the same. She'd at least had the advantage, the luxury, really, of becoming an adult before serious violence had walked into her life. Not like Marques. She could debate with herself forever over how well she'd handled it, was handling it, but she'd had resources, choices about how to cope. What did Marques have? His marching band and her.

"I'm sorry," Maureen said, "about what happened to Mike-Mike. It's a terrible, terrible thing and I'm sorry it happened. I would've stopped it if I could."

Marques turned his head, blinked away tears. "Me, too." He sniffled. Maureen felt him harden. "But that's the game, you know?"

"I don't know," Maureen said. "But I do know that you don't play the game, do you? That's not your life, you're not like that. Even if Mike-Mike and Goody wanted you to be."

"Mike-Mike didn't know nothing but what Goody told him he knew. And Goody think he's so hard, but look at him now. Runnin' like a bitch."

Maureen settled on her knees. Keep it simple, she thought. Baby steps. "The three of you were good friends?"

"Pffffffffff. We were boys, from like, way back in the day. From before the storm, even."

Back in the day, Maureen thought. Six years ago when you were six years old. What could Marques even really remember about that time? She couldn't recall having felt at twelve that she'd already lived a long life.

"We walked down the Convention Center together," Marques said. "We stuck together outside there for three whole days. The three of us on some ugly-ass piece of carpet that Goody cut out from inside with his knife. Like a fucked-up little raft. Made some badass niggers step off us, though, with that knife, like, *every* night. The three of us, taking turns standing guard. Everybody was sayin' not to mess with those crazy little niggers on the corner. Like, everyone, ya heard? We even got sent over to Houston together on this smelly bus." He shrugged. "We were livin' in that stadium, it was nothin' *but* New Orleans people, then some church people came in and messed it all up for us."

"They separated you?"

Maureen stood, easing over to a bench where she took a seat, begging Marques in her mind to follow, and to keep talking.

"They found out I had my grandmother looking for me in Baton Rouge. Made me go there. Alone. On another smelly damn bus."

He dropped his heavy knapsack off his shoulder, dragging it behind him as he sat beside Maureen on the bench.

"She put it on the Internet or something. I looked for her at the Convention Center, but never found her. I thought she might be dead. A lot of old people be dying out there."

"I'm real glad she wasn't dead," Maureen said, "and that you guys found each other again. Goody and Mike-Mike, they didn't have family?"

"Like uncles and cousins and shit, but they was in Houston."

"So they got to stay together in Houston, your friends," Maureen said. "And you had to come home to New Orleans."

"Baton Rouge first," Marques said. "For a couple of years, then I got to middle school and got kicked out and my grandma had some money from some other church people, so we came home. And then, you know, Houston sucked for Goody and Mike-Mike. Nothin' but bullshit and trouble, and gettin' hassled over school like I was dealin' with in Baton

Rouge, so then Goody's people here sent for him and he brought Mike-Mike back with him. And then we was all back together."

He grinned at the memory, like an old man remembering the guys he played college ball with. "The same old Josephine Street crew. Only Josephine Street was fucked up in the flood and the street wasn't like it was and none of us could live where we used to. So except for that."

"So you came home with your grandmother," Maureen said. "Who did the other guys come home to?"

Marques shrugged. "Me."

"You? They didn't have anybody else? It's been the three of you living pretty much hand to mouth on the streets since, what, 2009? Why don't I believe that? Who are these people that sent for Goody?"

Maureen had her own ideas about the answers to her questions, but she wanted to hear Marques say it. When Marques took a deep breath, Maureen held hers. He wanted to tell her more. She could feel it.

"Goody and Mike-Mike came home to do business with Bobby Scales," Marques said. "He'd been back awhile. Mr. Bobby is Goody's uncle. Mr. Bobby heard they was making trouble in Houston and volunteered to look out for them here in New Orleans." Marques shrugged. "I don't even know if Mike-Mike's people ever realized he'd left Houston. I don't know if they ever knew he left New Orleans after the storm. They was *all* fucked up since even before. Mr. Bobby had a house with electricity and stuff on Josephine, near where the flood wasn't so bad. Whoever owned it just never came back. He had other houses around that he hooked up the same way and used for stuff and for people to live in."

"People who did business for him lived in those houses," Maureen said. "People like Goody and Mike-Mike."

Marques nodded.

"And you?"

Marques shrugged.

"But listen to me, Marques. I think Bobby Scales is responsible for Mike-Mike's death. Goody knows it. You're too smart not to see it, too. You've known Scales was trouble for a long time, haven't you? The day I stopped Norman Wright at that green car, it was you who told me that car belonged to Scales. That was no slip of the tongue, was it? You told my partner even more about him that day on the playground. You knew Jackson and his girlfriend were holding for Scales. *You* called the cops to the Garvey Apartments, didn't you? For camouflage, so you could talk to us about him. So you could put us on to him without looking like a rat. It was all set up until Shadow saw you."

Marques's chin hit his chest. "Shadow ain't nothin'. He the rat. He just run around, rattin' on everything to Mr. Bobby."

"I know all about Shadow," Maureen said. "I know it's Scales you're afraid of. You're too smart not to be. He scares me, too, but not enough, and not as much as he thinks he does. And Shadow's not here now. I can help you, Marques, I got a lot of people on my side, but I need to know what you know about Bobby Scales to do it right."

Marques sank down lower on the bench, as if some internal apparatus that had been supporting him had failed and collapsed. "You got questions, ask him yourself."

"I will," Maureen said. "I'd be happy to. Tell me where I can find him. Just that one thing."

Marques pointed over Maureen's shoulder. "That's him right over there, watching us."

29

Maureen sprang to her feet.

Off to the side of the brass band stood a tall, slender black man with a shaved head, maybe eighteen, nineteen years old, in an untucked and spotless wifebeater T-shirt and a pair of brand-new baggy blue jeans. A huge elaborate black tattoo, a fleur-de-lis with wings, bloomed over his heart and across his collarbones, sending thick tendrils of ink down his ropy, muscled arms. He wore a diamond bracelet on his left wrist. He had long, thin fingers, the longest fingers Maureen had ever seen. He'd been standing there, blending in with the band and their friends, the whole time Maureen had been sitting in the square.

Spotted, Scales now made no attempt to hide. He moved another half step away from the band, as if to give Maureen a better look at him. He didn't smile. He didn't frown. She couldn't guess what he was thinking. She couldn't be sure he was thinking anything at all. The recorder clicked on in her brain. She scanned him for the physical details she could recall at a moment's notice, the ones that would ring a bell when she saw him from the cruiser at a three-block distance at night, the marker that he couldn't hide like the tattoos or remove like the bracelet. She found what she needed in his face. He had a smooth and wide forehead and high, squared cheeks. His eyes, tiny, dark pebbles, looked like his maker had grabbed him hard by the back of the head and then used his thumbs to push Scales's eyes far back into his skull.

The truth hit Maureen like a kick to the back of the knees: Scales had been waiting, too, like her, for Marques to get out of band practice. To do what with the boy, Maureen didn't even want to think about. Not to take him home. Not to take him for ice cream. Scales was cleaning up and Marques was next, was last, on the list. Maureen cursed herself for not somehow making Scales as separate from the others. He'd been there right in front of her. At least she had gotten to Marques first. With Marques standing beside her she was, for the moment, a step ahead.

Whatever Bobby Scales had in mind, it wasn't going to happen today.

Marques grabbed her arm.

"Stay here," she said. "Do not move from this spot. Mr. Elvin is gonna come over to you. He's gonna take you back inside."

Her eyes now locked on Scales, Maureen reached her hand behind her back.

Scales did the same.

Maureen broke free of Marques's grip and started walking toward Scales, leaving Marques where he stood. Marques said something, but the words didn't register.

Scales leaned toward her. Maureen watched his feet. He bounced one foot. He was deciding, fight or flight. Maureen quickened her steps. Scales didn't move. His hand stayed behind his back, his arm bent at the elbow and not moving. Don't do it, she thought. Do not pull a weapon here. Not with all these people around. The musicians backed away from Scales, raising their hands and their instruments, opening space around him. The tourists had stopped in their tracks, stupid as spooked herd animals, looking around as if maybe this were another Jackson Square street exhibition.

Maureen pulled her wallet from her back pocket. She flipped it open and raised her badge to Dodds as she strode past him. "Call nine-one-one. Now. Officer in need of assistance." She jerked her thumb over her shoulder. "Take care of Marques. Don't leave him alone."

She broke into a jog. She pointed one hand at Scales, raised her badge with the other. "NOPD. You, in the white T-shirt, stay where you are. Don't you move."

She watched Scales lick his lips, turn on those bouncing toes, and bolt up the middle of Chartres Street toward Canal, people staggering out of his way as he ran.

Maureen tucked her wallet through her belt and took off after him, half enraged that he'd run, half thrilled that he had, and fully relieved he hadn't pulled a gun on her in the heart of the French Quarter.

After one block she'd halved Scales's head start. He looked back once over his shoulder. Maureen could see the shock in his face that she'd closed the gap.

Scales had the build of an athlete, Maureen thought, but not the speed or the conditioning. She'd get him. The streets were narrow and tight. The Quarter, unlike her usual turf uptown, was laid out in a grid. It was full of people to get in the way. Scales had no alleys, no empty houses, no yards to cut through. The fences and walls were high, topped with spikes and broken glass. Not a lot of choices for him. Still, open bars and storefronts surrounded them. If he really had a gun on him, hostages and a standoff were a grim possibility.

After only three blocks, Scales was slowing. Too many joints, too many menthols. Too much fast food. Arms and legs pumping, Maureen gained on him. Another block and she'd have him. And when she caught him? Then what? Young and strong, he was no Norman Wright, he was no Little E, no Arthur from the Garvey Apartments. She'd have to be quick and smart.

She eyed the small of his back, targeting his tailbone. She'd nail it, full speed, with her left shoulder. That would send him flying, crashing to his face in the street. When she got her hands on him, when she got him down, she'd have to break something. Something important.

Scales hit a hard left turn up a cross street. He ducked under a balcony, cutting the corner close, like a ballplayer hitting first base and turning for second. He was headed for Decatur, a bigger and busier street full of cars.

Maureen, running at full speed and blind to the other side of the corner, cut it even closer, looking to gain ground. She wanted to get him before he got out into traffic.

The blow came from nowhere, catching her flush like a flying two-by-four across the throat. Her feet flew forward out from under her. She went down hard, in a heap of arms and legs, the back of her head striking the brick building behind her as she crumpled. The air burst out of her. She was flat on her back. Tears flooded her eyes. She had to get right, get on the defensive. She waited to get hit again. Her nose was running. Coughing, spitting, she rolled over on her stomach. Cover up, she thought. Cover up. But no more blows came. She got her arms and legs under her and pushed up on her hands and knees, fighting for her breath.

From this position, she realized, she could easily be shot in the head. She was presenting herself as a target to anyone behind her. She'd never see it, hear it, or feel it. Everything would just end. If it was gonna come, she thought, she'd be dead already.

She felt hands on her, grabbing at her back and shoulders. She lashed out with her fists. She missed. The hands stayed on her. She blinked, shaking her head. She had to clear her vision. The hands dumped her on her sore backside, leaned her against the building. She saw a lot of blue blur. A big bald head.

The sensations and images added up. The panic receded.

She realized she was drooling.

"Yo, Sixth District," a deep voice said. "We meet again. Looks like the graduation party is over."

"Fuck," Maureen said, her voice a rasp.

"What's your name?"

"I'm not concussed," Maureen said, coughing.

"Fine with me," the deep voice said. "I just don't remember your name."

"Coughlin. Maureen. Pleased to meet you. Again."

The bald cop handed her a handkerchief. "Hardin. Franklin."

Maureen wiped her eyes, her nose. She put her hand to the back of her head. It came away smeared with sticky blood, but not a lot of it. Wouldn't even need stitches. Her ponytail had cushioned that blow. She'd had more blood than that on her hands before. She wiped them on her jeans. She tried to get her feet under her and stand. Hardin held her down.

"Easy, easy," he said. "Try to relax. Everything's done for now."

Maureen closed one eye, bringing Hardin, on one knee beside her, into focus. She sniffed, coughed some more. "Tell me you got that mother-fucker."

Hardin shook his head. "No dice. We stopped for you when you got drilled. You went down *hard*."

He handed her a bottle of water. She rinsed her mouth and spat on the sidewalk. Swallowing hurt. She sat propped up against a boutique, a high-end shoe store. People had drifted out of the store and formed a loose cluster around her. Maureen felt for her badge, which she found on her belt. She searched the sidewalk for her shades. Hardin put them in her hand. She hung them on the front of her tank top.

"I need to get up," she said. "Everyone standing over me like this, it makes me . . . I'll lean. I need to get off the ground."

"I got you," Hardin said.

He helped her up. He cleared away the bystanders, at least to the other side of the street.

Maureen leaned against the building. Her breathing improved, but her heart, it beat like she was still sprinting. She patted her pockets, found her cigarettes. She pulled one out of the pack and put it in her mouth.

"You need to hurry with that," Hardin said, lighting it for her. "EMS will make you toss it."

"Call them back. Tell them not to bother. I'm fine." Maureen took a deep drag. "There was a boy, a young boy about twelve, in the square. His name is Marques."

"No boy that I saw," Hardin said, "and we came through the square. But I wasn't looking, either. That guy Dodds who called it in sent us after you. We were rolling in from the other side of the square. We got out of the car and started running. Two of us from over on Bourbon responded, too, but your perp turned the other way. He had a car waiting on Decatur, we think. It wasn't the guy you were chasing that took you out. He had a friend. You were ambushed."

"Did you get a look at him, the friend?"

"Black kid, early twenties. We put the word out, but don't get your hopes up. A lot of people match that description."

Maureen nodded, sucking on her cigarette. The hot smoke burned her throat, but her heartbeat responded. Her nerves mellowed. She wiped her eyes with the heels of her hands. That Hardin hadn't seen Marques didn't mean anything. He might've run right past him. Maureen hadn't given Dodds any indication there was a connection between Scales and the boy.

"The getaway car," Maureen said, "was it a maroon Escalade?"

"Indeed," Hardin said. "Friends of yours?"

"People of interest. A guy named Bobby Scales and another who goes by Shadow."

If what Hardin said was true about the ambush, Maureen thought, while she'd been staring at Scales, waiting to make her move, Shadow had been watching her. Of course he'd stayed out of sight. Maureen had seen him twice. She knew his face. He'd jogged ahead, hidden around the corner, and Scales had led her right to him. Maureen checked her memory of the chase. Not much use, that. She'd been so focused on Scales, there could've been clowns on unicycles a block or two ahead and she'd never have noticed. Maureen realized that during the chase, while she'd been impressed with her own speed, in truth Scales had let her hang close. He'd toyed with her. Like he and Shadow had in the Channel. Who could resist a free shot at a cop?

She should have seen it coming, all of it.

There was probably a third person at work in this, she thought, waiting in the car. Scales to snatch the boy, Shadow on the ground to look out and run interference, and a getaway driver. Pretty organized for a bunch of street thugs. She wasn't dealing with three young boys from the playground anymore, Maureen realized. She'd graduated.

"Can you send someone back to the Cabildo," Maureen asked, "and see if that boy is there? That's who Scales, the guy I was chasing, was after. That's why he was in the square in the first place. That boy needs protection. Scales is into some dirt and Marques knows about it."

Hardin nodded. "My partner's back at the unit, interviewing the band. If the kid's there, we'll hang on to him." He keyed the mic at his shoulder and made the call. "You're kind of fresh on the job to be doing plainclothes work."

Maureen drank more water, in small sips. "It's my day off. I was in the square, having a coffee, minding my own business."

"So it was dumb luck," Hardin said, "that you were there when this Scales character and his buddy show up to kidnap this boy."

"One hundred percent."

Hardin laughed. "Extraordinary. You finish field training yet?"

"One more shift."

"Man, your FTO must love you."

"We get along," Maureen said.

Hardin's radio crackled. He bent his head to listen. "No sign of this Marques kid," he said, shaking his head. "Dodds is with my partner. He said the kid took off running soon as you turned your back. You know where to find him?"

"I know one playground he likes," Maureen said. "But I get the feeling that Scales knows about that, too. Other than that, I have no fucking idea." She blew out a long sigh. She bent over, hands on her thighs. "Fuck me, I don't feel so good."

Another message came over Hardin's radio. Something about a shoplifting in another part of the Quarter. He walked a few steps away to listen to the rest of the call.

Maureen looked around, noticing the gawkers across the street, where the other cops had herded them. Spectators, fucking always. She should get moving. Fuck EMS, who were taking their sweet time. She had to call Atkinson. And Preacher. If she was going to have any chance of controlling this story, she had to get to him before news of her escapades did. She owed him the courtesy of telling him to his face that she'd disobeyed his orders again. Preacher, she thought. Man, he was gonna flip the fuck out on her. She'd smooth it out. She'd give him the same story she'd given Hardin. Preacher wouldn't believe it any more than Hardin did, but like Hardin, he'd pretend he believed. The tale was plausible enough to cover his ass over his trainee run amok. He's her training officer, he could claim, not her babysitter. None of her shit would get on him. Thank the Lord no one had gotten hurt but her. So far.

"She's a cop?" she heard someone in the street say, the barker from the restaurant two doors down. "She's police? Her? For real? Man, she 'bout got killed. Shouldn't she be bigger?"

Nice work, Coughlin, Maureen thought. You're a regular fucking supercop.

She touched her fingertips to her throat. She didn't need a mirror to know she'd been bruised. And right when her cheek had almost healed. Was this gonna last her whole career? Her lower back was tightening up. She felt a new ache emerging at her tailbone from where she'd hit the sidewalk. That would bruise, too, blooming like a thundercloud.

She pulled herself off the wall and walked over to Hardin, who was sending two late-arriving officers to the shoplifting on lower Decatur.

"Listen, Hardin," she said, "it's about time for me to get out of here."

"You really ought to get checked out. You did hit your head."

"I'm fine. I've had worse."

"Why am I not surprised?"

"I need to talk to my FTO about this fiasco," Maureen said. "I don't want him hearing about it from someone else first."

"It may be too late for that," Hardin said. "A foot chase in the Quarter with an off-duty probie who gets knocked on her ass by the perps? It makes the wire pretty quick. And I get the feeling he's gonna know it's you whether or not he hears your name."

"I need to make the effort," Maureen said. "Out of respect. Plus, I'm sure the story will be screwy by the time it gets to him."

"True enough," Hardin said. "So what about the kid?"

"I get the feeling he's long gone," Maureen said. "I think he lives in Central City. I'm sure he ran for home. But if you find him, could you hold on to him? Call Detective Sergeant Christine Atkinson in Homicide. That's who needs him. I was helping out."

"'Cause you just happened to run into him."

"Right."

"Okay. Atkinson. I know her." Hardin smiled. "The Spider. She knows what you're up to? That you're involved in her case?"

"More or less," Maureen said. "She's got two cases, probably related, and Marques is a witness in both. Maybe. We're not sure what he knows. This is why we need him."

"And Scales is a suspect in these killings."

"He's a name that keeps coming up," Maureen said. "And now he's a face."

"He's got a sheet?"

"Not under that name," Maureen said, "or not yet. But he's getting one. The older guy that got shot on Washington the other night, and the young kid under the overpass in the CBD. Atkinson thinks he's the main player in both."

"The one in the trunk of the car," Hardin said, his face grim. "Scales did that?"

"His first name was Michael."

"Give me three more minutes before you take off."

Hardin called over the remaining two officers. He pointed to the underside of the wraparound balcony on the corner. The shoe store had security cameras perched over its doorways, two on the Chartres Street side and another two on the cross-street side. Four cameras. Maureen's heart leaped. Scales had run right past all of them. Shadow had stood right beneath one if not more of them. From the video they could make photos. Things were heating up for Scales and Shadow. The loose strands were starting to form a web.

"First thing we're gonna do after we talk here," Hardin said, "is get a look at that video." He pointed a finger at the other officers. "That's what you two are doing this afternoon. You're gonna get us everything this store has about what happened on this corner. Make it part of your canvass. Go over to Decatur, both directions from the corner. Get the security footage from the stores. We're looking for plates on a maroon Escalade."

Hardin introduced the officers to Maureen, explained who she was. The officers listened, taking notes as Hardin talked. Maureen flashed back to her moments standing over the suspect on the balcony of the Garvey Apartments, when the other officers had surrounded her, waiting to see what she would do next. This was a different moment, a better moment.

"Now tell these officers what you told me," Hardin said, "and give us descriptions of Scales and his friend. Let's see what we can do about those two having a bad night."

30

Walking back to her car though the Quarter, Maureen called Atkinson, leaving her a message about the chase and the searches for Scales and Shadow, and for Marques. Next, she called Preacher, stepping into a doorway to make the call. She shifted her weight from one foot to the other, trying to ease her back. The effort didn't do any good. She dreaded the morning, after her body had had a night's sleep to tighten up.

"I had a feeling I'd be hearing from you," Preacher said. "You've been busy."

"I didn't go home like you told me to."

"I heard."

"I didn't do what I promised," she said. "I'm sorry. I went down to the Quarter. A couple of things happened down here we need to talk about. I'm on my way to my car." She paused, waiting for Preacher to speak. When he stayed quiet, Maureen said, "But I think we've gotten somewhere in the Scales case. Nothing illegal happened. Nobody got hurt, except for me. And I'm mostly okay."

"Sometimes, Coughlin," Preacher said, "you're like the daughter I never had. There's a reason that I never had that daughter. There's lots of reasons. Meet me, and we'll throw around some ideas about your future."

"Yes, sir. I'm guessing you're at the Mayan?"

"I wish," Preacher said. "I'm enjoying the hospitality of the Eighth District, over in the square sweating my ass off talking to the band director. But don't you worry, you'll be buying me a cigar tonight. Believe that."

"Yes, sir."

"I'm out of the car, Coughlin. You know how I feel about that." He hung up.

Maureen closed her phone, took a deep breath, and doubled back into the Quarter.

Maureen found Preacher leaning against his cruiser, parked where the brass band had stood earlier. The musicians clustered against the fence, horns and cigarettes in hand, scowls on their faces. As she approached, Maureen could smell the foul cigar that Preacher was smoking. Elvin Dodds was talking to Preacher. Neither man looked happy to see her.

Maureen worked up her best smile. "How much trouble am I in?"

"Not as much as Marques," Preacher said.

"Does this mean I get two thousand push-ups?" she asked.

Neither man laughed, or even smiled. Maureen tossed her smile aside.

"You could have come to me," Dodds said. "We could have done this inside. Safely. Like professionals. Like adults. We're supposed to be the adults here."

"I told Marques to stay put," Maureen said, turning to Preacher. "Mr. Dodds here was ten yards away. I wanted to grab Scales while I had him in front of me. He's the target, isn't he?"

"Marques panicked and ran," Dodds said, "before I even realized what was happening. Can you blame him? He's a frightened kid to begin with. It didn't start with this Bobby Scales stuff. He's been in trouble here before. He knows the rules about repeat offenders. The kid wants to march.

Wants it as bad as I've ever seen a kid want anything. He did every last one of those push-ups, and ten for good luck." Dodds held up a flat hand. "Even as a board. Great form for a little kid, too. He'd make a pretty good Marine."

"Where would he go?" Maureen asked. "Where would he run to?"

"I'm guessing he'd go home," Dodds said. "I don't know what other options he has. He doesn't hang with any of the other kids in the band. Not since Mike-Mike was asked to leave. We've been trying to change that, to get him to make more friends in the band, the whole 'you are who your friends are, make sure they're lifting you up, not dragging you down' stuff, but these kids, Marques isn't the only one, they're worse than old men about the old neighborhood. Everything is 'my hood' this and 'my crew' that. They were barely out of diapers when the storm hit. It's imitative of the older kids and the grown-ups, but the young ones do believe in it, hard. It's tough being a neighborhood kid with no neighborhood."

He held up the blue binder. "I have a last name and an address for Marques from when he registered. I don't know what it's worth."

Preacher flipped open his notepad. "Marques Greer. 2053 Josephine."

"The two thousand block," Maureen said. "That's not good, is it?"

"Not at all," Dodds said.

"The house where I grabbed up Little E," Preacher said, hitching up his pants, "is 2012. I'm not optimistic anyone lives at 2053 at all. We get this shit constantly, people throwing out addresses that flooded out. Like we weren't here. Like we don't know and aren't gonna figure it out. Sometimes it's even where they used to live. It'll happen to you, Coughlin. I promise."

"Marques told me," Maureen said, "that he came back to New Orleans with his grandmother, from Baton Rouge. We got a name for her? A phone number? Someone has to pay for this program, right?"

"Roots of Music isn't free," Dodds said, "but some of the kids, we enroll them on scholarships paid for by donation. We can only afford a few but we do as many as we can. Marques is a scholarship kid. So was Mike-Mike. They came in together."

"But you take down an emergency contact, right? You have that number."

"We do." Dodds put on his glasses and flipped pages in the binder. "Never used it. The thing with the push-ups we handled here."

When he found the right page, he held the binder out to Maureen. She shifted aside so Preacher could read over her shoulder.

"Has anyone tried this number?" Preacher asked. "That's a Texas area code."

Dodds turned pages again, finding a new one. He held the book back out.

"Marques and Mike-Mike left the same Texas contact number?" Maureen asked. "How would Marques have a Texas number? His grandmother never got past Baton Rouge."

"It's Mike-Mike's number," Preacher said, "the one on the cell phone his people gave him when he came from Houston."

"Why would Marques give that number," Maureen asked, "and not a New Orleans number for the grandmother?"

Dodds shrugged. "Mischief. Protection. He doesn't want his grandma knowing when he gets in trouble. Who knows?"

"Camaraderie, too," Preacher said. He tapped his fist over his heart. "Because they're boys. It's gangsta to be mysterious."

"These numbers are worthless," Dodds said, snapping the binder closed. "Pay-as-you-go, throwaway cells. When kids like Mike-Mike get sent back to New Orleans, they get a cell prepaid for two weeks, a month, maybe. Their people always promise to reload the account. They never do. If we tell the kids to come back when they get a real phone number, we won't see them again. We really don't want to let them go, or chase them away, once we've got them in the door."

"But it didn't strike you as odd that these two unrelated boys listed the same out-of-state contact number?" Maureen asked.

"Why would it?" Dodds answered. "Who would notice?" He held up the binder. "I got Mississippi numbers in here, Baton Rouge, La Place, Atlanta, Birmingham. If all we took were kids from two-parent homes with solid New Orleans addresses and phone numbers, we couldn't field a jazz quartet. The kids with no stability are the ones we *want*. They need the help. We didn't want to kick Mike-Mike out. We really didn't. It was maybe the toughest choice I've made since I took this job. But he was bad for the group. We had no one to reach out to for help with him."

"It is what it is," Preacher said. "A lot of the families that got scattered after the storm stayed scattered. Whoever handled Marques's paperwork inside Roots wouldn't look twice at a Houston cell-phone number attached to a grandmother moving back to town from Baton Rouge. Paperwork that says Houston on one line, Baton Rouge on another, and New Orleans on a third? That's normal."

"Jesus," Maureen said, "how does anyone keep track of anything around here?"

Preacher and Dodds traded glances, each giving the other a chance to answer.

Preacher stepped up. "Exactly like this. By driving around all day and paying attention, by talking to other people trying to pay attention and then threading the stories together. Legwork. That's the job, Coughlin. That's the city."

Maureen looked back and forth between Preacher and Dodds. She chewed her bottom lip. She knew what she wanted to ask: *Really? It's still like this? It's still this much of a clusterfuck? Katrina was six years ago.* But she knew better. The two men before her were not the audience for that question. She could take it to Waters, bitch to him about the chaos, the dysfunction, and the disorder later. He'd get a good laugh over it. And then he'd tell her to think about Ground Zero, about the complexities, the starts and stops, the backstabbing and foolishness, all that drama presided over by a soulless, soul-crushing bureaucracy in a city that *hadn't* been 80 percent underwater for six weeks. Instead of asking *Why is it like this?* she knew the right question to ask was *What do we do now?*

Before she could ask it, her phone buzzed in her pocket. She pulled it out and checked the number. Atkinson. Maureen had the feeling that here was her answer about what to do next.

She looked at Preacher. "It's Atkinson."

"Let's not have the detective sergeant getting kicked to voice mail," Preacher said. "Answer it."

Maureen flipped open her phone. "Coughlin."

"Where are you now?" Atkinson asked.

"In the Quarter. You got my message?"

"I did."

"We have an address for Marques, and a last name. 2053 Josephine."

"Meet me there," Atkinson said. "Bring Preacher."

She was gone before Maureen could agree. Of course, there was no question.

"Atkinson wants us to meet her there."

"Then there we two shall be," Preacher said.

"Atkinson came by this morning," Dodds said. "The kids hadn't gotten here yet. She didn't say what it was about. She said she couldn't wait."

"She was due in court," Maureen said.

"Has she found Marques?" Dodds asked.

"I fucking hope not," Maureen said. "She's a homicide detective."

Preacher raised his hand. "Easy, Coughlin. Settle." He handed a business card to Dodds. "You see, you hear from Marques, call us. Call Atkinson. Call the Eighth District, even. They know the story. Fuck it, call your wife and bring him home for dinner." His eyes flitted to Maureen, then back to Dodds. "Just don't let him out of your sight."

"Will do," Dodds said. "I'll try the Houston number. You never know. But I'll tell you this, I'd bet anything you can find him back here tomorrow at two in the afternoon for the next practice. He never misses. Never."

"I'll keep that in mind," Preacher said. "Let's get him through tonight first, then we'll worry about tomorrow."

"Thanks for your help," Maureen said.

She put out her hand. Dodds shook it.

"Good luck, Officer Coughlin," he said. "Welcome to New Orleans."

"Thanks," Maureen said. "I get that a lot."

She and Preacher climbed into the cruiser, Preacher driving. They didn't speak.

He hit the lights, then backed them out of the square and down Chartres Street. The first side street they hit, Preacher took them over to Decatur, where they made a right and traced the river toward Canal and a route uptown. Preacher stayed quiet as they bumped over the Canal Street streetcar tracks and drove Tchoupitoulas through the CBD.

"You're still pissed," Maureen said.

"What did I fucking tell you this afternoon?"

"You told me to go home. I know. I'm sorry."

Preacher slammed on the brakes, stopping the cruiser in the middle of the road. Other drivers swerved around them. Maureen was petrified. Of an accident. Or Preacher. She'd never seen him this angry. Was she about to get fired? He looked like he wanted to slap her.

"I also told you," Preacher said, "not six fucking hours ago, that this situation is about Marques and not about you."

"What're you talking about? I did everything I could to protect that kid. I took every precaution."

"You did everything you could," Preacher said, "to protect yourself. Sneaking over there like that, off-duty and out of uniform, trying to work around the teachers, and around me, and around Atkinson, trying to make yourself look good. You think I'm stupid? This ain't my first rodeo."

"It wasn't like that, Preach," Maureen said. "I swear. That wasn't my plan."

"The best chance we have of protecting that kid," Preacher said, "and anyone else that Scales has on his hit list, is catching Scales. And that kid is the best chance we have of catching that motherfucker. And now the kid is in the wind."

He resumed driving, shaking his head. "If I was you, I would find a real delicate way of telling Atkinson what you learned from Marques, so that she don't know it's you who spooked and lost her best witness. In case you haven't noticed, we're oh-for-two with those three boys. We are not doing well. We are not doing a good job."

"Aren't you forgetting that I saved Marques's life this afternoon?"

Preacher slammed on the brakes again. More screeching and swerving. Her stomach somersaulting, Maureen gripped the door handle hard.

"If Scales pulls a gun in the middle of Jackson Square," Preacher said, "and starts shooting, we're scrubbing blood off St. Louis Cathedral. Jesus H. Christ on a Popsicle stick, Coughlin, I don't even wanna think about it. And what did I tell you after the Arthur Jackson business? Suppose Shadow was hiding around that corner with a gun? It's dumb luck that your brain salad isn't splattered all over Chartres Street."

Preacher loosened the top button of his uniform shirt. "I can't take this, Coughlin. I can't. I feel like I'm gonna barf my meat pies all over the dashboard. Your way ain't always the best way. Every idea you have ain't a good one just 'cause you had it. Ain't no one ever told you these things before?"

"If I hadn't been there," Maureen said, shaken but defiant, "Scales would have Marques. And we probably wouldn't even know it."

Preacher started driving again. He was quiet for a long time.

"I know. Things worked out better than if you'd listened to me. It's just there are things you need to learn about being part of a team, about respecting authority and chain of command. You're not always gonna be so lucky. The next time might be a disaster. Odds are it will be. How long you think you're gonna last as a cop leaving messes for fucking ranking detectives to clean up?"

"I saved his life," Maureen said. "I did."

"Yes, you did. You got that going for you."

Maureen lit a cigarette. Her hands trembled. "So why do I feel so fucking shitty?"

"My little girl," Preacher said, "she's growing up."

31

Maureen stepped out of the patrol car onto Josephine Street and into a warm sprinkle of rain, more a mist than a shower. As she and Preacher wove their way through the lower Garden District and then Central City, she had watched the edge of a low thunderstorm pass like a magician's hand over New Orleans, dissipating the thick heat. The flat white sunlight of high afternoon had morphed in the humid early evening into a dense and golden liquid that coated everything around her: the struggling trees, the potholed and trash-strewn street, the broken-down cars, and the abandoned clapboard houses.

In the eerie fantastical light, Maureen had felt for a moment as if she were traveling through a wet painting. Her anxiety had dissipated with the heat. Preacher, too, had mellowed. Now standing in the street looking at the remains of the house at 2053 Josephine, she felt slammed back into her reality. Atkinson waited for them perched on the hood of her white car, oblivious to the rain, smoking a cigarette with her cowboy boots up on the bumper.

The wrecked, rectangular cottage on a slab had at one point, before the flood, been painted white, but six years of weather and neglect had turned the house a sad ashen and dingy gray, forlorn even in the gorgeous light of the sunset. Plywood boards, tagged with amateurish graffiti in dulled colors, covered the door and windows. To the right, the remains of another house sagged into itself, overgrown with crawling vines. Next door on the left was a scorched slab, blackened pipes sticking up through the concrete like bony fingers.

On the front wall of 2053, to the left of the front door, was painted the marking that Maureen had come to think of as a Katrina tattoo: the infamous spray-painted "X" inside a circle, with special markings inside the pie's slices for the search party, the date of the search, and, in the bottom triangle, the number of bodies recovered. According to the symbol she was looking at now, the ATF had searched the place on September 12. They'd found no bodies.

Maureen saw that on the other side of the front door from the "X" an animal rescue group had kept a running tally of the dates they'd left dog food. Every other day for a week. And then, under the tally's final date, was a note: *Two dogs found, one lost, one taken.* The rescue group had started to leave a phone number, but after four numbers had run out of paint. No great loss, Maureen figured. Wasn't likely that whoever had abandoned the dogs had returned to reclaim them. More recently, several city agencies had papered the front door with a variety of official notices.

"I've been thinking about how all this fits together," Atkinson said, walking over to Preacher and Maureen. "I think what we're dealing with is the second coming of the J-Street Family. Goody is Scales's nephew. Mike-Mike was Goody's lapdog and Marques was the third musketeer, either recruited or conscripted. It is, or was, the makings of a crew."

"Scales is J-Street?" Preacher asked. "I never even heard of him. And I knew those fuckers, every last one of them."

"You had no reason to know him," Atkinson said. "Not until now. He's coming of age before our eyes, making his move, recruiting every foot soldier he can find, now that the feds have the big dogs locked up and have moved on to other things."

"Like the NOPD, for instance," Preacher said.

Atkinson gave Preacher a rueful smile. "Feds are more interested in us than any J-Street leftovers these days, that's for sure."

She walked back to her car. Reaching in the driver's side window, she popped the trunk from under the dash. From the trunk she pulled a pry bar and a heavy long-handled flashlight. She handed the pry bar to Preacher, who turned and handed it off to Maureen.

"I'll stay here with the cars," Preacher said. "You go."

Maureen followed Preacher's gaze down the block, where she saw the house that must've been where Preacher had picked up Little E "rescuing" the puppy.

The house was actually in good shape, freshly renovated if not rebuilt from scratch. It was also the only place like it on the block. Teenagers hung on the front porch, the girls and boys segregated like shy students at an eighth-grade dance. The three girls huddled on the steps, chatting with one another while leaning over cell phones balanced on their knees. The four boys clustered at one end of the porch, draped like boneless sunning cats over the porch swing and the railing, doing their best to get the attention of the girls and ignore them at the same time. Maureen knew the girls were doing the same thing as the boys, and, she noted, were already better at it.

In the front yard, younger kids teased a gray-and-white puppy with a rope toy. Nothing cruel to it that Maureen could see. The kids, three girls and a boy, shrieked and giggled. They weren't much younger than Marques and his friends. The puppy leaped and yipped after the toy, its stubby tail a beating blur. It looked healthy enough. The animal certainly had energy to burn. She thought of the bloated, scarred animal that Preacher had confiscated from Little E. Maureen lit a cigarette. Over the flame of her lighter, she watched Preacher watch the house, his gaze fixed and intense. He made excuses about the car, but really it was the dog he wanted to watch.

Preacher pulled his flashlight from his belt, handing it over to Maureen. "I take it you don't have yours."

"Weapon?" Atkinson asked.

"Not carrying that, either," Maureen said. She worried Atkinson might leave her behind; no way Preacher would hand over his gun to her. "Sorry about that. I haven't been home since lunch."

"You see what I have to work with here," Preacher said.

"I'm sure we'll be fine," Atkinson said.

She crossed the sidewalk and stepped into the thigh-high grass surrounding the abandoned house. Maureen dropped her smoke in the street and followed.

"Watch out for the trash and bottles," Atkinson said.

As they closed in on the house, Maureen picked up a familiar sickly sweet odor. She stopped, breathed in deep to be sure. Something had died nearby, and not long ago, maybe in the house. They'd lost track of Marques only an hour or so ago, but Goody? Only hearsay put him in Baton Rouge. "Hold up."

Atkinson stopped, turned. "Don't worry, Maureen. I smell it, too. It's not a person."

Another thing to look forward to, Maureen thought. The varied bouquets of death and decay, and being able to sort them with a sniff. "What is it, then, that smell?"

"Rats, probably. Dead under the house, around the yard. The city probably came through, spread poison around. They do that when the vermin get especially bad." She started walking again. "Follow me around the back."

When she came around the rear of the building, a swarm of vicious mosquitoes descended on Maureen like an attack squadron of tiny vampires. She felt pinpricks up and down the back of her neck and her arms. Swearing, she dropped the flashlight and the pry bar in the grass, slapping at her exposed skin, aggravating her sunburn, and probably looking, she realized too late, like a rank amateur. Rotting animals and killer Amazon mosquitoes, she thought, and they hadn't even opened up the abandoned house yet. No wonder Preacher hadn't wanted to come. And she'd thought he was giving her time with the detective. The longer she knew Preacher, the smarter, the savvier, he got. She slapped at the back of her neck again. Atkinson's collared long-sleeved shirts in the summertime made a new world of sense.

Maureen snatched up the tools she'd dropped in the grass. "Sorry about that. I think I stepped on a nest."

"Light a cigarette," Atkinson said. "That'll help with the bugs."

Around the back of the house, pots, pans, glassware, utensils, kitchen appliances, lay scattered across the yard, as if the kitchen had sneezed its contents out the back door. A couple of upturned kitchen chairs. Had everything been washed out by the floodwaters, Maureen wondered, or thrown out months or years later in a bitter tantrum? Somebody had lived here once. They had left a life here, thinking they'd be back in a matter of days. Someone who'd done a lot of cooking, Maureen thought, looking over the detritus, and had kept two dogs. She wondered if they'd cooked for their dogs.

The evening light was dying and throwing shadows. Atkinson clicked on her flashlight. She shone it on the edges of the board over the back door. "This one isn't nailed down. Look at the dirt there on the porch. The board's been moved. Someone's been going in and out."

She stepped to the side of the doorway, tapped on the board with the flashlight handle. The thuds echoed dully inside the house. "NOPD. This building is condemned and scheduled for demolition. Anyone inside?"

Atkinson waited beside the doorway, listening. Maureen hoped to hear Marques's soft voice from inside the dark building. She wanted to see him slip out from behind the board.

"Anyone inside should come out now," Atkinson commanded, "with their hands where I can see them. This is the NOPD."

Her grip tight on the pry bar, Maureen waited, tense. The cigarette in her lips repelled the bugs from her face, but her arms and the back of her neck were getting devoured. She'd be a pint low before this adventure ended, but she was determined not to flinch or fade under the assault.

The jury remained out on the bulletproof vest, she thought, but she'd never come to work, never leave the house again in the summer without bug spray.

Atkinson turned to her. "Help me with this."

Together, they pulled the board aside, dropping it to the ground. Maureen almost ducked before the open doorway, but stopped herself. She didn't know what she'd been expecting to rush out of the darkness. Not a flurry of bullets, but a cloud of bats, maybe, or a swarm of flies.

Atkinson seemed to have anticipated nothing, which was what they got.

Maureen followed Atkinson into the kitchen. She'd been right about the death smell. Definitely worse outside or underneath the house. Not that the inside smelled that great. Decay, mildew, animal piss. They made a right out of the kitchen and headed down a short hall, deeper into the dark, the buckled linoleum floor cracking and creaking beneath their feet.

At the end of the hall was a room with no door. And in the hall the strong smell of something unmistakable. Not death. Doritos. No doubt about it.

Inside the room, two mattresses were laid against opposite walls, each covered with a single dirty sheet. Snack bags, take-out containers, and empty plastic soda bottles littered the room, a mini-landfill between the beds. In one corner of the room, a Coleman lantern stood atop a red cooler. The cooler had a water line stained around its middle, like a bathtub ring. A second lantern sat in the opposite corner. There's your kerosene for the car fire, Maureen thought.

Someone had tacked a tattered Saints flag halfway up one wall.

If she didn't consider what she'd gone through to get here, Maureen thought, this room was a typical young-boyhood hideout, the local version of a tree fort or a clubhouse—post-Katrina Central City–style. She shone her flashlight around the room.

They hadn't found Marques in person, but maybe they'd found where he'd been, and where he would come back to. She walked over to the lantern. Using her lighter, she easily got it going. Plenty of fuel. They had ready access to kerosene.

"See the height of that flag?" Atkinson said, shining her light on the gold helmet at its center. "That's a twelve-year-old's reach. This has got to be it."

"Our boys."

Atkinson pressed her lips together. Her eyes scanned the room. "I'd like some hard proof."

Maureen ran her flashlight over the mattresses. "Valuables, anything personal would be close at hand, right? Hidden within reach of the beds?"

"Or carried with the boys."

Maureen spotted something, papers peeking out from under one of the mattresses. She walked over and pulled the pages free. Sheet music. She couldn't read the notes, but the title printed across the top of the page said "Do Whatcha Wanna." She handed the papers to Atkinson.

"That's marching-band music." Atkinson kicked through the trash. She bent over, came up with a drumstick. "Who do we know who plays drums in a marching band?"

"Let's see what else we got," Maureen said.

She squatted at the foot of the mattress. She grabbed it by the corners and flipped it over, losing her balance and tumbling over on her backside.

"Well, look at that," Atkinson said.

Maureen righted herself, dusting the back of her jeans as she stood.

Framed in the circle made by Atkinson's flashlight was a handgun. Small-caliber.

"I've seen the ballistics from the Wright killing," Atkinson said, shaking her head, a sadness seeping into her voice. She glanced at Maureen, looked back at the gun on the floor. It had been under the same mattress as the sheet music. "We're looking at the murder weapon that killed Norman Wright."

"You're not changing your mind about who shot Wright, are you?" Maureen asked.

"No, I'm not," Atkinson said. "Chances are the dead one did the killing. It's kind of a sad axiom around here. Killing other people is a leading cause of death in New Orleans. I think Marques just hung on to the gun for protection after Mike-Mike died."

"Well, that's a break for you, I guess, in that case."

Atkinson shrugged. "I guess. We'll find prints for all three boys on it, but we'll match the gun to the residue on Mike-Mike's hands." She was quiet for a while. "I would've been okay tonight just finding Marques."

"Me, too," Maureen said. "The night's not over yet. What're the chances we find something in this trash that leads us back to grandma's house?"

"Slim to none, something tells me," Atkinson said, "and Slim left town."

Maureen got down on her knees, started sifting through the trash. She'd dug through worse in her day. "Maybe somebody put Slim on a bus back home from Houston."

32

When Maureen and Atkinson got out front, the cars were there, but Preacher was gone.

After a panicked moment, Maureen spotted him down the street, leaning on the picket fence and talking to the boys who'd come down from the porch. Nobody, not Preacher, not the boys, and certainly not the placid-faced girls on the steps, appeared tense or angry. The little kids had been rounded up and taken inside. Maybe they were short on bug spray over there, too.

She and Atkinson had found nothing else useful anywhere in the house.

"Maybe we can sit on the place," Atkinson said. She sounded unsure.

"Not worth it," Maureen asked, "or not doable?"

"I can't do it personally," Atkinson said. "I got other cases. He's gonna see a unit sitting out here from three blocks away. He'll see us long before we see him."

"Let me do it," Maureen said. "I'll go home and get my car. I'll bring a thermos of coffee. My weapon."

"No offense, but no fucking way," Atkinson said, chuckling. "I wouldn't put a seven-foot, ten-year vet out here alone overnight. Weapon or no weapon. If something happened to you? Everyone involved would be eaten alive if word got out that a trainee was left alone on an all-night stakeout. I need my pension." She raised her chin in Preacher's direction. "Let's see what your guru's accomplished." She put her fingers in her mouth and whistled.

Preacher turned at the sound. He waved. He shook hands with the boys, exchanging a few more words with them before heading back Maureen's way.

"Community policing at its finest," Preacher said upon his return.

He had copies of the photos of Mike-Mike and Goody in his hand. Maureen was stunned he said nothing about being whistled for, by a female no less.

"What'd you get?" Atkinson asked. "We know he's been here. We got nothing else."

"The past couple of weeks," Preacher said, "three boys have been in and out of the house." He held up the photos. "Goody and Mike-Mike had set up residency. The third came and went. Couple days here, couple days gone at a time."

"What else went on at the house?" Atkinson asked. "Were they dealing out of it?"

"That had stopped before the boys showed up," Preacher said. "They came after the house was taken off the market, so to speak."

He waved his arm at the wrecked vacants surrounding them. "According to the folks down the street, the city's come through finally and condemned these houses, slated them for teardown ASAP. Might happen next week, might happen next year. But the knuckleheads can't use 'em for business anymore when no one knows what kind of uniforms will be coming through when. And then, of course, should you be using the place for warehousing, the wrecking ball's not gonna wait for you to move your package out of the way."

"Weird," Atkinson said, turning in place, studying the houses. "When the city starts spreading paper on a block, the bodies usually drop in twos and threes. We get a real flash of real violence. Turf wars. Like Baghdad, fighting almost house to house, block to block. But Wright was our first trip to Central City in a while. People around Homicide were even starting to talk."

"I don't get it," Maureen said. "I don't get people shooting each other over empty houses any more than I get them killing each other over broke-down cars."

"These empty houses," Atkinson said, "have been a boon for the drug dealers since the storm. They provide limitless free space. For selling drugs, for hiding guns, sometimes for dumping bodies. They provide cover for deals and meetings. But now, finally, the city is starting to clear the blighted housing. When they move into a pocket like this, whatever crew has been working here has to clear out and set up again elsewhere. Most of the time, they don't have to go far, a few blocks maybe, but they almost always run into another crew's territory."

"And then comes the violence," Preacher said.

"So whoever was using 2053 had set up shop in a new location," Maureen said, "before the boys turned it into their clubhouse."

"We can probably see it from here," Atkinson said. "Stash houses and luxury condos are the only housing stock we're not short of in this town."

Maureen walked out into the middle of the street, looking up and down the block. She wasn't checking for the new stash houses, though. She was studying the parked cars.

A late-model SUV, not the maroon Escalade, with Texas plates sat parked outside the house full of kids. Otherwise, the half-dozen cars on the block were busted-out rattletraps. They were not unlike, Maureen thought, the green Plymouth near the heart of this whole mess. They looked drivable, but barely.

Patrolling Central City with Preacher, she'd noticed plenty of cars that resided curbside, parked on blocks or ramps. It was one of the reasons that Wright repeatedly hitting so obvious a target had confused her. He'd had no shortage of choices.

In the evenings and on weekend afternoons, groups of men of every age often gathered around the cars, their hoods and trunks and doors propped open. The men were ostensibly fixing the engine or doing bodywork, but really they drank beer, listened to music, smoked cigarettes and cigars, and socialized. Maybe that was why it took an awfully long time, months if not years, Maureen assumed, to fix an old car in New Orleans. To Maureen, the old cars comprised part of her district's social landscape. Seeing the men in their place around the old cars gave her a sense of order, a sense of peace, about the neighborhood. It was one of those signs that she was learning to read, a sign of normalcy.

Now she wondered if the old cars hadn't become something else entirely for the local criminal crews: camouflage.

"What about the cars?" Maureen asked. "What if instead of changing blocks or houses, Scales changed tactics when the notices went up? What if he started using these old cars parked everywhere as storage? He's new. He's short on muscle, right, if he's got kids like Marques, Mike-Mike, and Goody doing his dirty work? He could move the cars around whenever he wanted, without ever exposing the stash to the light of day. Why not have a mobile stash? Like a shell game. That way, you're not dependent on some asshole who smacks up his baby momma and draws the cops right to your stash. Is it that big a leap from a broken-down dishwasher to a beat-up Plymouth?"

She turned to Atkinson. "You told me when I first told you about those three boys that they were lookouts, that they were watching the car for Scales. A drug stash would be a hell of a reason for that, as well as the reason for Wright to be breaking into it. We said it that night. We just didn't understand the scale of it."

"I could see it," Atkinson said. "It's risky, but it's aggressive. Creative, if a better idea on paper than in reality. It's a young man's strategy."

"Like trying to kidnap a twelve-year-old," Maureen said, "and decking a cop in the middle of the French Quarter?"

"Damn," Preacher said. "How long was that Plymouth there? How many times did we drive past it? We never looked at it twice."

"Why would we," Maureen said, "until Wright got greedy, or desperate, and blew it?"

Just like Arthur Jackson, she thought, who lost control of himself and showed the world his biggest secret. She recalled Preacher discouraging her several times from going over to the car. She wondered if he remembered that, too. Probably, she figured. But now was not the time to play *I told you so* with her FTO and superior officer. There was probably never a good time for that.

"Okay, here's another thing about the house," Preacher said. "The past couple of days, it was down to one kid coming and going."

"Marques," Maureen said.

"Skinny kid," Preacher said, nodding. "Has a big backpack with drumsticks poking out."

"Have they seen him today?" Maureen asked.

"They haven't seen him since yesterday," Preacher said. "They came around looking for him last night, thinking he might want to stay with them, but he wasn't here."

"He's living out of that bag," Atkinson said. "Crashing somewhere at night. He's running, no doubt about it."

"So where was he last night?" Maureen asked. "He got himself to band practice this afternoon."

Atkinson's radio crackled in her car. "Hold that thought."

She trotted over to the car, leaving Maureen and Preacher alone.

"We gotta find that boy," Preacher said. "If I had to bet on it, I'd say that crew across the street isn't doing any dirt. They seem like good kids. But they're not stupid. If they'll talk to me, they'll talk to anyone that comes asking. It's one way to not choose sides. If he hasn't already, Scales will search through his backlog of real estate inventory looking for Marques."

"I hope we didn't give him away by coming here," Maureen said, looking up and down the block. She didn't see anyone, but that didn't mean someone didn't see her.

Preacher checked his watch. "We missed our chance to get Marques's name in roll call for the night shift. I'll get something sent out, anyway."

"We're not going to find one twelve-year-old boy," Maureen said, "by occasionally glancing out the window of a police cruiser. Not at night, not with so many places to hide."

"Hey, hey, a little faith here," Preacher said. "The others will put a lean on the whole neighborhood for this. It's summertime, people out on the street all night. We'll twist some arms. We'll make it happen."

"And me?" Maureen asked. "I go home and have dinner and go to sleep. Just another normal day at the office."

"Go home and drink a bottle of bourbon and pass out on the bathroom floor, then," Preacher said. "Climb up on your cross and hang there. Whatever gets you through the night, Coughlin. But just remember that it's not about you, what's happening here, it's about Marques. And you're not the only one out here, Tonto. You're one of many. You're a cog in a machine. We had this conversation." He chuckled. "Cog, Coughlin. Get it?"

"This shit is making me crazy," Maureen said. "I could strangle somebody. I can't believe I chased after this job. What was I thinking?"

"It's usually about now," Preacher said, shaking his head, "that the quitters come out. The bitter end of training. Like werewolves, the quitters can't help it, the failure just comes out of them, from deep inside, like an ancient curse. I call it"—he spread his hands in a theatrical gesture—"Rise of the Quitters' Moon."

"I am not fucking quitting," Maureen said. "Don't say that. I never quit. What? I can't be frustrated?"

"He's a smart boy," Preacher said. "He's made it this far. He outlasted his friends. He's got us and Bobby Scales running in circles."

"This isn't fucking *Survivor Central City*, Preach."

"You don't need to tell me how it goes in this town. Understand?"

Atkinson returned, radio in hand. "I gotta go. Some poor bastard got pistol-whipped out in Lakeview."

Maureen couldn't say Atkinson looked happy about it, exactly, but there was a charge to her, an energy in her stride that Maureen hadn't seen since the night they'd met under the overpass—which was the last time Maureen had been around her when she'd caught a body.

Is that gonna be me? Maureen wondered. Is murder gonna be what turns me on?

"Is the guy dead?" Preacher asked.

"They don't call me for the live ones," Atkinson said. "Believe." She scratched her scalp. "So we're nowhere with this kid. He's in the wind. Still. I fucking hate this."

"He's smart," Maureen said. "And we're gonna let the night shift at the Sixth know. They'll put a lean on it."

"A lean?" Atkinson asked. More voices over her radio. "Whatever. Sounds impressive."

"She's got a lot to learn, the kid," Preacher said. "Lots of lingo to get down."

Atkinson pointed with her radio antenna at Preacher, and then at Maureen.

"Anything happens, anything, I want to hear. I'll make sure the Eighth puts someone on the Cabildo tomorrow. He shows up for marching band, we won't miss him this time. Maybe we can get Scales at the same time, put a fucking bow on the whole thing."

She turned on her boot heel and headed back to her car. She revved the engine, hit the lights, and sped off up Josephine Street.

"You should see the look on your face, Coughlin," Preacher said. "I know it's a job thing, 'cause I'm chock-full of wisdom and therefore hip to such things, and it's not like nobody can tell you're ambitious, but do yourself a favor and don't let any of the young fellas on the job see you look like that at another female. Especially not one with a rack like that. Some of your coworkers, they're not like me; they lack intellectual finesse."

Maureen let all that go. Her mind was elsewhere. She followed Preacher back to the car, trailing by a yard, watching her feet on the asphalt, one after the other: right, left, right, left.

"Relax, Coughlin. You'll see her again." Preacher opened the cruiser's driver's side door. "Seriously, I think it's safe to say you found yourself a rabbi. And quick, too. Might be a record, you ask me."

"The marching band," Maureen said.

She looked up from her feet, blinking over the car at Preacher as if unsure of who he was or why they stood where they did. She wondered if her push-up form was as good as Marques's. She'd never had anyone to teach her. Her old track coach hadn't been much help with that. He'd never had anyone to teach him, either. He was a priest. He'd never been an athlete, or, like, say, in the military.

"I think Atkinson's right," Preacher said. "We don't find Marques tonight, then we find him tomorrow. He's smart enough to know we'll look for him there. He knows the place to be is with us." He frowned, worry on his face. "Get in. I'll take you back to the Quarter for your car."

"You heard Dodds talking about Marques," Maureen said. "You were there. You heard what he said."

"Indeed," Preacher said.

Maureen could see his gears turning. He was trying to catch up to her thought process.

"What kind of kid," Maureen said, "does Marines-ready push-ups? What kind of kid wants nothing more than to march?"

Preacher's eyebrows arched. "I know. Doesn't make sense. Especially with the friends he chose. When I was that age I was perfecting my jerk-off stroke, not my push-up form."

"Think about it," Maureen said. "What's the Roots of Music provide? Uniforms, discipline, tests, tasks, peers. Knowing where to go and what to do every day."

"I know, I know. It all contradicts. I have no answers. Kids are a mystery." He hitched up his pants. "You wanna get dinner?"

Maureen almost snapped at him. Suddenly he'd become an idiot? It had to be now? She remembered that she'd seen things that he hadn't. She'd had a conversation that he'd missed, because he'd stayed in the car.

"Take me to Mother Mayor's place," Maureen said. "I need to talk to her."

Preacher checked his watch. "Come on, Coughlin. That was where we started. It did nothing for us."

"This is different," Maureen said. "Believe me. Take me there, or take me to my car and I'll go alone. You know I will."

"Are you, like, threatening me with something?" Preacher asked. "Because that's what it sounds like. Haven't we discussed your tone?"

"Please, Preacher," Maureen said. "Give me one more hour. Call it in, make something up, or don't. It's not a secret. Whatever you think is best. But do this with me."

"A cigar," Preacher said, "and a bottle of brandy."

"Done."

"No, port, instead. And no bullshit rotgut, either. I know you worked in a bar. I know you know the good stuff."

"Done, done, done. You've got an extra set of cuffs?"

"Coughlin, should I even ask what for?"

Maureen jumped in the cruiser. "Can we go?"

"The young," Preacher said, climbing into the car. "Always in a hurry."

33

Maureen knocked on Mother Mayor's front door. She'd been knocking for a while. Someone from down the block had already yelled through the dark for them to leave the poor old woman alone. Preacher sat on the hood of the cruiser, his arms crossed, his hat back on his head. This was Maureen's play and he was letting her have it. She knew that, and was grateful for it. She also knew that he was skeptical of her getting in the door. But he'd radioed the Sixth anyway and had two units stationed around the corner in case anyone headed out the back door of Mother's house. Preacher was no fool. He wasn't too proud to prepare for contingencies.

The Golden Rule: Cover Your Ass. Believe.

"New Orleans Police Department, ma'am," Maureen said, knocking on Mother's door. She rang the bell. "Officer Coughlin, ma'am. We talked earlier in the week."

She waited some more. She would've worried about Mother Mayor—it wasn't impossible that Scales also knew what Maureen had figured out—but walking up the front steps she'd heard a TV that now, minutes later, she didn't hear. Someone was in there. Someone was home. She thought maybe she'd seen a shadow in the living room. But no one came to the door. Maureen felt that familiar simmer beginning in her gut—the temperature rising on her temper. She ran her tongue across her front teeth, back and forth, back and forth, like the arm of a metronome. Patience was what she needed now. The spider, she thought. Be the spider. Wait. See. Don't get caught in your own threads.

"I've got all night," Maureen said. "Really, I do, Mother. I have nothing else to do with the rest of my goddamn life but stand on this stoop and make unpleasant noise. I'll wait."

Tonight, she missed her uniform. Even the vest. She missed the extra size it gave her.

Maureen thought she might back down off the stoop. She could talk to Preacher. They could invent another way to find out if Marques was inside Mother Mayor's house. But Maureen couldn't fight it. She sucked at waiting. Always had. Low-cut Chuck Taylors or not, she wanted to kick that fucking door down. She needed to know if she was right about Marques and Mother Mayor. And she needed to know right now.

The knuckle where her pinky met her hand was tender and swollen from hitting the door. She slapped the door with the flat of her hand so hard her palm stung.

"I am trying to fucking help you!"

She raised her arm again. The door flew open.

Mother Mayor gasped, wide-eyed at the sight of Maureen's raised open hand. She drew back as if expecting a slap. "What do you *want?*"

Maureen pulled her badge from her belt. She held it up to Mother's face like damning evidence. "New Orleans goddamn Police Department. I've been knocking forever. You're lucky you still have a front door."

"Coughlin." Preacher's voice, calm, from behind her. Someone deep in Maureen's head made a note of it, and filed it away. "Easy."

"I have nothing to say to you," Mother said. "And watch your mouth. In fact, get off my stoop."

"Where is he?" Maureen said. "Your grandson, Marques? Where is he?" She stood up on her tiptoes, trying to look around Mother and into the house. "Is he here?"

"Go," Mother Mayor said. "Go now."

But she didn't step back and close the door. Instead, she leaned around Maureen, eager to catch Preacher's eye. "Officer, are you responsible for this young lady? I'll call the district and report the both of you. I have the number on speed dial."

"I'm sure you do," Preacher said.

He hauled his weight off the car. He crossed the sidewalk, set his foot on the bottom step of Mother Mayor's stoop. "Ma'am, if your grandson is Marques Greer, as Officer Coughlin seems to think, and with good reason I might add, and if the boy is here with you, we very much need to talk to him."

"Did Marques tell you," Maureen asked, "that someone tried to kidnap him today? In the middle of Jackson Square. Did he tell you that I saved him?"

Maureen could hear Preacher's heavy breathing behind her. He'd moved up a step. She moved the slightest bit to one side, giving Preacher a more direct look at Mother Mayor.

"Mother, you know me," he said. "You don't like me, but you know me. If I'm out of the car, and working late, it's because something important is happening. This ain't shoplifting or picking pockets. This ain't fighting in the playground."

"My grandson doesn't do any of those things. He's a good boy."

And there it was.

Nothing to it, as far as Preacher was concerned. Unreal, Maureen thought. Like a Jedi fucking mind trick.

At least, Maureen thought, she'd been right that Marques was Mother Mayor's grandson. She was the one who'd brought him home from Baton Rouge while his mother served overseas. She'd probably raised him. She'd known he was in trouble the first time Maureen had come around. That was why Mother had refused to give her name. Maureen was willing to wager there were more photos of Deandra and her son in the house, hidden from curious eyes.

Did she know Marques had been in the car that had Mike-Mike's body in the trunk? Had Scales already been to her door looking for Marques?

Maureen bit down into her bottom lip, nearly hard enough to draw blood. Just shut up. Just wait. Be smart. Keep your mouth shut half a minute longer.

"The lady officer here is a tad overenthused," Preacher said. "She's excitable, to say the least. We're working on that. She's new. But she's a smart woman and a hard worker. She wants to do the right thing. She thinks your grandson is in very real, very now trouble, with us and with people worse than us. I do, too. We can help him. They can't. They only want to hurt him. It doesn't get any simpler than that. You know this."

From her doorway, Mother Mayor looked away from Preacher, scanning the block. Maureen followed her eyes. Shadows hung everywhere, in doorways and in windows, the occasional orange glow of a cigarette tip revealing half of a face on a porch or out on the sidewalk. She wondered if Mother Mayor was searching the block for Scales, or if she was weighing the judgment of her neighbors. Maureen imagined the neighbors didn't often get a chance to pass judgment on Mother. They'd want to take advantage of the opportunity. They'd see her opening her door for the police. Word would get back to Scales, if he wasn't already one of the shadows out on the street.

Mother Mayor stepped back from the door. "Come in, officers."

Preacher said nothing, his head down as he came up the stairs, as if to look away from Mother Mayor's surrender. Maureen said, "Thank you."

From the look on Mother Mayor's face, Maureen noticed as she passed, you'd think the old woman had opened her door to Katrina's floodwaters all over again.

Stepping into the living room, Maureen wondered if she should call Atkinson now, thinking that maybe a detective's authority would lend urgency to the proceedings. Unless, a quieter voice told her, unless getting up in Mother's authority was the exact wrong thing to do. Wouldn't be the first time, Maureen knew, that she had made the wrong choice. It wasn't what Preacher had done. He'd been firm, but gentle, respectful. His approach was getting results.

She'd wait till they were sure, then. She'd wait to see how things played out.

"We'd very much like to talk to the boy," Preacher said. "Here, in your living room. With you in the room."

Maureen noticed he wasn't even asking anymore if Marques was there, quietly and effortlessly ending the game they'd been playing. Not asking questions removed the option of easy lies for Mother. The only sound in the house was the asthmatic rattle of Mother Mayor's air conditioner, the machine working overtime in the next room.

Maureen nearly hit the ceiling when Preacher's name crackled loud over his radio. "Jesus. Fuck." She hadn't realized she'd been so tightly coiled.

Preacher threw her a look. He adjusted the volume on his radio, keyed the mic on his shoulder, and gave the cop on the other end, named Spivey, the go-ahead.

"Movement around the back of the house," Spivey said. "Careful in there."

That got everyone's attention.

"How many?" Preacher asked. "More details would help."

His voice was calm, but his body had tensed. He turned to step away from the women, but with three people standing in it, Mother Mayor's living room was about full. Preacher had nowhere to go. He couldn't hide the conversation.

"Mother," Maureen said, "is your back door locked?"

Mother nodded.

"You're sure?" Maureen asked. "You're positive?"

The glare from Mother Mayor answered her question.

"One, maybe two individuals," Spivey said.

"Descriptions?" Preacher asked. "Height? Age?"

"Can't confirm. It's dark as fuck back here."

"Do you have a light in the back?" Maureen asked.

Mother Mayor nodded.

"No one goes in the kitchen," Preacher said. "Everyone stays right here."

Mother took a step toward a side window. Maureen reached out and snatched her arm. She prepared herself for the haymaker sure to follow, but Mother didn't throw it.

"The curtains," Mother said.

"Too late for that," Maureen said. "Stay here in the center of the room. Stay away from the windows."

"Where are you exactly?" Preacher asked Spivey.

Static instead of an answer, then: "Hold on a sec, Preach."

More static over the radio. Mother clutched tight fistfuls of her dress.

"We're gonna fan out on the block," Spivey said. "Stay away from the windows."

Maureen, her hand on Mother's elbow, deepened her breathing, making sure to keep it quiet. She stayed conscious of her heart rate, waiting for the cold teeth of a headache to start chewing on the back of her brain. Nothing so far.

Where was Marques hiding in the house? Maureen wondered. Upstairs? The bathroom? Or was he that moment climbing out a window? He had to know better than that. And who was that creeping in the yard? Scales? Shadow? Other cohorts? Could be neighborhood kids trying to get a peek in Mother's window for a look at the action. Or was it Marques himself out there?

Preacher took a moment to pat his brow with a bandana. "Do you have any idea at all," he asked Mother, "who could be outside? They appear to be trying to sneak into your yard."

"I don't know," Mother said.

"Is it Marques out there?" Maureen asked.

"You should let me go in the kitchen," Mother said.

This was not good, Maureen thought. This situation was all kinds of bad and getting worse. Nervous cops on the prowl outside, searching in the darkness for unknown, unidentified persons. She'd heard the stories, plenty of them. Kids in the shadows, a sudden movement or something in their hand, dead in their tracks in the wrong place at the wrong time with the wrong cops. Maureen felt her pulse quicken its pace. Any faster and her heart would trip over its own feet and go flying.

She couldn't be a wild card. She couldn't add to the entropy. She needed to march straight on toward the one fact they absolutely had to have: the current whereabouts of Marques Greer.

"Mother," Maureen said, "I need you to tell me the absolute truth. Is Marques in the house?"

She waited. Mother said nothing. And neither did Preacher. Maureen pointed to the window. "Who is out there?"

"I already answered that question," Mother said.

"Your back door isn't locked," Maureen said, "is it?"

"I already answered that one, too." Mother lifted her chin. "I think I need to talk to a real police officer."

"You leave the back door open for your grandson, don't you?" Maureen said. "So he can sneak in and out for food, maybe even the shower and his bed, and you can claim to be none the wiser."

"That's not true. I would never treat Marques like a criminal. He's a sweet boy."

"If that is Marques out there," Maureen said, "creeping around in the dark, he now has five or six twitchy cops stalking him. They're sweaty, they're bug-bit, and they're getting more pissed by the second. Don't you think you should tell us if your grandson is out there? Aren't you smarter than this?"

"He's not out there," Mother said.

"If he gets shot," Maureen said, "you are responsible for the consequences. For all of them, the whole bucketful, and not just what happens to him, but what happens to all of us, and this whole neighborhood. They'll blame us, but you'll know the truth. And I know for a fact you won't have the nerve to tell it, will you? Not even to your daughter."

"It's not him," Mother said. "He knows better."

"Then where is he?" Maureen asked.

"I really think," Mother said, "that there should be a lawyer here. I want a lawyer here."

"Nobody's been arrested," Maureen said. "We're not here to hurt Marques. We're trying to help him."

"So I should trust you?" Mother asked. "Why? Because you're white? Or is it because you're the police?" She shook her hands at the ceiling, shouting. "Praise Jesus and lawdy, lawdy, lawdy, here come the white woman gon' save all the little black babies."

"There can be a lawyer tomorrow," Maureen said, not rising to the bait. "There can be a lawyer later."

"So you say." Mother put her hands on her hips, defiant to the last. "Your shit is *tired*, little girl."

Fuck this, Maureen thought. Time to take it to the next level. She had the extra set of handcuffs from the car in her back pocket. She could cuff Mother Mayor, set her on the couch, and search the house herself. If Mother insisted on a scene, Maureen would hang a laundry list of charges on the stubborn bitch. How about aiding and abetting, harboring, accessory after the fact, for starters? Not that Mother wouldn't love being busted, being paraded out the front door and into the squad car. She'd eat it up. The neighborhood martyr.

One more deep breath, then, Maureen thought. One more shot at letting sense prevail.

"Where is Marques?" she asked.

And then, without thinking, before she got an answer, Maureen reached behind her back for the cuffs. She heard the barest whisper of a "shit" from Preacher.

Mother Mayor, who had witnessed her share of arrests, had recognized the move.

"Oh no! Oh no you DID NOT!"

No sense in not pulling them now, Maureen thought. She raised the cuffs over her head. "WHERE IS HE?"

Maureen caught motion—a shape, a shadow—in the corner of her eye.

"I'm right here."

Maureen lowered the cuffs.

Marques, haggard and dirty, his face a defiant echo of his grandma's, stood in the doorway between the two rooms. "I'm right here."

Mother Mayor cupped her hands over her mouth and nose. "Why, baby? Why? They're gonna take you away. What about your momma? What if we can't find you this time? What if we can't bring you home?"

Marques wore a long white T-shirt over blue basketball shorts. His sneakers were filthy. The T had a photo screened on the front, a picture of Mike-Mike with a small gun in one raised hand and a fan of dollar bills in the other. Photoshopped, Maureen realized, to imitate another infamous photo that had circulated around the city a couple of years ago. The picture was faked, Maureen thought, but the dates beneath it were not: Sunrise 1997–Sunset 2011.

I waited tables, she thought, almost as long as Mike-Mike was alive. That's no kind of life.

"I didn't know he was in the car," Marques said.

He can't even bring himself, Maureen thought, snapping back to reality, to talk about the trunk. She tucked the handcuffs back into her jeans.

"I swear I had no idea," Marques said.

"I know," Maureen said.

"I didn't. Mr. Bobby just said get rid of the car. He said Mike-Mike was off doing him a favor."

"I know. You don't have to tell me this right now, Marques."

"Get it out of the 'hood and torch it, he said. It was my idea to do it by the firehouse."

"I know."

"He promised us fifty bucks. Each. We was gonna give Mike-Mike a cut, me and Goody, soon as we found him. 'Cause we were boys, you know?"

"It's okay," Maureen said. A lie.

It wasn't okay, of course, and she knew it, and it wasn't going to be okay, and everyone in the room knew it. They were like people in a waiting room, trying to swallow a terminal diagnosis. Things had completely gone to shit. It might very well turn out that the fire had killed Mike-Mike. That right there, no matter what Marques claimed to know, would destroy his life. But the kid was twelve and petrified. What else was she going to tell him, other than it was okay? If someone had told me that lie when I was twelve, she thought, and given me even some false hope, my whole life might've turned out different, or at least a lot less messy.

The first shots hit—two *thunks* into the front of the house—like a heavy ball or bricks thrown against the wall. Then the telltale crack of gunfire—the terrifying sound lagging a fraction of a second.

The next two bullets exploded through the front window.

Nobody screamed. But everyone moved.

Preacher tackled Mother Mayor, the two of them thumping hard to the floor, landing in a heap. Maureen dove after Marques, who had turned to flee. She snatched at his ankle, tripping him, sending him sprawling across the kitchen floor, his palms squeaking on the linoleum as he slid. Panicked voices shouted over Preacher's radio. Multiple sirens erupted outside. Yelling. More gunshots. Nothing hit the house this time.

Maureen didn't hear Preacher answer his radio.

Answer them, Preach. Answer.

In front of her, Marques lay on the kitchen floor. Maureen could hear him fighting for breath. She scrambled after him, called his name. He didn't answer. She grabbed one of his legs, pulling him toward her as she threw her body over his.

Two more shots hammered the side of the house.

A drive-by. Scales. Had to be. She called out, "Is anyone hit?" No answer. "Preacher?"

Marques struggled and squirmed underneath her. A good sign. If he'd been shot, he wouldn't be able to fight her. She didn't feel blood underneath her in his clothes or on his skin. She didn't see any leaking out of him onto the floor. Terror made him strong and frantic, but she kept him pinned, covering his limbs with hers. She knew he'd explode out the back door and hit the streets running if he got away from her.

"Preacher?"

A serious coughing fit, maybe Preacher, maybe Mother, Maureen couldn't tell. Then, finally, Preacher's voice: "Fuck. We're good. We're okay. You?"

"Same," Maureen said.

"Stay the fuck down. The both of you."

"You're okay, Marques," Maureen said, teeth clenched. She struggled to sound soothing. She wasn't any good at it under normal circumstances, forget while getting shot at. "You're okay. Relax. We're okay."

Unless someone kicks in that back door, she thought, staring hard at it and praying that Mother Mayor hadn't lied about locking it. Somebody comes through that door with a gun and we are dead. Maybe she could somehow get between Marques and the door, shove him into the living room, buy him a few seconds. After that, what? All of them were toast. She swallowed hard, her throat dusty and arid.

"It's all right, Marques," Maureen said, staring down the back door. "We're gonna be fine. We'll be outta here soon. Your grandma's all right, Marques. They missed."

Marques settled underneath her. More from exhaustion, she figured, than anything she'd said. Thank God. He was wearing her out.

"Get *off*, yo."

Maureen eased her weight off of him, settling on the floor beside him, one hand pressed firmly into the small of his back. She felt brave enough to draw her legs underneath her.

"Stay down. Stay still."

Kneeling, she kept her head low, letting her mind run in place of her feet. Maureen felt comforting warmth spreading in her belly. She smiled. Scales would be fucking furious. They'd managed to double fuck him. Not only had he missed a second chance to get Marques, but this time the cops had snagged the boy instead, and he knew it. Scales had rolled up, guns blazing, right into what amounted to a trap. Who cared if it happened by plan or by accident, she thought, as long as he got caught? And she wanted him caught tonight.

She could be part of it. She was three feet from the back door. She could be out that door in under two seconds. In the mix. In the chase.

The seconds kept ticking by.

Under her hand, Maureen felt Marques try to rise to his knees. She pushed him back down. The boy, she told herself, the boy is the reason you're here. Do your job. Protect him. Don't go chasing the wrong target yet again.

The sirens of the police pursuit faded into the distance. Loud voices crackled over Preacher's radio. Maureen listened to the chase carry on without her. She leaned back on her hands and let out a long exhale. She slid herself out of the way on her backside as Mother Mayor crawled into the kitchen.

Mother threw herself over Marques, gathering him to her like a bundle of laundry and squeezing hard enough to wring him out. She sobbed. Marques said nothing, letting himself be held. He all but disappeared into his grandmother's arms.

Maureen lay down on her back, staring up at the ceiling. Holy shit. She was exhausted.

Two cops burst through the front door, guns drawn, yelling for no one to move.

This time Mother Mayor screamed. Maureen rose up on her elbows. Fucking cowboys. Don't do this, she thought. Don't turn this into one big lawsuit.

"For fuck's sake," Preacher said. "Are you kidding me? The fucking cavalry arrives."

He sat on the floor with his back propped against the living room wall. He was pale, Maureen noticed, and breathing more heavily than usual, but he seemed okay overall. She had a feeling it was the cigars more than the bullets that had him ailing.

"In here is the one place there wasn't any shooting," Preacher said.

"Put those guns away, you sweaty pricks. There's women and children in here. We're in one piece and we'd like to stay that way. Believe."

The two cops holstered their weapons, apologizing. They waited for orders.

"Don't move," Preacher told them. "Don't mess nothing up. Go back outside."

Without a word they stepped back outside.

"Fucking amateurs," Preacher said. He pulled his handkerchief from his pocket, patted at the sweat on his head. "Coughlin, make yourself useful for a change. Get over here and help me up."

34

Maureen stood with Atkinson in the street outside Mother Mayor's house, the two of them awash in colored lights and surrounded by busy people in and out of uniform. They smoked cigarettes and surveyed the damage from the drive-by. The holes in the front wall of the house were hard to see in the night, two dark spots high up on the vinyl siding. Tomorrow, in the daylight, somebody would get up on a ladder for a better look at the damage. The front window, completely shot out, was the obvious and immediate problem. Imagine all the mosquitoes getting in, Maureen thought. And those flying roaches, too, drifting through the night like helicopters with broken rudders.

Maureen watched as neighbors descended upon Mother Mayor's property and took over the glass clean-up, inside and outside the house. The women supervised while the men worked. Plywood boards were carried over from neighboring yards and sheds and propped up against the side of the house, ready to cover the window as soon as the broken glass had been removed. They'd keep the bugs and the weather out, Maureen thought, but the inside of Mother Mayor's place would be even dimmer now. Those thin, flat boards perfect for covering windows and doors, Maureen had learned, were never in short supply in this town. Neither were tools or ladders. Or neighbors, for that matter, who at least helped clean up while gossiping about how the mess got made.

A few feet away, Preacher sat alone on the back bumper of an ambulance, his uniform shirt open over his white T-shirt after getting checked out, his color returning as he nursed a bottle of water. Maureen knew he was already thinking about his next cigar.

Mother Mayor was inside the house, in the kitchen with Marques and two investigators from the juvenile division. Protecting Marques, not only from the streets but also from the potential caprices and cruelties of the system, had begun. It was going to be a long process.

Atkinson crushed out her cigarette in the gutter, her blond hair and pale face turning blue then red then blue again in the whirling emergency lights.

"What's the word on Scales?" Maureen asked.

"They beat the pursuit first to Carrolton Avenue and then onto the I-10, where they blew east at over a hundred miles an hour. Smoked us easy. The state police are aware. They won't get caught. Not tonight."

"Was it the Escalade?"

"One of those new Camaros," Atkinson said. "Stolen like the Escalade, I'm sure. It's that ugly burnt-orange color. One of my neighbors drives a Honda that color. I don't get it."

"Should make it easy to find," Maureen said.

Atkinson checked her watch. "Oh, the flames shooting up in the sky as it burns will probably help with that, too. We'll find the car by midmorning, what's left of it, at least. I don't think he's putting twelve-year-olds on the job this time, though."

"What's next for Marques?" Maureen asked.

"The juvenile officers will leverage his status as a witness and as a victim against his role, whatever it was, in Mike-Mike's death and any drug business. They'll try to get him a break."

"And then you'll do what?" Maureen asked.

"I'll let them," Atkinson said. "If I have my way, Marques doesn't even miss band practice tomorrow. Whether Scales killed Mike-Mike with his own hands or tricked Marques and Goody into burning their friend to death, he is the one responsible for that murder. Wright's, too, as far as I'm concerned. Scales is the one I want. He did his best to turn Marques into a criminal. There's no reason for me to do the same thing by locking Marques up with people just like Scales."

"Seems to be plenty of them out here on the streets, too."

Atkinson shrugged. "Indeed. But without them, what would women like you and me do with ourselves?"

"Will Marques get to stay with his grandmother?" Maureen asked.

"I don't see why not," Atkinson said. "If only because the process of taking him away from her would last until he was eighteen anyway, the way this city works. The farther he gets from me, though, the less power I have over his fate."

"Not me," Maureen said. "This is my district. I'll be around here nearly every day."

Atkinson released a long, low whistle. "Be careful with that. Don't go appointing yourself anyone's savior, no matter how bad he seems to need it. He's got a mother who's a soldier, and a force of nature for a grandmother. He's got backup."

"For all the good it's done him so far."

"The one with no family," Atkinson said, "is the one in the morgue. You're not a social worker. You wanna help Marques? Put cuffs on Bobby Scales."

"And the battle goes on," Maureen said. "At least we've got him on the run. The more energy he's got to spend hiding from us, the less he's got to spend on Marques."

"We've definitely given him some bigger and badder worries," Atkinson said. "What do you make of this shooting? Tell me what you think."

"I don't know how he expected to hit anyone inside the house," Maureen said, "popping off two shots at a time. He couldn't see us from the street. The shooter used a handgun, probably. Revolver. We found no shells in the street." She frowned. "Lousy choice of weapon. I'd think he'd want a semiauto, if not a full. Aim and squeeze off two shots. Aim again, squeeze off two more. Hard to do in a moving car, thank God. Either overconfident or amateurish."

Or, a new thought told her, they hadn't planned on a drive-by at all.

"Could be that Scales hadn't anticipated us tracking Marques to his grandma's house," Maureen said. "So he had to adjust on the fly when he spotted the cruiser out front. The drive-by was a last-second choice. A pride saver or a frustration move. Not even Plan B, probably. But he had to do something."

"Not bad," Atkinson said, nodding. "We'll know more, maybe, when we pull the bullets from the house. Let me know which detective in your district ends up with this one. I'm gonna want a powwow."

Preacher had wandered over from the ambulance. He hitched up his pants. "Ladies," he said, with a nod. "Glad we all survived Officer Coughlin's idea of a day off."

"Whaddaya think, Preach?" Maureen said. "I got sunburned and eaten alive by mosquitoes. I uncovered a major new drug-dealing strategy. I got punched in the throat. I got shot at. Can we call this my last day of training or what?"

Preacher gave Atkinson a long look. The detective sergeant dropped her eyes and raised her hands. "This has nothing to do with me. I'm so not involved here."

Preacher turned to Maureen. "Except for the drug thing, Coughlin, none of that other stuff is *supposed* to happen. It's shit you're supposed to avoid."

"C'mon, Preacher," Maureen said. "You don't think I earned a break?"

"I think we got rules in this department, Coughlin. I think we got strict regulations and procedures. What kind of example would I be setting if I let you slip through early? You owe me a day. I want it. You're going to do it." He put his arm around Maureen's shoulder. "Without rules, Coughlin, everything descends into chaos. You know this."

"Believe," Atkinson said.

A call came over the radio Atkinson held in her hand. She raised the radio and responded. She turned to Maureen, her eyes ablaze. "Decomp in Armstrong Park. Some guy walking his dog found a throat slash. Pretty ripe, I hear. Wanna come see?"

"You know what?" Maureen said. "Just this once I think I'll pass. I need a bath, and some sleep."

Atkinson patted Maureen on the back. "Stay in touch. Five, seven quick years, we'll get you a shield in no time. That way you won't have to miss out on the good stuff."

"I can't wait," Maureen said.

35

The following afternoon, Maureen and Preacher sat in their cruiser, Preacher behind the wheel. They were parked in the Irish Channel, the working-class neighborhood between the Garden District and the river, their light bar flashing while they babysat a small park at Second and Annunciation Streets. The gates of Annunciation Park, Preacher had explained to Maureen as they drove over, had been locked for years, throughout the early 2000s. They'd been locked for so long, he said, that when the city finally decided after Katrina to redevelop and reopen the park, the parks department had to clip the locks with bolt cutters because nobody in the city government could find the keys.

Today, they parked with the lights whirling so anyone wondering would know that the NOPD had officially claimed that territory for the neighborhood. They were paying it special attention. It was a new tactic the department employed, encouraging patrols to take their breaks at the parks in order to discourage the dealers and the gangs from reclaiming the land.

The city had sunk a lot of federal money into the new parks and play-grounds. Nobody wanted schoolkids stepping on crack vials or finding bullet holes in the new slides.

Something about the flashing lights, Preacher said, made everyone take a cop car more seriously. Maureen agreed that the city's kids needed safe spaces to be kids.

Her last day on the clock as a trainee had been as uneventful as the day before had been exciting. She and Preacher wrote some traffic tick-ets. They took reports at two separate fender benders. They had a long lunch and drank a lot of coffee. Right before stationing themselves at the park, they'd spent a large chunk of the afternoon managing the car-pool lane at the swanky private school in the Garden District. Maureen had even gotten her own bright orange mesh vest and hand-help stop sign. It was her turn. She did her best to be personable. The kids were no prob-lem. The parents were another story entirely. It was soccer-mom bumper cars with late-model SUVs.

Maureen lowered the windows of the cruiser as Preacher fired up a ci-gar. He puffed away, eyelids drooping, as he worked on the *Times-Picayune* crossword. Maureen had a hot coffee from the CC's and a smoke of her own going. A warm breeze blew through the car, ruffling the pages of Preacher's newspaper. Sparrows chirped on the sidewalk, fussing over bread crusts someone had tossed away.

Her arm out the window, cigarette burning in her fingers, coffee cup in her other hand, Maureen watched a thirtyish couple exercise their two dogs, a big yellow one and a small brown one, in the park. "There are leash laws, correct?" she asked.

Preacher looked up from the paper, squinted at the couple. "I'm sure there are. Usually, unless we get a complaint or we need a reason to talk to someone, we let it go."

"I figured that," Maureen said. "I was just checking."

"Indeed," Preacher said, returning to his puzzle. "Good looking out."

The brown dog, some kind of midsized shepherd mix, Maureen figured, inspected the edges of the park, her nose to the ground, her tail wagging. A determined investigator, she seemed intent on sniffing every dandelion and blade of grass from top to bottom. Her owners called to her repeatedly and halfheartedly. Every now and again, the dog snatched something from the weeds and chowed it down, always, to Maureen's amusement, throwing a guilty look back at her owners after she had swallowed her prize, as if she knew she shouldn't be doing what she was doing but also knew there was nothing her owners could do to stop her.

Clever girl, Maureen thought.

The yellow dog was a different creature. She chased a tennis ball over and over again, attacking each pursuit with explosive enthusiasm, bolting after her quarry as if each throw were the first ball she'd ever chased, as if she'd only just then discovered how far and how fast she could run. The way the dog ran with such utter abandon, tail high, long legs a blur, ears pinned back, pink tongue flying loose from her toothy smile, filled Maureen with a strange envy. She knew it was just a dog at play she was watching, but *joy* was the only right word available for what she was witnessing.

"I wanna feel like that," Maureen said.

"Like what?"

"Like that big yellow dog over there."

"You wanna feel easily entertained?"

"What? No. Damn it, Preach."

Preacher smiled. "You're so gonna miss me, Coughlin."

"It's not like I'm never gonna see you again," Maureen said. "Geez, you make it sound like we're breaking up."

She turned away, not wanting Preacher to see the grin she felt curling the corners of her mouth, or the color in her cheeks. If he knew he'd gotten a rise out of her, he'd never let her live it down.

The couple in the park had corralled and leashed the dogs. As the foursome headed toward the exit nearest the cruiser, the brown dog trotted merrily in front of the group, satisfied, it appeared to Maureen, with the day's take in treasures. The yellow dog lagged a bit behind, droopy and panting, but wearing her own aura of weary contentment, carrying her now dirty and slimy ball in her jaws.

Maureen turned back to Preacher. His face was melancholy. Experience told her he was acting. Instinct told her he was not.

"What the hell, Preach?" she asked. "You're being all weird. Seriously."

"I was watching you," he said, "while you watched that yellow dog run. That's what you looked like, chasing Mike-Mike through the park. Pure. On fire."

"That's nice," Maureen said, "but I failed. I didn't catch him."

"No, you didn't," Preacher said. "But while you were running, you were all in. You were committed. You were a thing of beauty."

"Thanks, Preach."

Preacher grinned. He put his cigar in his mouth, turning it like he was winding a watch. "What? No harassment jokes?"

"Not this time."

"Speaking of time," Preacher said, "we're about all done here. Congrats, Coughlin. Your training is over."

"Any final words of wisdom," Maureen asked, "before I hurtle off alone into the great beyond?"

"You owe me a bottle of top-shelf fucking port, Officer. I forget nothing."

He leaned forward in the driver's seat, moving to turn the key, but he didn't start the car. He turned to Maureen.

"What I was trying to say with that 'thing of beauty' crapola was this: Doing this job, Coughlin, in this fucking city, it's going to break your heart. I don't mean the royal you, I mean you in particular. More of us than you think take our twenty and check out relatively unscathed. Maybe we shouldn't, maybe that speaks ill of our hiring standards. Who the fuck knows?

"But you, you're special. Your heart's gonna get crushed into a thousand tiny sparkly little shards. And then the city's gonna force-feed you the wreckage and then laugh at you while you cough it back up. It won't hold your hair back for you while you're hanging over the bowl, neither. It's not that kind of town. Make some friends. Keep them close. And when shit gets deep, far beyond what you can stand, just hold fast and don't give up." He shrugged. "It ain't poetical, but it is what it is."

"I love this job," Maureen said. "I love this city. I'm ready."

"I know," Preacher said. "That's what I'm trying to tell you, that's your problem right there." He started the car. "You're doomed, like the rest of us who live here. At least try to enjoy it, and keep your pension, too, if you can."

Maureen turned as the couple and the dogs passed close by the car. The man smiled at her. "Evening, Officer."

"Evening, y'all," Maureen said, raising her hand in a wave. "Beautiful dogs. Y'all have a nice night."

"Y'all," Preacher said, laughing. He threw the cruiser into drive. "Already. You're so fucking done. You're a lifer if I ever saw one."

Maureen raised her coffee cup. "Believe."

ACKNOWLEDGMENTS

Although depicted fictionally in this book, the Roots of Music is a real organization and marching band doing fantastic and important work with the youth of New Orleans. Learn more about it, its success, and how to help it continue here: www.therootsofmusic.com.

Other organizations doing great work to support New Orleans youth through education and musical tradition include Trumpets Not Guns (trumpetsnotguns.com), the Tipitina's Foundation (tipitinasfoundation.org), and the Louis "Satchmo" Armstrong Summer Jazz Camp (louisarmstrongjazzcamp.com).

Thanks to the McDonald, Lambeth, Murphy, and Loehfelm families for their continued love and support; the usual band of New Orleans reprobates and raconteurs, including Jarret Lofstead for inspiring one of my favorite lines; Handsome Willy's Patio Bar & Lounge; the Parkview Tavern; CC's, Mojo, and the Reservoir coffeehouses; NOLAFugees Press|Productions; Laura Lippman, John Lescroart, Colin Harrison, and John Connolly for holding the door open; my wonderful editor, Sarah

Crichton, and all the supertalented (and impossibly patient) people at FSG and Picador; the Garden District and Maple Street bookshops.

Love and gratitude to my agent, Barney Karpfinger, and his killer staff at the Karpfinger Agency. The best in the business.

Musical inspiration provided by Galactic, Truth Universal, the Rebirth Brass Band, the Soul Rebels Brass Band, Dr. John, Anders Osborne, Pleasure Club, Kate Bush, Otis Taylor, the Kills, the Gutter Twins, Metric, the Twilight Singers, Band of Skulls, Tori Amos, Gaslight Anthem, Garbage, the Dead Weather, the Tragically Hip.

A fond farewell to the late, lamented Rue de la Course of Magazine Street.

All my love to my extraordinary wife, AC Lambeth, for her strength, talent, vision, inspiration, and faith.

A NOTE ABOUT THE AUTHOR

Bill Loehfelm was born in Brooklyn and grew up on Staten Island. In 1997, he moved to New Orleans. He is the author of the novels *The Devil She Knows*, *Bloodroot*, and *Fresh Kills*, which won an Amazon Breakthrough Novel Award. Loehfelm lives in New Orleans with his wife, the writer AC Lambeth.